U0005188

好讀出版

# 王爾德
# 短篇小說集II

Selected Works of
Oscar Wilde

## 王爾德

Oscar Wilde

陳筱宛＝譯

CONTENTS

2

王爾德短篇小說集 II

3

# 謎樣女子的祕密

這張臉的主人心中藏有祕密，
但說不上來那祕密是好或壞。
這張臉的美是由許多神祕感營造出來的美，
這種美其實是心理感受，
而不是外貌的賞心悅目。

一天下午，我坐在和平咖啡館外頭，觀看巴黎人生活的奢華與寒酸；啜飲著苦艾酒，我對眼前這番驕傲與貧窮共存的奇特景象感到詫異。這時，聽見有人喊我名字，轉身，看見了莫奇森勛爵。我倆從大學畢業後就再也沒見過面，而那已是將近十年前的事了；我很開心能再次遇見他，我們熱情地握手寒暄。

當年在牛津，我們是很要好的朋友，我非常喜歡他，他人長得帥，個性開朗活潑，是個值得尊敬的人。我們一票朋友總調侃地說，要不是這個人總是堅持說實話，他肯定是最棒的朋友了；不過，我想實情是，我們都因他的坦率而更加欽佩他。

但隨即我發現他變了許多，他看起來焦躁不安、滿心困惑，似乎懷疑著什麼事。我想，那跟時髦的懷疑論無關，因為

莫奇森是最最堅定的托利黨黨員，對摩西五經亦如對上議院那般忠貞不渝；因此，我斷定事情肯定跟女人有關，便問他結婚了沒。

「我對女人不夠了解。」他答道。

「我親愛的傑瑞德，」我說，「女人是用來愛，不是用來理解的。」

「我沒辦法去愛一個無法信任的對象。」他回答。

「傑瑞德，我想你一定是遇上什麼謎團了，」我驚嘆道，「說給我聽聽。」

「我們去兜兜風吧，」他答道，「這裡人太多了。不，別搭黃色的馬車，選個別的顏色——那裡，那輛墨綠色的不錯。」不一會兒，我們的馬車便快步走下大街，朝瑪德蓮大教堂的方向前進。

「咱們要上哪兒去？」我問道。

「噢，你愛去哪裡就去哪裡！」他回答，「要不，去森林附近那間餐廳吧。我們可以在那裡吃飯，然後聊聊你的近況。」

「可是我想先聽聽你的故事，」我說，「把那件困擾著你的事告訴我吧。」

他從口袋取出一只附有銀色搭鉤的摩洛哥皮革小盒，遞給了我。打開盒子，我看見裡頭有張女子的照片——女子高䠷纖瘦，一雙迷濛的大眼和一頭奔放的秀髮格外引人注目；她全身裹著厚重的皮草，看起來像個能預知未來的人。

「你對這張臉有何看法？」他說，「它誠實嗎？」

我仔細端詳著照片，感覺這張臉的主人心中藏有祕密，卻說不上來那祕密是好或壞。這張臉的美是由許多神祕感營造出來的美，這種美其實是心理感受，而不是外貌的賞心悅目；此外，那抹輕輕略過唇角、似有若無的笑意，則含蓄得不像是真

正的溫柔。

「怎麼樣，」他耐不住性子追問道，「你認為呢？」

「她是穿著貂皮大衣的蒙娜麗莎，」我回答，「先讓我多了解了解她吧。」

「晚一點好了，」他說，「等吃完晚飯後。」接著，他便開始談論起其他的事。

等到侍者為我們送上咖啡和香菸後，我提醒傑瑞德他承諾過的事。傑瑞德從椅子站起身，在房裡來來回回走了兩三趟，最後在一張扶手椅坐下，告訴我底下的故事——

「有天傍晚，大約五點鐘左右，我走在龐德街頭。街上發生了一起嚴重的馬車相撞事故，整個交通幾乎因此癱瘓。有輛小型黃色單頭馬車停在人行道旁，不知怎地引起了我的注意。經過那輛馬車時，我發現從裡往外張望的，正是下午我給你看的那張照片的臉。我立刻為之神魂顛倒。那一夜，還有隔天，我一直想著那張臉。我在那條可恨的巷道徘徊，仔細地查看每輛馬車，癡心盼著那輛黃色馬車再次出現，卻偏偏找不到我那美麗的陌生人，最後甚至開始認為她只是一場夢罷了。

「大約一個星期後，我和德拉斯泰爾夫人共進晚餐。原訂八點開席，可是一直到八點半，我們仍在客廳等候其他賓客。最後，僕役推開門，通報艾洛伊夫人到了——她，居然是我尋尋覓覓的那名女子。艾洛伊夫人緩緩走了進來，看起來像一道披著灰色薄紗的月光，而且最教人開心的是，主人要我護送她入座。

「待眾人坐定，我隨口攀談著：『艾洛伊夫人，前幾天，我好像在龐德街看見你了。』她面上霎時血色盡失，低聲向我說道：『請求您別大聲嚷嚷，您說的話全被人聽見了。』

「我氣自己為何起了個這麼糟的開場白，便趕緊草草轉入法國戲劇的話題。她的話不太多，總是以悅耳的聲音低語，

彷彿怕有人聽見似的。我不顧一切、胡裡胡塗地墜入了愛河，誰教全身上下籠罩著難言神祕感的她，激起了我最熾熱的好奇心。

「吃完晚飯不久，她便匆匆離去；臨去前，我問能否登門拜訪，她遲疑片刻，環顧四周，確定附近沒人後才說：『好，明天下午四點三刻。』而後我纏著德拉斯泰爾夫人打聽艾洛伊夫人的事，卻僅得知孀居的她住在公園道的一幢漂亮屋子，以致於當在場某個科學迷開始發表『寡婦，是婚姻關係中最適者生存的典範』云云爾長篇大論時，我便起身告辭回家。

「第二天，我準時抵達公園道，男管家卻說艾洛伊夫人剛剛外出了。我悶悶不樂地前往俱樂部，心中滿是困惑；幾經思量，寫了封信問她是否允許我擇日再訪。等了好幾天，全無回音，最後終於收到一封短箋，說她週日下午四點會在家，末了還附帶特別注明──『請別再寄信到此地。詳情容後面告。』週日，我見到了她，當天她迷人得無懈可擊。可是正當準備離開之際，她開口央求，假如我還會寫信給她，請把信寄到格林街的惠塔克書房，由克諾斯太太轉交：『我無法在自己家裡收信，我有苦衷。』

「這一季，我常常與她會面，而那種神祕的氣氛從未離開過她周身。有時，我認為她是受到某個男人的控制，但她看起來如此難以親近，讓人實在很難相信這個想法是正確的。我很難下任何結論，因為她就像博物館展示的那些奇怪結晶體，這一刻清澈透明，下一刻又煙霧迷濛。

「最後我決心開口向她求婚。我受夠了每次造訪，還有幾次寫信給她，她都要不斷故弄玄虛、吊人胃口。我捎信到惠塔克書房，問她下週一六點能否見我。她說好，我歡天喜地，開心極了。當時我心想，撇開那種神祕感不談，我對她真的一片癡心；而今我明白，一片癡心正是神祕感成致。不，不對，我

・7

謎樣女子的祕密 The Sphinx Without a Secret

愛的是那女子本身。那些神祕莫測讓我好生困擾,快把我逼瘋了。為什麼命運要這樣玩弄我?」

「所以你發現真相了?」我大喊。

「恐怕是如此,」他回答,「你得自行判斷。」

他繼續往下說:「當週一來臨時,我和叔父共進午餐;下午四點左右,我人在馬里朋路上。你知道我叔父住在攝政公園那一帶。我想去皮卡底里,便走捷徑,穿越許多陌巷。突然間,我看見艾洛伊夫人走在前頭,戴著厚厚的面紗,步行速度飛快。她走到街底最後一間房子,上了臺階,掏出一把大門鑰匙,開門走了進去。『原來謎底藏在這裡。』我對自己說,接著便趕緊上前研究那棟屋子。那似乎是出供人租住的地方。她的手帕不小心掉在門前石階上,我撿起來,收進口袋中。接著開始思考該怎麼做,我得出了結論,認為自己無權暗中查探她的私生活,便駕車前往俱樂部。

「六點整,我依約去見她。她斜倚在沙發上,穿著一件銀絲紗質的午茶裝,上頭鑲了一整圈她常戴的某種奇特月光石。她看起來相當迷人。她說:『真高興見到你。我一整天都沒出門,快悶壞了。』我不可置信地盯著她瞧,並從口袋取出手絹,遞給她。我平心靜氣地說:『艾洛伊夫人,今天下午你把這個掉在卡姆諾街了。』她驚惶地看著我,卻無意接下那條手帕。

「我問:『你去那裡做什麼?』她反問:『你有什麼權利質問我?』我回應著:『憑著深愛你的男人應有的權利。我來這裡,是想求你嫁給我。』她把臉埋進雙手間,突然淚流滿面,泣不成聲。

「我繼續強調:『你一定要告訴我實話。』她站起身,直勾勾地瞅著我,說:『莫奇森勛爵,我沒有事能告訴你。』

「我大聲嚷道:『你分明是去見某人,這就是你的祕密。』她臉色霎時變得慘白,說:『我去那裡並沒有和任何人

碰面。』

　　「我指責道：『難道你不能說實話嗎？』她態度堅決：『我說的是實話。』我氣瘋了，不知道自己還對她說了些什麼，但肯定是很難聽的話。最後，我衝出那棟房子。

　　「第二天，她寫了封信給我，我原封不動地退回，接著便和亞倫・柯維爾動身前往挪威。一個月後我回到倫敦，在《晨間郵報》讀到的第一則新聞就是艾洛伊夫人香消玉殞的訊息——她在歌劇院著了涼，不過五天，便死於肺充血。我足不出戶，誰也不見。我愛她愛得那麼深、那麼瘋狂。老天爺啊，我是如此愛慕著她！」

　　「所以，你去了那條街，進了那間屋子？」我說。

　　「對。」他回答。

　　他描述著當時情景：「有一天我實在忍不住，再也受不了自己疑心的折磨，便去了卡姆諾街。我敲了那扇門，來應門的是個模樣正派的婦人。我問她，是否有房間可以出租。婦人回答：『有的，先生。客廳應該可以租給您，我已經三個月沒見到那位小姐了，既然她租金還沒付，理應可以租給您。』

　　「我拿出照片問：『是這位小姐嗎？』婦人驚呼：『沒錯，就是她。您知道她什麼時候回來嗎？』我回道：『她死了。』婦人說：『噢，先生，您說的不是真的吧！她可是我最好的房客。她付我一週三基尼，為的只是偶爾來我家客廳坐坐。』

　　「我問：『她來這裡跟誰見面嗎？』但婦人向我保證事情並非如此，說她總是獨自前來，從未與任何人會面。

　　「我忍不住大喊：『那她到底來這裡做什麼？』婦人回答：『先生，她只是坐在客廳裡讀書，有時喝點茶。』我不知該做何回應，只好給了婦人一枚金鎊，便離開了。好了，告訴我，你怎麼看這件事？你不會相信那婦人說的是實話吧？」

　　「我相信。」我說。

「那麼艾洛伊夫人究竟去那裡做什麼？」他不死心地問。

「我親愛的傑瑞德，」我回答，「艾洛伊夫人只是一個熱中於懸疑神祕的女子。她租下這些房間，為的是享受戴著面紗上那兒去、想像自己是個女英豪的快感。她熱愛祕密，可惜她本人是個沒有謎題的人面獅身像。」

「你真這麼想？」他又問。

「我敢肯定是如此。」我答道。

他拿出摩洛哥皮革小盒，打開它，凝視著照片，最後他說：「我真想知道實情究竟是什麼。」

# The Sphinx
# Without
# a Secret

One afternoon I was sitting outside the Cafe de la Paix, watching the splendour and shabbiness of Parisian life, and wondering over my vermouth at the strange panorama of pride and poverty that was passing before me, when I heard some one call my name. I turned round, and saw Lord Murchison. We had not met since we had been at college together, nearly ten years before, so I was delighted to come across him again, and we shook hands warmly. At Oxford we had been great friends. I had liked him immensely, he was so handsome, so high-spirited, and so honourable. We used to say of him that he would be the best of fellows, if he did not always speak the truth, but I think we really admired him all the more for his frankness. I found him a good deal changed. He looked anxious and puzzled, and seemed to be in doubt about something. I felt it could not be modern scepticism, for Murchison was the stoutest of Tories, and believed in the Pentateuch as firmly as he believed in the House of Peers; so I concluded that it was a woman, and asked him if he was married yet.

'I don't understand women well enough,' he answered.

'My dear Gerald,' I said, 'women are meant to be loved, not to be understood.'

'I cannot love where I cannot trust,' he replied.

'I believe you have a mystery in your life, Gerald,' I exclaimed; 'tell me about it.'

'Let us go for a drive,' he answered, 'it is too crowded here. No, not a yellow carriage, any other colour — there, that dark green one will do'; and in a few moments we were trotting down the boulevard in the direction of the Madeleine.

'Where shall we go to?' I said.

'Oh, anywhere you like!' he answered — 'to the restaurant in the Bois; we will dine there, and you shall tell me all about yourself.'

'I want to hear about you first,' I said. 'Tell me your mystery.'

He took from his pocket a little silver-clasped morocco case, and handed it to me. I opened it. Inside there was the photograph of a woman. She was tall and slight, and strangely picturesque with her large vague eyes and loosened hair. She looked like a clairvoyante, and was wrapped in rich furs.

'What do you think of that face?' he said; 'is it truthful?'

I examined it carefully. It seemed to me the face of some one who had a secret, but whether that secret was good or evil I could not say. Its beauty was a beauty moulded out of many mysteries — the beauty, in fact, which is psychological, not plastic — and the faint smile that just played across the lips was far too subtle to be really sweet.

'Well,' he cried impatiently, 'what do you say?'

'She is the Gioconda in sables,' I answered. 'Let me know all about her.'

'Not now,' he said; 'after dinner,' and began to talk of other things.

When the waiter brought us our coffee and cigarettes I reminded Gerald of his promise. He rose from his seat, walked two or three times up and down the room, and, sinking into an armchair, told me the following story:—

'One evening,' he said, 'I was walking down Bond Street about five o'clock. There was a terrific crush of carriages, and the traffic was almost stopped. Close to the pavement was standing a little yellow brougham, which, for some reason or other, attracted my attention. As I passed by there looked out from it the face I showed you this afternoon. It fascinated me immediately. All that night I kept thinking of it, and all the next day. I wandered up and down that wretched Row, peering into every carriage, and waiting for the yellow brougham; but I could not find ma belle inconnue, and at last I began to think she was merely a dream. About a week afterwards I was dining with Madame de Rastail. Dinner was for eight o'clock; but at half-past eight we were still waiting in the drawing-room. Finally the servant threw open the door, and announced Lady Alroy. It was the woman I had been looking for. She came in very slowly, looking like a moonbeam in grey lace, and, to my intense delight, I was asked to take her in to dinner. After we had sat down, I remarked quite innocently, "I think I caught sight of you in Bond Street some time ago, Lady Alroy." She grew very pale, and said to me in a low voice, "Pray do not talk so loud; you may be overheard." I felt miserable at having made such a bad beginning, and plunged recklessly into the subject of the French plays. She spoke very little, always in the same low musical voice, and seemed as if she was afraid of some one listening. I fell passionately, stupidly in love, and the indefinable atmosphere of mystery that surrounded her excited

1
3

謎樣女子的秘密　The Sphinx Without a Secret

my most ardent curiosity. When she was going away, which she did very soon after dinner, I asked her if I might call and see her. She hesitated for a moment, glanced round to see if any one was near us, and then said, "Yes; tomorrow at a quarter to five." I begged Madame de Rastail to tell me about her; but all that I could learn was that she was a widow with a beautiful house in Park Lane, and as some scientific bore began a dissertation on widows, as exemplifying the survival of the matrimonially fittest, I left and went home.

'The next day I arrived at Park Lane punctual to the moment, but was told by the butler that Lady Alroy had just gone out. I went down to the club quite unhappy and very much puzzled, and after long consideration wrote her a letter, asking if I might be allowed to try my chance some other afternoon. I had no answer for several days, but at last I got a little note saying she would be at home on Sunday at four and with this extraordinary postscript: "Please do not write to me here again; I will explain when I see you." On Sunday she received me, and was perfectly charming; but when I was going away she begged of me, if I ever had occasion to write to her again, to address my letter to "Mrs. Knox, care of Whittaker's Library, Green Street." "There are reasons," she said, "why I cannot receive letters in my own house."

'All through the season I saw a great deal of her, and the atmosphere of mystery never left her. Sometimes I thought that she was in the power of some man, but she looked so unapproachable, that I could not believe it. It was really very difficult for me to come to any conclusion, for she was like one of those strange crystals that one sees in museums, which are at one moment clear, and at another clouded. At last I determined to ask her to be my wife: I was sick and tired of the incessant secrecy that she imposed on all my visits, and on the few letters I sent her. I wrote to her at the library to ask her if she could see me the following Monday at six. She answered yes, and I was in the seventh heaven of delight. I was infatuated with her: in spite of the mystery, I thought then — in consequence of it, I see now. No; it was the woman herself I loved. The mystery troubled me, maddened me. Why did chance put me in its track?'

'You discovered it, then?' I cried.

'I fear so,' he answered. 'You can judge for yourself.'

'When Monday came round I went to lunch with my uncle, and about four o'clock found myself in the Marylebone Road. My uncle, you know, lives in Regent's Park. I wanted to get to Piccadilly, and took a short cut through a lot of shabby little streets. Suddenly I saw in front of me Lady Alroy, deeply veiled and walking very fast. On coming to the last house in the street, she went up the steps, took out a latch-key, and let herself in. "Here is the mystery," I said to myself; and I hurried on and examined the house. It seemed a sort of place for letting lodgings. On the doorstep lay her handkerchief, which she had dropped. I picked it up and put it in my pocket. Then I began to consider what I should do. I came to the conclusion that I had no right to spy on her, and I drove down to the club. At six I called to see her. She was lying on a sofa, in a tea-gown of silver tissue looped up by some strange moonstones that she always wore. She was looking quite lovely. "I am so glad to see you," she said; "I have not been out all day." I stared at her in amazement, and pulling the handkerchief out of my pocket, handed it to her. "You dropped this in Cumnor Street this afternoon, Lady Alroy," I said very calmly. She looked at me in terror but made no attempt to take the handkerchief. "What were you doing there?" I asked. "What right have you to question me?" she answered. "The right of a man who loves you," I replied; "I came here to ask you to be my wife." She hid her face in her hands, and burst into floods of tears. "You must tell me," I continued. She stood up, and, looking me straight in the face, said, "Lord Murchison, there is nothing to tell you." — "You went to meet some one," I cried; "this is your mystery." She grew dreadfully white, and said, "I went to meet no one." — "Can't you tell the truth?" I exclaimed. "I have told it," she replied. I was mad, frantic; I don't know what I said, but I said terrible things to her. Finally I rushed out of the house. She wrote me a letter the next day; I sent it back unopened, and started for Norway with Alan Colville. After a month I came back, and the first thing I saw in the Morning Post was the death of Lady Alroy. She had caught a chill at the Opera, and had died in five days of congestion of the lungs. I shut myself up and saw no one. I had loved her so much, I had loved her so madly. Good God! how I had loved that woman!'

'You went to the street, to the house in it?' I said.

'Yes,' he answered.

'One day I went to Cumnor Street. I could not help it; I was tortured with doubt. I knocked at the door, and a respectable-looking woman opened it to me. I asked her if she had any rooms to let. "Well, sir," she replied, "the drawing-rooms are supposed to be let; but I have not seen the lady for three months, and as rent is owing on them, you can have them." — "Is this the lady?" I said, showing the photograph. "That's her, sure enough," she exclaimed; "and when is she coming back, sir?" — "The lady is dead," I replied. "Oh sir, I hope not!" said the woman; "she was my best lodger. She paid me three guineas a week merely to sit in my drawing-rooms now and then." "She met some one here?" I said; but the woman assured me that it was not so, that she always came alone, and saw no one. "What on earth did she do here?" I cried. "She simply sat in the drawing-room, sir, reading books, and sometimes had tea," the woman answered. I did not know what to say, so I gave her a sovereign and went away. Now, what do you think it all meant? You don't believe the woman was telling the truth?'

'I do.'

'Then why did Lady Alroy go there?'

'My dear Gerald,' I answered, 'Lady Alroy was simply a woman with a mania for mystery. She took these rooms for the pleasure of going there with her veil down, and imagining she was a heroine. She had a passion for secrecy, but she herself was merely a Sphinx without a secret.'

'Do you really think so?'

'I am sure of it,' I replied.

He took out the morocco case, opened it, and looked at the photograph. 'I wonder?' he said at last.

# 坎特維爾大宅之鬼

你必須為我的罪惡哭泣，因為我沒有眼淚；
同時還要為我的靈魂祈禱，因為我沒有信仰。
如果你能永保體貼、善良與溫柔，
那麼死亡天使將會憐憫我。

## 1

美國公使海瑞姆·B·歐提斯先生買下坎特維爾大宅的時候，每個人都告訴他，他做了一件非常愚蠢的事，因為眾人皆知那個地方——鬧鬼。甚至在他們開始討論交易細節時，非常在乎名望體面的坎特維爾勛爵本人都認定，向歐提斯先生說明這項事實是他應盡的義務。

「我們自己都不想住在這樣的地方，」坎特維爾勛爵說，「因為我的姑婆波爾頓公爵遺孀有天在晚餐前更衣時，突然發現有雙骷髏手掌搭在她的肩膀上，嚇得她痙攣發作，從此再也沒有真正恢復過健康。歐提斯先生，我覺得我有義務告訴您，我家族裡有好幾個在世的親人都看過那鬼魂；就連教區牧師——身為劍橋大學國王學院院士的奧各司特斯·丹皮爾牧師

也撞見過它。發生了公爵遺孀那樁不幸意外後，年輕的僕役全都不肯繼續留下來，坎特維爾夫人則時常夜不成眠，因為在夜裡，走廊和書房總會傳來邪門的怪聲。」

「大人，」這位公使回應道，「我會把家具和那個鬼魂一併列入估價。我來自一個現代的國家，凡是能用錢買得到的東西，一樣不缺。既然我們活躍敏捷的年輕小夥子在舊世界裡狂歡作樂，重金挖走你們的最佳女演員和歌劇首席女伶；我想，如果歐洲真有鬼魂出沒，我們的公立博物館肯定會在很短的時間內將它買下，並在各地巡迴展示。」

「雖然那鬼魂可能會抗拒貴國極富創新精神的劇團經理們，所設想的各種提議，但它確實存在。」坎特維爾勛爵面帶微笑說道，「整整三個世紀以來，精確來說，是打從一五八四年起，它可是眾所周知，遠近馳名，總是會在我們家族所有成員快過世前現身。」

「噢，家庭醫師不也是如此嗎！可是，大人，這世上並沒有鬼魂這種東西，而且我想大自然的規律也不會為了英國貴族而暫時不起作用。」

「您在美國肯定非常崇尚自然，」坎特維爾勛爵答道，儘管他其實不大明白歐提斯先生的最後一句評論是什麼意思。「倘若您不介意屋子裡有鬼，那就沒有問題。只是您一定要記得，我曾警告過您。」

會面後不出幾個星期，這宗買賣順利完成，公使和他的家人在這一季結束之際搬進了坎特維爾大宅。

歐提斯夫人的閨名為盧克雷蒂亞·R·塔班，雲英未嫁時住在紐約西五十三街，是個豔冠群芳、遠近馳名的紐約美女，而今雖已步入中年，但風韻未減，靈動明眸和絕佳體態依舊。許多美國女子離開家鄉後，誤以為表現出一副長期健康欠佳的姿態才算是歐洲美人，可是歐提斯夫人從未落入這類錯誤迷

思。她體格健美，活力充沛。其實從許多方面來看，她都是個十足的英格蘭人，而且極好地證明了我們和今日美國在各方面都是一樣的，只可惜——語言不同。

這個家的長子名叫華盛頓。對於雙親在為自己洗禮時，因一時愛國心的驅使而取了這個名字，一直覺得很懊惱。這名長相俊美的年輕金髮男子早已開始從事外交工作——他在紐波特賭場一連三季帶頭跳起類似法國花式舞的複雜舞步，在倫敦甚至是出了名的善舞。唯一的弱點是貪逐女色和渴求貴族爵位。除此之外，他可是非常明智。

維吉妮亞·E·歐提斯小姐是個年方十五的小女孩，像頭小鹿般動作靈巧、楚楚可憐，一雙藍色大眼閃耀著自由的光采。她是個了不起的女騎士，有回騎著矮種馬與老畢爾頓勛爵比賽繞行坎特維爾大宅的園林兩圈，結果正好在阿基里斯的雕像前，以超前一匹半的馬身長度贏得了比賽。這事兒讓年輕的柴郡公爵開心得不得了，當場向她求婚，但當晚立刻被他的監護人送回伊頓，哭得一把鼻涕一把眼淚。

排行在維吉妮亞之後的，是常被人喚作「星條旗」的雙胞胎，因為他們老是挨鞭子，身上常有一條一條的痕跡。這對調皮可愛的男孩，是這個家撇開可敬的公使不談，唯二堅貞支持著共和黨的成員。

由於坎特維爾大宅距離最近的火車站亞思科還有七英里遠，歐提斯先生打電報讓一部四輪遊覽馬車來接他們，一家人興致高昂地展開這趟兜風之旅。

這是個宜人的七月傍晚，空氣中飄蕩著淡淡的松木香。偶爾，他們會聽見斑尾林鴿用甜美的聲音育雛，或是在沙沙作響的蕨叢深處窺見雉雞光滑的胸膛。小松鼠則在他們一行路過自己身旁時，從櫸樹間使勁地盯著他們瞧；兔群鑽過枯枝、躍過長滿苔蘚的小圓丘，匆匆跑開，放眼望去到處都是牠們的白尾

巴。然而，當馬車轉進坎特維爾大宅前面那條路時，突然間烏雲密布，空氣似乎被古怪的沉默凍結，一大群禿鼻烏鴉無聲飛過他們的頭上。在抵達大宅之前，斗大的雨珠已然落下。

站在臺階上迎接他們的是個衣著整齊的老婦，她一身黑色絲綢，戴頂白色軟帽，還穿著圍裙。她是女管家阿姆尼太太，在坎特維爾夫人的執意請求下，歐提斯夫人才同意讓她保有原本的職務。當歐提斯一家人走下馬車時，阿姆尼太太向每個人行了屈膝禮，同時用一種奇特、古雅的方式說：「恭迎大駕，有失遠迎，幸勿見罪。」

他們由她領著，穿過出色的都鐸王朝時期大廳，來到了書房。這是個狹長低矮的房間，牆面鑲滿黑櫟木，盡頭則是一大扇彩繪玻璃窗。他們看見桌上已備妥熱茶，於是脫下大衣，紛紛入座，開始四處張望，阿姆尼太太則在旁伺候。

突然間，歐提斯夫人瞥見壁爐旁的地板上有塊暗紅色汙漬，她完全沒意識到那代表了什麼，便開口對阿姆尼太太說：「那邊地板上好像沾了什麼東西。」

「沒錯，夫人，」這名年紀很大的女管家低聲回答，「血漬一向都沾在那個點上。」

「多可怕呀，」歐提斯夫人驚呼，「我可不想要客廳裡有血印。一定要馬上把它清理乾淨。」

這名老婦露出微笑，用同樣低沉神祕的口吻解釋；「那是愛蓮諾‧坎特維爾夫人的血。一五七五年，她的丈夫賽門‧坎特維爾爵爺就在那個位置殺了她。賽門爵爺比她多活了九年，後來卻在非常神祕的情況下忽然消失無蹤。他的屍首從未被人找到，但他罪孽深重的魂魄至今仍在這大宅裡徘徊不去。這血漬廣受觀光客和後人的青睞，萬萬不可隨意抹除。」

「哪有這種事，」華盛頓‧歐提斯高聲說道，「平克頓牌的冠軍除汙劑和模範清潔劑能馬上徹底清除它。」在驚嚇過度

的女管家還來不及出聲干預之前，他毫不猶豫地直接跪在地板上，用一小根看起來像是黑色化妝品的東西迅速擦去地面的污點。不過短短幾分鐘，就再也看不見血漬的痕跡了。

當華盛頓環顧四周，迎上家人敬佩折服的眼光時，更是得意洋洋地宣稱：「我就知道平克頓肯定有效。」可是他話都還沒說完，一道駭人的閃電讓這個陰暗的房間頓時變得明亮，一陣可怕的隆隆雷聲嚇得這家人全都跳了起來，阿姆尼太太則暈了過去。

「真可怕的氣候！」美國公使一邊點燃長型方頭雪茄，一邊冷靜地說道，「我想，這個古老國度的人口太多，以致於沒有足夠的好天氣讓人人都能同享。我一直深信，移居他國是解決英格蘭問題的唯一對策。」

「親愛的海瑞姆，」歐提斯夫人大喊，「怎麼辦，管家太太昏倒了。」

「就像損壞賠償一樣，把它記在她的帳上，」公使回答，「以後她就不會再昏倒了。」幾分鐘後，阿姆尼太太果真醒了。當然，她非常非常地苦惱，並嚴正警告男主人提防禍事將會降臨這個家。

「老爺，我親眼看過那些事發生，」她說，「那會讓任何基督徒的寒毛直豎。因為發生在這宅邸的可怕事情，讓我不知有多少個夜晚都不敢闔眼入睡。」公使夫婦友善地向這名老實的婦人再三保證，他們並不怕鬼。最後，在祈求老天保佑她的新雇主並談妥加薪事宜後，老管家即步履蹣跚地走回自己的房間。

# 2

暴風雨肆虐了一整晚，但沒有發生任何特別值得注意的事。然而，翌日清晨，當這家人下樓吃早餐時，赫然發現那塊恐怖的血跡再次出現在地板上。

「我想這不是模範清潔劑不夠力，」華盛頓說道，「因為我用在所有的東西上都很有效。這肯定是那個鬼魂在搞鬼。」於是，他第二次動手將那塊汙漬擦掉，可是隔天清晨它又恢復原狀。儘管夜裡公使都會親自鎖上書房，把鑰匙帶到樓上，但隔天清晨汙漬仍舊如常出現。這下子，歐提斯一家莫不對此感到好奇。公使開始懷疑自己否定鬼魂的存在是否太過獨斷；歐提斯夫人則表達她想加入超自然學會的意願；華盛頓寫了封長信給麥爾斯和帕德默兩位先生，想探討「一旦涉及犯罪，血腥汙漬將經久不變」這個主題。但那天晚上，關於幽靈是否真實存在的所有疑惑，全解除了。

　　那是個晴朗溫暖的日子，趁著傍晚的涼意，歐提斯一家外出兜風，直至九點才回到家，並吃了頓簡單的晚餐。席間的聊天話題並未涉及鬼魂，也就是說，他們並沒有會見到鬼魂的心理準備——據說那常發生在超自然現象出現之前。

　　後來，我從公使那兒得知，當晚餐桌上談論的，不過是有教養的美國上流階級很尋常的談天主題，像是——身為女演員，芬妮・戴溫波特小姐的表現遠比莎拉・伯恩哈特①更為優異；就算是最棒的英格蘭餐館，也不容易吃到綠玉米、蕎麥餅和玉米片；波士頓對世人性靈發展的重要性②；鐵路旅遊中行李託運系統的優點；相較於倫敦人慢吞吞拉長調子說話的方式，紐約腔悅耳多了。談話中，隻字未提超自然話題或賽門・坎特維爾爵爺。

　　晚上十一點，所有人準備上床就寢。大約半個小時後，燈光全部熄滅。過沒多久，公使被房門外走廊傳來的奇怪聲響吵醒，聽起來像是金屬撞擊的鋃鐺聲，而且似乎愈來愈靠近。他立刻起身劃了根火柴，想知道現在是幾點。此時正好是一點鐘。他相當鎮定，先檢查自己的脈搏，確認自己完全沒有發燒。那奇怪聲響仍舊持續著，同時又多了明顯的腳步聲。公

使穿上拖鞋，從化妝箱中取出一只橢圓形小瓶，接著打開房門。在昏暗的月光下，他看見一名形貌很恐怖的老翁站在他面前——老人的雙眼像燒紅的煤炭；披散在肩頭的灰色長髮糾結成團；一身款式古舊的服裝既破爛又骯髒，他的手腕和腳踝戴著沉重的手銬與鏽蝕的腳鐐。

「老太爺，」公使說，「請您務必為那些鎖鍊上油，因此，我給您帶來一小瓶坦莫尼日升潤滑油。據說只要使用一次就能徹底見效，產品外包裝紙上還印了好幾則使用見證，推薦者是敝國幾位很著名的牧師。我把它放在燭臺旁留給您用。倘若您覺得合用，我很樂意再多為您準備幾瓶。」說完這些話，公使將小瓶子擱在一張大理石桌上，便關上房門睡覺去了。

這個坎特維爾大宅之鬼氣壞了。他先是愣了片刻，接著拿起瓶子，往光滑的地板狠狠砸去。他發出低沉的呻吟，飛過走廊，渾身散發出一種恐怖的綠光。然而，當他抵達巨大的橡木樓梯頂端時，一扇門被猛然推開，出現了兩個矮小的白袍人影，接著一個大型枕頭颼地掠過他的腦袋瓜！此時顯然沒有迷惘或悵然若失的餘地，他只能匆促利用四度空間做為遁逃的手段，穿過壁板消失不見，隨後整間屋子變得無比安靜。

一回到位於大宅左廂的小密室，他便斜倚著一道月光，讓自己的呼吸平穩下來，並嘗試理解目前的處境。在這從未間斷的三百年輝煌鬼魂生涯之中，他何曾遭遇過如此惡劣的羞辱。

他回憶起公爵遺孀穿著蕾絲織品、戴著鑽石站在鏡子前，被他嚇得昏厥倒地；還有那四個女僕，他只不過從某個閒置空房的窗簾後朝她們咧嘴微笑，就嚇得她們歇斯底里；還有教區牧師，有天晚上比較晚離開這個家的書房，他便將對方手上的蠟燭吹熄，結果害牧師長期為精神錯亂所苦，從此得接受威廉・顧爾爵爺③的照顧；以及年長的德特雷慕雅夫人，有天清晨醒得特別早，沒想到卻看見一具骸骨坐在火爐旁的安樂椅上

閱讀她的日記，後來便因腦部發炎而臥床六個星期，在調養過程中，她變得虔信上帝，甚至與那醜聲遠播的懷疑論者伏爾泰斷絕往來。

他還想起那個可怕的夜晚，當敗德的坎特維爾勛爵被人發現倒在臥房的更衣間時，喉嚨裡卡了一張方塊傑克，就快要窒息身亡；臨死前，他招認自己在克洛克佛德會所④騙了查爾斯‧詹姆士‧福克斯五萬英鎊，靠的正是那張紙牌，而且他發誓是大宅之鬼逼他吞下它的。

還有那個男管家，只因看見一隻綠色手掌輕拍窗玻璃，便在廚房的食品貯藏室飲彈自戕；還有還有，美女史都費歐德夫人為了遮掩烙印在她白皙皮膚上的五個指印，無時不刻得戴著黑色絲絨脖圍，但最後仍在國王街底的鯉魚池投水自盡。

他過去的所有豐功偉業突然全都浮上心頭。他沉溺在真正藝術家那種強烈的自我中心裡，細細回想自己最有名的表現。他想起自己最近一次扮演「紅魯本——又名，被勒死的帥哥」這角色，以及以「憔悴的吉比恩——貝克斯里荒原的吸血鬼」一角初登場。還有某個美好的六月傍晚，他只不過在網球場上用自己的骨頭玩九柱保齡球，卻掀起軒然大波的種種往事，這一切都讓他不禁苦笑。在經歷這光輝的一切之後，這些不知天高地厚的可恨美國人竟然跑來叫他用什麼日升潤滑油，還朝他的腦袋瓜丟枕頭！真教人難以忍受。更別提，歷史上從來沒有哪個鬼魂遭受過這樣的待遇。因此，他決心要復仇！他陷入深思，直到天色微亮方止。

# 3

第二天早上，歐提斯一家聚在一塊兒吃早餐時，花了好多時間討論這個大宅之鬼。美國公使發現對方沒有收下自己的禮物時，心裡自然有點不快，他說：「我並不想讓那個鬼受到任

何人身傷害。況且，考慮到他在這座宅邸已經住了那麼久，你們向他丟枕頭實在很不禮貌。」這是個公允的評論，只可惜雙胞胎聽了，卻突然爆出一陣大笑。「另一方面，」公使繼續說道，「假如他真的拒絕使用日升潤滑油，我們就必須解下他身上的鎖鍊。房門外有那麼大的噪音實在很難入睡。」

不過，在這週剩下的幾天裡，鬼魂並沒有騷擾他們，唯一引起大家注意的是，書房地板上的血漬持續再現。這件事確實有些蹊蹺，因為公使晚上總會將書房房門鎖上，而且窗戶也都牢牢地閂上。不僅如此，那汙漬呈現出的變色龍般顏色變化也讓大夥議論紛紛——有好幾個早晨，它是暗淡的紅色（接近印度紅的赤褐色），接著它成了朱紅色，然後是濃豔的紫色；還有一回，當他們根據自由美國人歸正聖公會的簡單儀式，下樓進行家庭禱告時，發現它竟然變成了鮮豔的祖母綠。這些多采多姿的變化自然逗得這家人非常開心，因此每天晚上都會針對這件事隨意打賭。唯一一個沒有加入這場鬧劇的人是小維吉妮亞，不知道為了什麼，她每次看見那血跡，表情總是非常悲傷，當它變成祖母綠的那個早上，她甚至差點哭出來。

鬼魂第二次現身是在週日晚上。就在他們上床後不久，突然被大廳傳來的一陣可怕巨響嚇了一跳。他們衝下樓，發現一套巨大的古老盔甲與底座分離，摔落在石板地上，而一旁坐在高背椅上搓揉自己膝蓋、一臉痛徹心脾的，正是坎特維爾之鬼。隨身帶著豆子槍的雙胞胎立刻朝他發射兩顆彈丸，而唯有在描紅習字簿上長期仔細地練習，才能達到這般射擊精準度。美國公使則拿出左輪手槍指著他，並按照加州的規矩要求他高舉雙手！

鬼魂發出無比憤怒的尖叫聲，接著像陣薄霧般橫掃過他們身邊，連帶弄熄了華盛頓·歐提斯手上的蠟燭，讓這家人徹底陷入黑暗之境。等到爬上階梯頂端，鬼魂才定下心來，決定使

出他著名的惡魔笑聲。這一招他用過好幾回，每一次都十分管用。據說它讓芮格勛爵的假髮一夜花白，還讓坎特維爾夫人聘用的三名法國家庭教師提早辭職走人。因此，他用盡力氣笑出最駭人的笑聲，直到古老的拱形屋頂不斷發出巨大聲響。

可是，令人喪膽的回聲都還沒有消失呢，一扇門被推開，身穿一襲淡藍色晨衣的歐提斯夫人走了出來，對著他說：「我想你身體可能不大舒服，所以幫你準備了一瓶多柏醫生牌藥酒。這藥對治療消化不良的效果很好。」鬼魂憤怒地盯著她瞧，並準備讓自己變身為一頭大黑狗，這項技能是他聲名遠播的理由，不過家庭醫師總認為，那只是坎特維爾勛爵的伯父——湯瑪斯・霍騰閣下長久以來的愚蠢妄想罷了。可是，逐漸逼近的腳步聲讓他遲疑不決，最後，鬼魂放棄施行他的惡意企圖，而化為淡淡的磷光，搶在雙胞胎走近之前消失無蹤，只留下一聲深沉的教堂墓地式呻吟。

回到自個兒房間的那一刻，老鬼完全崩潰了，陷入非常猛烈的焦躁不安中。雙胞胎的低級玩笑，和歐提斯夫人令人不快的唯物主義當然都無比惱人，但真正最教他苦惱的是，他竟然無法撐起那套鎧甲！他原本期望美國人就算再先進時髦，看見穿著盔甲的幽靈總該覺得毛骨悚然吧！倘若這理由還不夠合理，至少此舉也是出於尊重他們國家的國民詩人郎費羅，畢竟那些優雅迷人的詩作⑤總在坎特維爾一家人進城時，伴他消磨許多疲憊的時光。再說，那是他的盔甲。他曾經穿著它在坎諾沃斯馬上比武大會中贏得重大勝利，甚至還獲得童貞女王⑥本人的高度讚許。然而，今晚他想穿上它的時候，卻被巨大護胸甲與鋼製頭盔的重量徹底壓垮，害他重重摔倒在石板地上，不僅一雙膝蓋嚴重破皮，右手指節也撞傷淤青。

這件事發生後，有好些日子他病得很嚴重，除了持續維護血跡的存在，他幾乎沒踏出房門半步。經過好一陣的休養照

料，他恢復了健康，決心第三度嘗試嚇唬美國公使及其家人。

　　他選定在八月十七日，星期五現身，當天甚至花了很多時間梭巡翻找自己的衣櫃，最後決定戴一頂飾有紅羽毛的大型寬邊軟帽，用一條裹屍布裝飾手腕和頸部，再帶上一把生鏽的匕首。接近傍晚時分，外頭颳起疾風暴雨，風勢是如此強勁，吹得這間老宅的所有窗戶與門扇全都不斷搖晃，嘎嘎作響。事實上，這正是他所鍾愛的那種天氣。

　　他的行動計畫如下——悄悄潛入華盛頓・歐提斯的房間，從床尾朝華盛頓嘰哩咕嚕地瞎扯一番，接著按照慢版音樂的節奏朝他自己的喉嚨捅三下。他對華盛頓懷抱特殊恨意，因為這傢伙總習慣用平克頓牌模範清潔劑，清除著名的坎特維爾血跡。動手收拾這個魯莽愚蠢的青年，讓他陷入悲慘的恐懼情狀後，接下來便前往公使夫婦的臥房，他打算將濕冷的手放在歐提斯夫人額頭上，同時用尖利憤怒的氣音朝她心生戰慄的丈夫，附耳道出這棟老宅可怕的祕密。

　　至於小維吉妮亞，他還拿不定主意該怎麼做。她從來沒有冒犯過他，更別提她人長得美，個性又溫和。他心想，從衣櫃發出幾聲低沉的呻吟便綽綽有餘了；倘若那樣還沒能吵醒她，他可能會用自己那顫動不已的手指在床罩上抓撓。

　　關於那對雙胞胎，他決心要給他們一個教訓。第一件事當然就是坐在他們胸口，製造出讓人喘不過氣來的噩夢感。其次，由於他們的床舖幾乎緊鄰著彼此，他打算以冰冷的綠色屍首形體站在兩張床舖中間，直到他們嚇得屁滾尿流、無法動彈為止。最後，則是迅速脫掉裹屍布，睜著一顆骨碌碌的眼珠，憑著褪色泛白的骨頭在房間四處爬行，這可是「蠢丹尼——又名，自殺屍骨」的扮相，過去他不只一次靠這個角色製造出成功的效果，這足以和他另一個知名角色「瘋子馬汀——戴面具的神祕人物」相提並論。

晚間十點半的時候，他聽見這家人準備就寢。來自雙胞胎的狂放尖聲大笑讓他煩惱了好一會兒，這兩個無憂無慮的小男生睡前顯然不忘自娛。不過到了十一點一刻，所有的聲音靜了下來。當午夜報時響起，他自信滿滿地展開了行動。貓頭鷹不斷拍打著窗玻璃，渡鴉從紅豆杉上發出低沉沙啞的叫聲，風兒則像迷惘的靈魂在大宅裡到處徘徊嗚咽。

　　歐提斯一家沉沉睡去，渾然不覺大禍臨頭。儘管風強雨驟，他仍舊清楚聽見美國公使規律的鼾聲。他鬼鬼祟祟地從壁板後頭走出來，一抹邪惡的笑容浮現在他那殘酷瘤皺的嘴邊。當他躡手躡腳走過那扇巨大的凸窗前，月娘躲進了雲後。他和他妻子的家族紋章刻在那扇凸窗上，塗著天藍色和金色，以為裝飾。

　　他像個惡靈般持續滑行了好一陣，當他通過時，彷彿就連黑暗都討厭他。他一度認為自己聽見有束西在叫喊，因而停下腳步；但那只是紅色農場上某條狗追捕獵物的長聲吠叫。於是他繼續前行，口中喃喃唸著怪異的十六世紀詛咒，同時在午夜的空氣中不斷迅速揮舞那把生鏽的匕首。最後終於抵達走廊轉角，轉過去就能通往倒楣的華盛頓臥房。他在那裡駐足了一會兒，強風吹亂了他滿頭的灰長髮，把他身上的裹屍布弄得更加駭人。

　　這時，十二點一刻鐘響，他感覺是時候了。他暗自輕笑，走過那個轉角，結果卻發出一聲恐懼的哀號，立刻嚇得向後退，用那雙瘦骨嶙峋的修長雙手掩住自己蒼白的臉龐——在他正前方，站著一個可怕的幽靈，動也不動地活像尊雕像，巨大醜陋如瘋子的夢！它的頭又禿又亮；它的臉又圓又肥又白；五官扭曲成永恆的獰獰笑容。雙眼射出猩紅色光線，長著一張血盆大口，一套跟他類似的駭人破爛服裝，披裹在巨大的形體上。它胸前別著一張用仿古字母符號書寫的怪異告示，似乎是

某種羞恥清單，某種瘋狂罪愆的記錄，某種作奸犯科的可怕行事曆；同時，它的右手還高舉著一把閃閃發亮的鋼劍。

他從來沒有見過鬼，自然感到無比的恐懼，在匆匆瞥了那個凶惡幽靈第二眼後，便飛也似地逃回自己的房間。沒想到在快速跑下走廊時，他竟然被自己的長裹屍布絆倒，隨身攜帶的那把生鏽匕首最終掉進了公使的長統靴中，次日清晨被男管家發現。

一回到自己的套房，他便撲倒在一張硬板小床上，把臉埋在衣服底下。然而，一會兒之後，勇敢的坎特維爾老鬼還是想展現自己的權威，決定天一亮就要去找那個鬼談一談。因此，當黎明即將以銀色勾勒山丘的輪廓時，他便動身前往撞見那可怕幽靈的地點。他鼓勵著自己，畢竟二鬼聯手勝過單打獨鬥，更何況有了新朋友的幫助，他就有把握一定能好好教訓那對雙胞胎。

誰知，到了那個定點，他卻看見一幅可怕的景象。這幽靈肯定遇上了什麼事，因為從它空洞雙眼射出的光完全消失了，閃閃發亮的劍從它手中落下，而且還以一種勉強又不舒服的姿勢斜倚著牆。當它的頭滑到地上滾動著，整個身體幾乎橫臥下來時，他衝上前去，用手臂使勁抓住它，結果令他震驚的是，自己竟抱住了一件白色麻紗床帷，躺在他腳邊的則是一支長柄地板刷、一把切肉刀，還有一顆空心蕪菁！由於無法理解這奇特的轉變，他急忙抓來那張告示牌，在昏暗的晨光中讀著那些可怕的字眼——「老鬼才是唯一真正原創的幽靈。謹防仿冒。其他全是假貨。」

整件事快速閃過他的腦海。他被耍了，他遭人設計，他竟然被騙倒了！他的眼神又回復了原本自信的神情，使勁咬住自己無牙的牙齦，同時高舉乾枯的雙手，以老派的用語起誓：「雄雞二啼後，血債必定要討還，屠殺將悄然而至……」

還來不及說完整段可怕的誓言，遠處農莊的紅瓦屋頂便傳來一聲雞鳴。他發出一聲低沉苦澀的長笑，等待著。他等了好幾個小時，可是那隻公雞不知為何卻再也沒有啼叫。最後在七點半的時候，女僕出現了，他只好放棄原訂計畫，躡手躡腳地走回自己的房間，思索著自己一廂情願的期盼與令人費解的難題。

他非常喜愛古代騎士團，因而查閱了幾本相關書籍，結果發現書上那些凡是與他立下相同誓言的每個場合，雄雞總是會啼第二次。「這隻淘氣的雞肯定會下地獄，」他喃喃自語，「有一天我會拿著結實的矛，在山谷裡追著牠跑，讓牠為我啼出一聲『死亡降臨』的啼聲。」接著，他鑽進一具舒服的鉛製棺材中，一路睡到傍晚。

# 4

第二天，老鬼覺得非常虛弱、非常疲憊。過去四週以來的緊繃情緒開始產生了影響。他心神不寧、極其煩躁，連最輕微的噪音都能讓他嚇一大跳。他一連五天都待在房裡，最後甚至決定放棄維護書房地板血漬這件事——假如歐提斯這家人不想要那個血痕，顯然代表他們不值得享有它。他們無疑是追求物質存在、水準極低的那種人，根本沒有能力欣賞靈異現象的象徵價值。

幽魂現身和靈異事件可就完全不同了，而且那不是他可以說改就改。每週在走廊上現身一次，還有每個月的第一和第三個星期三從凸窗發出嘰哩咕嚕聲音是他神聖的職責，他可不願有失尊嚴地逃避自己的義務。說他過去的人生非常邪惡，這話絕對不假，但從另一方面來說，只要處理跟超自然有關的任何事情，他可是再認真負責不過。因此，接下來的三個星期六，他照常在午夜到凌晨三點之間穿越走廊，並盡可能採取一切預防措施不被人看見或聽到。他脫下靴子，盡可能輕手輕腳地踩

過被蟲蛀蝕的老舊地板，穿上寬大的黑色絲絨斗篷，並仔細使用日升潤滑油為自己的鎖鍊上油。我必須承認，他可是費了好大一番功夫才讓自己接受、改用這種保護模式——有天晚上，他甚至在這家人吃晚餐時，潛入公使夫婦的臥房，帶走那瓶潤滑油。起初他覺得有點受辱，隨後便明智領會到這項發明有許多好處，而且在一定程度上符合他的需求。

　　然而，儘管一切順心，他仍持續受到騷擾。走廊上不斷出現橫越的細繩，害他在黑暗中被絆倒。有一回，他扮成「黑艾札克——哈格利樹林的獵人」時，不小心踏上了一片塗滿奶油的滑坡，導致嚴重跌跤；滑坡從掛毯室的入口延伸到橡木樓梯頂端，那是雙胞胎打造的「傑作」。這項侮辱之舉深深觸怒了他，他決心做最後一次努力，以維自己的尊嚴和社會地位，因此決定在第二天晚上以他著名的「魯莽的魯柏特——無頭伯爵」扮相，前去拜訪這兩個無禮的年輕伊頓公學學生。

　　他已經超過七十年不曾以這個裝扮現身了；事實上，自從他靠這副扮相嚇得美麗的芭芭拉‧莫迪胥小姐花容失色後，就不曾再用過。莫迪胥小姐受到驚嚇後，很突然地與現任坎特維爾勛爵的祖父解除婚約，改與英俊的傑克‧卡索頓私奔到格雷特納綠地⑦成婚；她宣稱這世上沒有什麼東西，能誘使她嫁入一個「任憑如此駭人的幽靈，於暮色蒼茫時分在露臺徘徊」的家庭。隨後不久，可憐的傑克在旺茲沃思公共草地與坎特維爾勛爵決鬥時丟了小命，莫迪胥小姐則在同年年底心碎而死，病故於唐橋井。因此從任何角度來看，這次的行動可算是非常成功。

　　然而，這副扮相需要極為困難的「化妝」（假如我可以用此種戲劇表演詞彙，來描述「超自然界」其中一項最大的謎團，或者用更科學的說法是「更高的自然世界」），得耗費他整整三個小時張羅準備。終於，一切全都準備就緒，他對自己的樣貌很滿意——搭配服裝的大型皮革馬靴比他的尺寸稍大了些，

並且只找到一對馬槍當中的一支；不過整體而言，他很滿意。

於是在凌晨一點一刻，他滑出壁板，悄悄走下走廊。抵達雙胞胎住的那間房間時（我得提一下，這間房因房裡幃幔的顏色而被命名為「藍色臥房」），他發現房門僅虛掩著。他猛地推開房門，希望來個令人難忘的出場，結果一大壺水倒在他身上，淋得他渾身濕透，水壺更是只差幾英寸就打中他左肩。在同一時刻，他聽見四柱床那邊傳來壓抑的尖聲大笑。他的精神大受打擊，因而用盡全力逃回自己的房間，翌日則因患了重感冒而臥床。整個事件唯一讓他感到安慰的是，幸好他沒有帶著頭去，否則後果可能不堪設想。如今，他已完全放棄想嚇唬這個粗魯無禮美國家庭的念頭，並設法求全地讓自己穿著鑲有滾邊的無聲拖鞋在走廊上爬行；用一條紅色厚圍巾包住喉嚨免得受風寒；並隨身攜帶一把小型火繩槍，以防遭到雙胞胎的攻擊。

然而，最後一擊發生在九月十九日。他下樓，來到宏偉的大廳，內心很確定無論如何自己在那裡不會受到騷擾。牆面原本高掛著坎特維爾家族的畫像，如今換成了美國公使夫婦的大型沙龍照，他自顧自地對著照片指指點點，嘲諷取樂。他只簡單穿了件俐落的壽衣，上頭還帶有教堂墓地的點點霉斑，手上提了盞小提燈，還拿著一把教堂司事的鏟子。其實，這副扮相是坎特維爾家族有充分理由得牢記、也是他最著名的模仿角色「無墳的約拿——雀西穀倉的盜屍者」，因為它是坎特維爾家族與鄰居拉佛德勛爵發生爭吵的真正起因。此時大約凌晨兩點一刻，就他能確定的範圍而言，沒有人被吵醒。當他悠閒地朝書房走去，想查看血跡是否還有丁點殘留，突然間從黑暗的角落竄出兩條人影朝他跳來，雙手高舉過頭瘋狂揮舞，還朝他的耳朵放聲「噓」他！

在那樣的情況下，驚慌失措是再自然不過的事，他急急衝向樓梯，沒想到華盛頓·歐提斯已經拿著園藝噴霧器在那裡等

著他；由於四面八方皆受敵人圍堵，幾乎陷入絕境，他只好從巨大的燒柴鐵爐逃走；幸運的是，當時爐中沒有點火，接著取道排煙管和煙囪。回到自己的房間時，他不僅全身覆滿煙塵，心情也騷動不安，灰心絕望。

這起事件之後，再也沒人見過他夜間巡遊。雙胞胎多次埋伏，打算偷襲他，而且每天晚上都在走廊上撒滿堅果外殼（此舉惹來雙親和眾僕役的惱怒不快），卻一無所獲。顯然坎特維爾之鬼的情感受到嚴重傷害，心灰意冷，不想再現身了。公使因而恢復他撰寫民主黨史的大業，此事已進行了多年。歐提斯夫人則舉辦了一場精采的烤蛤蜊宴，讓全郡仕紳無不為之驚豔——男孩們打曲棍球、玩尤克牌和撲克牌，從事各項美國國技；維吉妮亞則由年輕的柴郡公爵陪同，騎著她的矮種馬在鄉間小道上閒逛，這位公爵特地前來坎特維爾大宅消磨他最後一週的假期。眾人普遍認為那個鬼魂已經離開了，公使還為此寫信給坎特維爾勛爵，對方回信表示很高興聽到這個消息，並向公使可敬的妻子致上最高的祝賀。

其實，歐提斯一家人被騙了，因為老鬼仍舊在大宅中，儘管如今幾乎是個廢人，但他並未打算罷手，尤其在他得知賓客中有年輕的柴郡公爵這號人物後。

柴郡公爵的叔公弗朗西斯・史帝爾頓勛爵，曾與卡伯利旅長打賭一百個基尼，說自己願和坎特維爾之鬼擲骰子，結果次日清晨他被人發現全身麻痺地躺在棋牌室地板上，儘管後來仍活到很高的歲數，但自那之後除了「雙六」，無法開口說出任何話語。當時出於尊重這兩個貴族家庭的感受而努力不讓這件事傳揚出去，但依舊鬧得人盡皆知；關於這件事的完整始末，可以在塔透勛爵的攝政王及其友人回憶錄的第三卷找到。

因著這段往事，老鬼自然急於證明他對史帝爾頓家族的影響力不減當年。其實，他與那個家族算是遠房親戚，他的大堂

姊由於再婚，嫁給了德畢魯凱雷先生，而所有人都知道，那位年輕的柴郡公爵正是他的直系後裔。因此，他計畫以「吸血鬼修士——冷酷無情的本篤會修士」這個遠近馳名的扮相，出現在維吉妮亞的小情人面前。這個扮相十分恐怖，曾在一七六四年的最後一天晚上被史塔厄普夫人瞧見。她放聲發出最刺耳的尖叫，結果導致極嚴重的中風；並在剝奪坎特維爾家族這個與她最親的近親繼承權後，隨即將所有財產留給她在倫敦的藥劑師，之後不出三天就病故了。然而到了最後一刻，出於對雙胞胎的畏懼，老鬼還是無法跨出自己的房間，而年輕的柴郡公爵就這麼安穩地睡在皇家臥房那張巨大羽毛罩篷底下，夢見他的維吉妮亞。

# 5

　　幾天後，維吉妮亞和她的鬈髮護花使者前往卜洛克利卓原騎馬，穿越樹籬時，身上的騎馬裝勾破了好幾處。因此，回到家後，她決定從後方樓梯上樓，免得被人看見。當跑過掛毯室時，房門恰好開著，她覺得自己看見裡頭有人，以為是母親的女僕（對方時常把工作帶來這裡做），於是她往內探頭，想請女僕幫忙縫補衣服的破洞。教她大出意料的是，那人竟是坎特維爾鬼魂本尊！他坐在窗邊，看著轉黃的樹木在空中翻飛得斑駁金黃，還有紅葉在長長的林蔭道上狂舞。他隻手撐著自己斜倚的頭，整個人散發出一種極度抑鬱的態度。真的，他看起來是如此孑然無依，如此萎靡不振，讓小維吉妮亞打消拔腿逃走、將自己反鎖在房內這第一個念頭。她心中轉而充滿悲憫之情，決定嘗試安慰他。她的腳步是如此輕盈，而他的憂思是如此沉鬱，致使他渾然不覺她在場，直到她開口對他說話。

　　「我對你很過意不去，」她說，「不過，我弟弟明天就會回伊頓去了。接下來，只要你安分守己，就不會有人來打擾你。」

「要我安分守己真是太荒唐了，」他環顧四周，驚訝地發現冒險向他提出建議的，是個漂亮的小女孩，於是他應道，「這太荒謬了。我必須讓自己身上的鎖鍊錚錚作響，透過鑰匙孔發出呻吟聲，在夜半時分四處走動——如果你指的是這些事的話，那是我存在的唯一理由。」

「那才不是什麼生存的理由，你知道你自己向來都很邪惡。阿姆尼太太在我們剛搬來的第一天就告訴我們，你親手殺了自己的妻子。」維吉妮亞駁斥。

「沒錯，我承認。」他大發脾氣地說道，「但那純粹是家務事，與外人無關。」

「殺害任何人都是滔天大罪。」維吉妮亞回道。她有時會顯露出一種討人喜歡的清教徒嚴肅態度，這繼承自她過去的新英格蘭祖先。

「噢，我恨透了那種廉價又嚴苛的抽象道德感！我的妻子非常平庸，從來漿不好我的輪狀皺褶領，廚藝也一竅不通。啊，有一次我在哈格利樹林獵到一頭雄偉的兩歲雄鹿，你知道她是怎麼料理牠的嗎？無論如何，現在那都不重要了，因為那已經過去了。況且，雖然我殺了她，但我認為我妻舅把我活活餓死，也算不上什麼仁慈之舉。」老鬼氣憤地說。

「活活餓死你？噢，鬼魂先生，我是說賽門爵爺，您肚子餓嗎？我的包包裡有份三明治，您想吃嗎？」

「謝謝你，不用了，我現在永遠不必吃東西了，但還是非常謝謝你。比起你家其他那些不友善、野蠻沒教養、行為不端正的家人，你實在善良多了。」老鬼溫聲道。

「別這麼說！」維吉妮亞一邊跺腳，一邊喊道，「野蠻沒教養又不友善的人是你才對，至於行為不端正，你很清楚你從我的盒子裡偷了顏料，試圖恢復書房裡那可笑的血跡。起初，你拿走我所有的紅色系顏料（包括朱紅色），害我再也無法描

繪日落；接下來，你拿走祖母綠和鉻黃；最後，除了靛青和鋅白，我已經沒有別的顏色可用，所以只能畫月下場景——那教人看了有多鬱悶啊，而且還很難畫。雖然我覺得非常困擾，但我從來沒有揭發你。這整件事實在太可笑了，試問有誰聽說過祖母綠的血液呢？」

「這個嘛，你說得沒錯。」老鬼的語氣變得相當軟弱，「但我還能怎麼辦呢？如今，要取得貨真價實的血液是很不容易的，況且是你哥哥先用他的模範清潔劑發動這整件事，我實在看不出有什麼理由我不該用你的顏料。至於顏色，這始終是品味的問題；比方，坎特維爾家族擁有藍血，而且是全英格蘭最藍的血液⑧。不過，我明白你們美國人不在乎這種事。」

「你根本不了解美國，你能做的最佳選擇就是移居美國，拓展你的心胸。我父親會很樂意提供你免費的船票，儘管每一種烈酒⑨的關稅都很高，但打點海關不是難事，因為海關官員全是民主黨人。等到了紐約，你肯定會大紅大紫。我知道那裡有很多人願意花十萬美金買個祖父，當然樂於用更高的價錢買下家族幽靈。」維吉妮亞回道。

「我想我不會喜歡美國的。」老鬼嘆道。

「我猜，是因為我們沒有廢墟，沒有奇珍古玩吧。」維吉妮亞挖苦地說。

「沒有廢墟！沒有異寶奇珍！」老鬼應道，「但你們有海軍和粗鄙。」

「晚安。我這就去跟爸爸央求，讓雙胞胎多放一個星期的假。」

「維吉妮亞小姐，求你別去，」他大喊道，「我好孤單，好不快樂，我真的不知道該怎麼辦。我想好好睡一覺，卻辦不到。」

「那太荒謬啦！你只要上床躺好，吹熄蠟燭不就得了。有時候，保持清醒才是非常困難的事呢，尤其是上教堂的時候。

但入睡這種事根本一點難度也沒有。啊，就連小嬰兒都知道該怎麼做，而他們還算不上聰明呢。」維吉妮亞不可置信地說。

「可是我已經有三百年沒睡覺了，」他哀怨地說道，這話聽得維吉妮亞一雙漂亮的藍眼睛因吃驚而睜得老大。「這三百年來，我不曾入睡，我好累。」

維吉妮亞露出擔憂的嚴肅神情，她的雙唇像玫瑰葉子般抖個不停。她走向他，在他身旁跪下，抬頭望向他蒼老枯槁的臉龐。

「可憐的鬼魂，」她低聲說道；「你沒有地方可以安眠嗎？」

「在松樹林外的遠處，」老鬼用低沉又出神的聲音說，「有座小花園。那兒的青草長得又長又密，到處都是鐵杉花的白色星芒，還有夜鶯徹夜高歌。一整晚牠吟唱不絕，清冷透明的月娘往下俯瞰，紅豆杉會張開它巨大的臂膀保護安眠者。」

維吉妮亞的雙眼被淚水濡濕了，她把臉埋在雙手當中。「你說的是死亡花園。」她低聲說道。

「沒錯，死亡。死亡必定是非常美麗的事。躺在鬆軟的泥土地中，任憑青草在你頭上擺動，聆聽著寂靜之聲。既沒有昨日，也沒有未來。忘卻時間，寬恕生命，平靜安寧。你可以幫助我。你可以為我打開死亡之屋的大門，因為愛永遠伴隨在你左右，而且愛的力量比死更強大。」老鬼懇求著。

維吉妮亞不停地顫抖，一股冰冷的恐懼感流遍她全身，靜默持續了片刻。她感覺自己彷彿困在一場可怕的噩夢中。

接著老鬼又開口說話了，他的聲音像風的嘆息：「你看過書房窗戶上的古老預言嗎？」

「噢，我看過很多遍，」小女孩抬起頭大聲說道，「我知道得一清二楚。它是用奇特的黑色字體寫成，不太容易辨認。內容只有短短六句——『當一個成功而受人喜愛的女孩贏得罪人口中的祈願，當無法結果的杏樹開花結果，有個小孩為他流

淚，整座大宅都將安靜沉默，和平將降臨坎特維爾。』不過，我不明白它們指的是什麼。」

「那意思是說，」老鬼哀傷地解釋著，「你必須為我的罪惡哭泣，因為我沒有眼淚；同時還要為我的靈魂祈禱，因為我沒有信仰。如果你能永保體貼、善良與溫柔，那麼死亡天使將會憐憫我。你會在黑暗中看見可怕的朦朧影像，還會聽見邪惡的聲音在你耳中低語，但它們傷害不了你，因為地獄的力量無法擊敗小孩的純潔。」

維吉妮亞默不作聲，鬼魂低下頭看著她低垂的金髮，無比絕望地扭絞著雙手。突然間她站起身來，臉色無比蒼白，眼中卻散發奇異的光彩。「我才不怕，」她堅定地表示，「我會懇求天使饒恕你。」

他發出一聲微弱的開心歡呼，從自己的座位起身，牽起她的手，微傾他老派的優雅之姿，並親吻它。他的手指冷如冰，而他的唇熱如火。褪色的綠色掛毯上繡著小小獵人，他們吹響飾有流蘇的號角，並向她揮動雙手，敦請她別往前走，他們放聲喊道：「小維吉妮亞，回去，快回去！」可是老鬼把她的手抓得更緊了些，她則閉上雙眼不去看他們。長著蜥蜴尾巴、瞪大了眼睛的駭人動物，從雕花壁爐架朝她眨眼並低聲咕噥著：「當心哪，小維吉妮亞，要小心提防，我們可能再也看不到你了。」可惜老鬼滑行得更快了，因此維吉妮亞並沒有聽見他們的警告。

當他倆抵達房間的盡頭，他停下腳步，嘀嘀咕咕地說了些她無法理解的字眼。維吉妮亞睜開雙眼，看見眼前那道牆像一片霧那樣緩緩消失，露出了一個巨大的黑色洞穴。一陣刺骨寒風襲來，她感覺到有什麼東西正在拉扯她的洋裝。老鬼喊道：「快點，動作快點，否則就太遲了。」剎那間，壁板在他倆背後完全關上，掛毯室裡空無一人。

# 6

　　約莫十分鐘後，午茶的鐘響了。維吉妮亞沒有下樓，歐提斯夫人派男僕上去叫她。過了一會兒，男僕回來稟報，說到處都找不著小姐。由於維吉妮亞習慣每天傍晚到花園裡摘花裝飾餐桌，歐提斯夫人起初一點也不驚慌，可是等到六點鐘響，維吉妮亞仍舊杳無蹤影，她這才真正開始焦慮。她讓男孩們到外頭找維吉妮亞，他們夫妻則搜索屋內的每個房間。六點半的時候，男孩們回來了，說到處都找不到維吉妮亞的蹤跡。

　　此刻，他們全都惶惶不安，卻不知該怎麼辦才好。這時，公使突然想起幾天前，他允許一群吉普賽人在大宅的園林紮營露宿，因此立刻帶著長子和兩名農僕動身前往黑色丘陵凹地，他知道他們打算在那裡露營。那位年輕的柴郡公爵焦慮得快要抓狂，他懇求公使准許他一同前往，但公使擔心發生打鬥而不許他跟。

　　當他們抵達時，發現吉普賽人已經離開，但顯然走得相當倉卒，因為營火尚未完全熄滅，有些盤子還留在草地上。他派華盛頓和兩名農僕細細搜索這個區域，自己則跑回家，打電報給郡內的所有巡官，請他們留意一個小女孩被流浪漢或吉普賽人綁架了。

　　公使隨即命人牽來馬匹，同時堅決要求妻子與三個男孩坐下來吃晚餐，而後在馬夫的陪伴下，騎著馬走下亞思科路。然而，還沒離開幾英里遠，就聽見背後有人騎馬飛奔而來，他回頭張望，看見年輕的公爵騎著他的矮種馬接近，滿臉脹紅，沒戴帽子。

　　「實在很抱歉，歐提斯先生，」男孩喘得上氣不接下氣，「可是只要沒找著維吉妮亞，我就吃不下任何東西。請您不要生我的氣，如果去年您答應我們訂婚，可能就不會有這場騷動

了。拜託，您不會叫我回去吧？我不能回去！我不願回去！」

公使忍不住對這名年輕英俊的無賴微笑，為這年輕人對自己女兒的傾慕深受感動，因此從自己的駿馬俯身，親切地拍拍工爵的肩膀，說：「噢，賽索，如果你不願回去，我想你得跟我來，但是我必須在亞思科幫你買頂帽子。」

「噢，別管我的帽子了！我只求維吉妮亞平安！」年輕的公爵笑著大聲嚷道，接著一行人便朝火車站奔馳前進。公使在火車站詢問站長，是否曾在月臺上看見符合維吉妮亞形貌的女孩，卻得不到任何相關的消息。不過，站長通知了沿線各站，並保證將嚴加留意有無她的形影。

接著，公使在一間正要打烊的亞麻織品零售店，為年輕的公爵買下一頂帽子，便直接騎馬前往大約四英里外的貝克斯里。有人告訴他，這個村莊是吉普賽人經常出沒的地方，旁邊就是一處大型公共草地。他們喚醒村裡的警察，卻沒能得到任何資訊。騎馬找遍了整片公共草地後，他們調轉馬頭，往家的方向走。回到大宅已是晚間十一點左右，不僅精疲力竭，也悲痛欲絕。他們發現華盛頓和雙胞胎提著提燈在門房那裡等待，因為整條路非常黑暗。沒人找到維吉妮亞的半點蹤跡。

那些吉普賽人在卜洛克利草原被攔下來時，並未見到維吉妮亞和他們在一起，而他們之所以突然離開，是因為記錯了丘頓市集的日期，怕趕不上，才匆匆拔營上路。他們聽說維吉妮亞失蹤這件事也覺得很難過，由於非常感謝公使允許他們在園林中紮營，便決定派四個人留下來幫忙找人。鯉魚池已經被抽乾，整座宅邸也被徹底搜索過，但依舊一無所獲。顯然無論如何，這天晚上他們是找不到維吉妮亞了。公使和男孩們全都意志消沉、悶悶不樂地走向大宅，馬夫則牽著兩匹馬和那匹矮種馬尾隨在後。

走進大宅，他們看見一群六神無主的僕役，可憐的歐提

斯夫人則躺在書房沙發上,在恐懼和焦慮的雙重折磨下,幾乎要發瘋了,年邁的女管家在她額頭上灑了些提神好聞的香水,以紓緩她的情緒。公使立刻堅持夫人必須吃點東西,便指示僕人為所有的人準備晚餐。這是教人食不下嚥的一餐,幾乎沒有人開口說話,就連一向調皮搗蛋的雙胞胎也嚇壞了,因為他們非常喜歡自己的姊姊。等他們全都用餐完畢,公使不顧年輕公爵苦苦哀求,命他們所有的人進房睡覺,因為這天晚上已經沒辦法再多做些什麼了。等到明天一早,他會打電報給蘇格蘭警場,請他們立刻派些探員過來。

當他們陸續離開飯廳之際,鐘塔開始傳來午夜的報時聲,最後一聲鐘響後,他們聽見一陣砰然巨響和一聲突如其來的尖叫聲;一陣轟隆隆的落雷撼動整間屋子,空氣中傳來一首不屬於這塵世的音樂。樓梯頂端有塊鑲板飛了回來,發出巨響,維吉妮亞竟從那堆落在地上的東西當中走了出來,她看上去臉色蒼白且滿身灰塵,手中還拿著一只小珠寶盒。剎那間,他們全都衝到她身邊。歐提斯夫人激動地緊抓住她的手臂,公爵狂熱地吻得她透不過氣來,雙胞胎則是繞著這群人瘋狂地跳著戰舞。

「老天!孩子,你上哪兒去了?」公使相當生氣地質問著,認定她在玩某種愚蠢的鬼把戲。「賽索和我騎馬跑遍全國各地去找你,你母親嚇得要死。以後不許再這樣惡作劇了。」

「除了對付鬼魂!除了對付鬼魂!」雙胞胎雀躍地邊叫邊跳。

「我親愛的,感謝老天,終於找到你了;從今以後,你絕不許再離開我身旁一步。」歐提斯夫人低聲說著,她親吻這個顫抖的孩子,並且順了順她糾結的金髮。

「爸爸,」維吉妮亞沉著地說,「我一直跟那個鬼魂在一起。如今他死了,您一定要來看看他。過去他作惡多端,但是他真心懺悔從前的種種作為。他在臨死前交給了我這盒漂亮的珠寶。」

全家人驚愕地瞪著她，一聲不響，但她的態度很嚴肅認真，說完便轉身帶領大家穿過壁板的孔洞，走下一條狹窄的祕密走道；華盛頓則從餐桌上隨手抓了一根點著的蠟燭，尾隨著她。最後，他們來到一扇巨大的橡木門前，上頭滿是生鏽的釘子。當維吉妮亞伸手輕推，它便倚著沉重的鉸鍊往內打開，接著他們發現自己身在一間低矮的小房間內，裡頭有著拱形的天花板和一扇很小的鐵窗。一副巨大的鐵環嵌在牆上，被鎖鍊拴住的是一具可怕的骸骨，它在石板地上竭盡所能地伸展，似乎想用它削瘦的細長手指嘗試抓取那組老式的大木盤和廣口水罐，偏偏它們正好放在它搆不著的地方。那水罐顯然曾經裝了水，因為裡頭滿是綠黴。大木盤上除了一層灰，什麼也沒有。維吉妮亞跪在那副骸骨旁邊，小手交握，開始靜靜地禱告；其他人則驚訝地凝視這慘不忍睹的悲劇，這屋子裡的祕密如今在他們面前公開了。

「啊！」雙胞胎的其中一個突然驚呼了起來。他一直往窗外望，期望確認這個房間位在大宅的哪一側。「啊，那棵枯萎的老杏樹開花了耶，我可以在月光下清楚看見它的花。」

「上帝原諒他了。」維吉妮亞鄭重地表示。當她站起身，一束柔和的光照亮了她的臉龐。

「你真是個天使！」年輕公爵讚嘆道，他用手臂圈住她的脖子，溫柔地親吻她。

# 7

這些離奇事件發生四天後，一隊送葬行列在晚間十一點左右從坎特維爾大宅出發。靈車由八匹黑駿馬拉動，每一匹的頭上都戴著一大簇搖曳的鴕鳥羽毛，而沉重的棺木上頭則覆蓋著一襲深紫色的棺罩，飾以用金色繡線繡成的坎特維爾家族盾形紋章。眾多僕役手持點燃的火炬走在靈車和四輪大馬車旁，整

支送殯隊伍盛大而莊嚴，讓人留下深刻印象。

坎特維爾勛爵是主祭，他特地從威爾斯前來參加喪禮，並且和小維吉妮亞同坐第一輛馬車。接下來是美國公使夫婦，再來是華盛頓和三個男孩。最後一輛馬車坐的則是阿姆尼太太，眾人普遍認為，既然她五十多年來一直飽受大宅鬼魂的驚嚇，當然有權去看他最後一眼。

教堂墓地一角已經挖好一個很深的墓穴，恰好位在紅豆杉下方，教區牧師奧各司特斯・丹皮爾以最隆重的方式誦讀葬禮禱告文。禮成之後，眾僕役根據坎特維爾家族奉行的一項古老習俗，熄滅了手上的火炬；而當棺木緩緩降下到墓穴中時，維吉妮亞走上前，將一只用白色與粉紅色杏花打造而成的大型十字架花圈放在棺木上。就在這一刻，月亮從雲朵後方走出來，銀色月光靜靜灑落在這座小墓園的每個角落，遠處矮林傳來一隻夜鶯的輕聲啼唱。維吉妮亞想起鬼魂所描述的死亡花園，淚水不禁模糊了她的雙眼，乘馬車返家的路上，她幾乎一個字也沒說。

次日清晨，趁坎特維爾勛爵動身進城之前，公使找他談談該如何處置鬼魂留給維吉妮亞的那些珠寶──它們全都無比瑰麗，尤其其中一條威尼斯風格的紅寶石項鍊，無疑是十六世紀精湛工藝的典範。它們是如此價值連城，公使因而相當遲疑該不該同意自己的女兒收下這些珍寶。

他說：「大人，我明白在這個國家，永久管業權⑧不僅適用於土地，也適用於動產。我很清楚，這些珠寶理應是您家族的傳家寶。因此，我必須拜託您將它們帶到倫敦去，請將它們視為在某種奇特情況下回到您手上的財產。小女還只是個孩子，我很高興能這樣說──她對這種無益的奢華配件還不太感興趣。內人告訴我，雖然她不是什麼厲害的藝術品專家，不過年輕時曾有幸在波士頓度過好幾個冬天，因此還算識貨，她說

這些珠寶值很多錢，倘若出售，肯定能賣得高價。

　　「基於這些情況，坎特維爾勛爵，我想您一定了解我無法同意我的家人繼續保有它們。況且，無論這些無用的華麗飾物與小玩意兒對英國貴族而言有多適合或多必要，它們和成長於樸實無華環境的人實在格格不入，我只相信不朽與共和的簡樸原則。

　　「或許我該提一下，維吉妮亞很渴望您能允許她保留那只盒子當作紀念品，以此緬懷您那位誤入歧途的不幸但祖先。由於它非常老舊，年久失修，您也許能應允她的請求。於我而言，我得坦承我很驚訝，沒想到我的孩子會同情任何樣態的中世紀時期古人，我只能將它歸因於──維吉妮亞，是內人有次出訪雅典後，回到倫敦郊區後不久便產下她的這件事實。」

　　坎特維爾勛爵非常認真聆聽這位可敬公使的長篇大論，還不時撫弄自己灰白的鬍鬚，以掩飾他藏忍不住的微笑。當公使終於說完之後，他由衷握了握對方的手，說道：「我敬愛的先生，您可愛的千金為我不幸的祖先賽門爵爺提供了非常重要的協助，我和我的家人全都非常感謝她無與倫比的勇氣和膽量。這些珠寶顯然屬於她。更何況，我相信如果我敢沒心沒肺地把它們從她手中拿走，那邪惡的老傢伙肯定會在兩個星期內從墳墓裡爬出來，把我扭送冥府。至於說它們是傳家寶嘛，傳家寶絕不可能沒在遺囑或法律文件中被提及，但根本沒人知道這些珠寶的存在。

　　「我向您保證，我跟您的男管家一樣無權得到它們，況且等到維吉妮亞小姐長大後，我敢打包票，她肯定會很開心有漂亮的飾品可戴。此外，歐提斯先生您忘了，之前您不是將家具和鬼魂都列入估價當中嗎，所以屬於那鬼魂的任何東西也就同時轉讓給您了。無論賽門爵爺晚上會在走廊上做出什麼舉動，就法律觀點來說，他早就死了，而您則是透過購買取得了他的

財產。」

公使對於坎特維爾勛爵拒絕接受自己的提議感到非常苦惱，再三央求他重新考慮，可惜這位脾氣絕佳的貴族態度相當堅定，最後甚至反過來促成公使同意讓自己女兒保有鬼魂饋贈她的禮物。

一八九〇年春天，年輕的柴郡公爵夫人成婚之際，在女王的第一會客室被引介給其他人的時候，她身上配戴的珠寶成了眾人豔羨的共通話題。維吉妮亞得到了小冠冕，那是對所有善良美國小女孩的獎勵，並在男方達到法定年齡時嫁給了她孩提時的戀人。他倆如此登對並且深愛著彼此，除了鄧不勒頓侯爵夫人和美國公使，眾人莫不為他們結為連理感到開心。

原來，鄧不勒頓侯爵夫人一直努力想為自己七個待字閨中的女兒逮住柴郡公爵，並為此至少舉辦了三場昂貴的晚宴。至於美國公使，說來也怪，他私底下其實非常喜歡這名年輕公爵，但理論上他並不贊成封侯賜爵這套制度，用他自己的話來說，那便是——「受到喜愛享樂的貴族階級團團包圍，置身在萎靡不振的影響之下，不禁讓人憂慮真正的共和簡樸原則可能會被遺忘。」儘管如此，他的反對完全無效，而且我相信，當女兒倚著他的手臂，一同走過漢諾威廣場聖喬治教堂的紅毯時，全英格蘭再也找不到一個比他更驕傲的男人了。

新婚燕爾的公爵夫婦度完蜜月之後，來到了坎特維爾大宅。抵達的當天下午，他們散步來到松林旁邊孤獨的教堂墓地。當初，決定賽門爵爺墓碑碑文該寫些什麼時曾遇上很大的困難，最後決定只刻上這位老先生的名字縮寫，以及書房窗戶上的那首詩。公爵夫人帶來一把漂亮的玫瑰花，將它們撒在墳頭，他們在墳前佇足良久，接著走進老修道院傾頹的聖壇。公爵夫人選了根橫倒的柱子坐下，丈夫則躺在她腳邊，一邊抽著菸，一邊抬頭凝視妻子美麗的雙眼。突然間，他扔掉手上的

菸，握住她的手，說道：「維吉妮亞，為人妻的不該有祕密瞞著丈夫。」

「親愛的賽索，我沒有祕密瞞著你呀！」

「有，你有。」他笑著說，「你從來沒有告訴我，當時你和那鬼魂關在一起時，究竟發生了什麼事？」

「賽索，我從來沒跟任何人說過這件事。」維吉妮亞正色道。

「我知道，但你可以告訴我。」

「賽索，請別要求我這麼做，我不能跟你說。可憐的賽門爵爺，我虧欠他很多。拜託，賽索，別笑，這是真的。他讓我看見什麼是生命，什麼是死亡，還有為什麼愛能超越生與死。」

公爵坐起身，深情地親吻自己的妻子。「只要我能擁有你的心，你儘管保有你的祕密。」他低聲說道。

「賽索，你會永遠擁有的。」維吉妮亞凝視著他。

「有一天你會說給我們的孩子聽，對吧？」公爵微笑地說。

維吉妮亞羞紅了臉。

譯注

① 芬妮・戴溫波特小姐（Miss Fanny Davenport，1850～1898），英裔美籍舞臺劇女演員。

　 莎拉・伯恩哈特（Sarah Bernhardt，1844～1923），法國舞臺劇暨電影女演員。

② 波士頓素有「太陽系樞紐」、「宇宙中心」（The Hub）的美名。王爾德藉此諷刺那備受尊崇、驕傲自滿的波士頓文學與文化圈。

③ 威廉・顧爾爵爺（Sir William Gull，1816～1890），是十九世紀英格蘭著名的醫師。一八七一年，因成功治癒威爾斯親王的傷寒而獲封為從男爵。他曾在倫敦的蓋氏醫院（Guy's

Hospital）擔任主管，對醫學界貢獻至鉅且多，像是增進醫界對黏液水腫、截癱、神經性厭食症等等的認識。

④ 克洛克佛德會所（Crockford's），倫敦最早的紳士俱樂部之一，創立於一八二八年，結束於一八四五年。由於這個會所的消遣活動集中於博奕，聲名並不是太正面。

⑤ 亨利・華茲華斯・郎費羅（Henry Wadsworth Longfellow，1807～1882），美國詩人。這裡影射的是〈盔甲裡的骷髏〉（The Skeleton in Armour）一詩。

⑥ 指伊莉莎白一世。

⑦ 十八世紀的英格蘭，人們必須年滿二十一歲，得到父母同意，且經牧師證婚，婚姻方才生效。同一時間，蘇格蘭的規定則相對寬鬆，只要年滿十六歲，在一個見證人面前立下誓言，婚姻即可成立。格雷特納綠地（Gretna Green），正是最緊鄰英格蘭的蘇格蘭小鎮，因地利之便，成了當時著名的私奔者結婚天堂。

⑧ 藍血，指的是貴族血統。

⑨ Spirit，這裡有兩層意思，暗指「鬼魂」。

⑩ 永久管業權（mortmain），是指土地一旦轉讓給社團（如教會、慈善團體等）後，就不能再被轉讓的一種土地占有狀態。這種情形通常會損害領主的利益，因此英格蘭自一二一五年起便立法防止土地淪為永久管業，直到一九六○年才完全廢止這項規範。

# The Canterville Ghost

## 1

When Mr. Hiram B. Otis, the American Minister, bought Canterville Chase, every one told him he was doing a very foolish thing, as there was no doubt at all that the place was haunted. Indeed, Lord Canterville himself, who was a man of the most punctilious honour, had felt it his duty to mention the fact to Mr. Otis when they came to discuss terms.

'We have not cared to live in the place ourselves,' said Lord Canterville, 'since my grandaunt, the Dowager Duchess of Bolton, was frightened into a fit, from which she never really recovered, by two skeleton hands being placed on her shoulders as she was dressing for dinner, and I feel bound to tell you, Mr. Otis, that the ghost has been seen by several living members of my family, as well as by the rector of the parish, the Rev. Augustus Dampier, who is a Fellow of King's College,

Cambridge. After the unfortunate accident to the Duchess, none of our younger servants would stay with us, and Lady Canterville often got very little sleep at night, in consequence of the mysterious noises that came from the corridor and the library.'

'My Lord,' answered the Minister, 'I will take the furniture and the ghost at a valuation. I come from a modern country, where we have everything that money can buy; and with all our spry young fellows painting the Old World red, and carrying off your best actresses and prima-donnas, I reckon that if there were such a thing as a ghost in Europe, we'd have it at home in a very short time in one of our public museums, or on the road as a show.'

'I fear that the ghost exists,' said Lord Canterville, smiling, 'though it may have resisted the overtures of your enterprising impresarios. It has been well known for three centuries, since 1584 in fact, and always makes its appearance before the death of any member of our family.'

'Well, so does the family doctor for that matter, Lord Canterville. But there is no such thing, sir, as a ghost, and I guess the laws of Nature are not going to be suspended for the British aristocracy.'

'You are certainly very natural in America,' answered Lord Canterville, who did not quite understand Mr. Otis's last observation, 'and if you don't mind a ghost in the house, it is all right. Only you must remember I warned you.'

A few weeks after this, the purchase was completed, and at the close of the season the Minister and his family went down to Canterville Chase. Mrs. Otis, who, as Miss Lucretia R. Tappan, of West 53rd Street, had been a celebrated New York belle, was now a very handsome, middle-aged woman, with fine eyes, and a superb profile. Many American ladies on leaving their native land adopt an appearance of chronic ill-health, under the impression that it is a form of European refinement, but Mrs. Otis had never fallen into this error. She had a magnificent constitution, and a really wonderful amount of animal spirits. Indeed, in many respects, she was quite English, and was an excellent example of the fact that we have really everything in common with America nowadays, except, of course, language. Her eldest son, christened Washington by his parents in a moment of patriotism, which he never ceased to regret, was a fair-haired, rather good-looking young man, who had qualified himself for American diplomacy by leading the German at the Newport Casino for three successive seasons, and even in London was well known as an excellent dancer. Gardenias and the peerage were his only weaknesses. Otherwise he was extremely sensible. Miss Virginia E. Otis was a little girl of fifteen, lithe and lovely as a fawn, and with a fine freedom in her large blue eyes. She was a wonderful amazon, and had once raced old Lord Bilton on her pony twice round the park, winning by a length and a half, just in front of the Achilles statue, to the huge delight of the young Duke of Cheshire, who proposed for her on the spot, and was sent back to Eton that very night by his guardians, in floods of tears. After Virginia came the twins, who were usually called 'The Stars and Stripes,' as they were always getting swished. They were delightful boys, and with the exception of the worthy Minister the only true republicans of the family.

As Canterville Chase is seven miles from Ascot, the nearest railway station, Mr. Otis had telegraphed for a waggonette to meet them, and they started on their drive in high spirits. It was a lovely July evening, and the air was delicate with the scent of the pine-woods. Now and then they heard a wood pigeon brooding over its own sweet voice, or saw, deep in the rustling fern, the burnished breast of the pheasant. Little squirrels peered at them from the beech-trees as they went by, and the rabbits scudded away through the brushwood and over the mossy knolls, with their white tails in the air. As they entered the avenue of Canterville Chase, however, the sky became suddenly overcast with clouds, a curious stillness seemed to hold the atmosphere, a great flight of rooks passed silently over their heads, and, before they reached the house, some big drops

5
1

坎特維爾大宅之鬼 The Canterville Ghost

of rain had fallen.

Standing on the steps to receive them was an old woman, neatly dressed in black silk, with a white cap and apron. This was Mrs. Umney, the housekeeper, whom Mrs. Otis, at Lady Canterville's earnest request, had consented to keep on in her former position. She made them each a low curtsey as they alighted, and said in a quaint, old-fashioned manner, 'I bid you welcome to Canterville Chase.' Following her, they passed through the fine Tudor hall into the library, a long, low room, panelled in black oak, at the end of which was a large stained-glass window. Here they found tea laid out for them, and, after taking off their wraps, they sat down and began to look round, while Mrs. Umney waited on them.

Suddenly Mrs. Otis caught sight of a dull red stain on the floor just by the fireplace and, quite unconscious of what it really signified, said to Mrs. Umney, 'I am afraid something has been spilt there.'

'Yes, madam,' replied the old housekeeper in a low voice, 'blood has been spilt on that spot.'

'How horrid,' cried Mrs. Otis; 'I don't at all care for blood-stains in a sitting-room. It must be removed at once.'

The old woman smiled, and answered in the same low, mysterious voice, 'It is the blood of Lady Eleanore de Canterville, who was murdered on that very spot by her own husband, Sir Simon de Canterville, in 1575. Sir Simon survived her nine years, and disappeared suddenly under very mysterious circumstances. His body has never been discovered, but his guilty spirit still haunts the Chase. The blood-stain has been much admired by tourists and others, and cannot be removed.'

'That is all nonsense,' cried Washington Otis; 'Pinkerton's Champion Stain Remover and Paragon Detergent will clean it up in no time,' and before the terrified housekeeper could interfere he had fallen upon his knees, and was rapidly scouring the floor with a small stick of what looked like a black cosmetic. In a few moments no trace of the blood-stain could be seen.

'I knew Pinkerton would do it,' he exclaimed triumphantly, as he looked round at his admiring family; but no sooner had he said these words than a terrible flash of lightning lit up the sombre room, a fearful peal of thunder made them all start to their feet, and Mrs. Umney fainted.

'What a monstrous climate!' said the American Minister calmly, as he lit a long cheroot. 'I guess the old country is so overpopulated that they have not enough decent weather for everybody. I have always been of opinion that emigration is the only thing for England.'

'My dear Hiram,' cried Mrs. Otis, 'what can we do with a woman who faints?'

'Charge it to her like breakages,' answered the Minister; 'she won't faint after that'; and in a few moments Mrs. Umney certainly came to. There was no doubt, however, that she was extremely upset, and she sternly warned Mr. Otis to beware of some trouble coming to the house.

'I have seen things with my own eyes, sir,' she said, 'that would make any Christian's hair stand on end, and many and many a night I have not closed my eyes in sleep for the awful things that are done here.' Mr. Otis, however, and his wife warmly assured the honest soul that they were not afraid of ghosts, and, after invoking the blessings of Providence on her new master and mistress, and making arrangements for an increase of salary, the old housekeeper tottered off to her own room.

## 2

The storm raged fiercely all that night, but nothing of

particular note occurred. The next morning, however, when they came down to breakfast, they found the terrible stain of blood once again on the floor.    'I don't think it can be the fault of the Paragon Detergent,' said Washington,    'for I have tried it with everything. It must be the ghost.' He accordingly rubbed out the stain a second time, but the second morning it appeared again. The third morning also it was there, though the library had been locked up at night by Mr. Otis himself, and the key carried upstairs. The whole family were now quite interested; Mr. Otis began to suspect that he had been too dogmatic in his denial of the existence of ghosts, Mrs. Otis expressed her intention of joining the Psychical Society, and Washington prepared a long letter to Messrs. Myers and Podmore on the subject of the Permanence of Sanguineous Stains when connected with Crime. That night all doubts about the objective existence of phantasmata were removed for ever.

The day had been warm and sunny; and, in the cool of the evening, the whole family went out for a drive. They did not return home till nine o'clock, when they had a light supper. The conversation in no way turned upon ghosts, so there were not even those primary conditions of receptive expectation which so often precede the presentation of psychical phenomena. The subjects discussed, as I have since learned from Mr. Otis, were merely such as form the ordinary conversation of cultured Americans of the better class, such as the immense superiority of Miss Fanny Davenport over Sarah Bernhardt as an actress; the difficulty of obtaining green corn, buckwheat cakes, and hominy, even in the best English houses; the importance of Boston in the development of the world-soul; the advantages of the baggage check system in railway travelling; and the sweetness of the New York accent as compared to the London drawl. No mention at all was made of the supernatural, nor was Sir Simon de Canterville alluded to in any way. At eleven o'clock the family retired, and by half-past all the lights were out. Some time after, Mr. Otis was awakened by a curious noise in the corridor, outside his room. It sounded like the clank of metal, and seemed to be coming nearer every moment. He got up at once, struck a match, and looked at the time. It was exactly one o'clock. He was quite calm, and felt his pulse, which was not at all feverish. The strange noise still continued, and with it he heard distinctly the sound of footsteps. He put on his slippers, took a small oblong phial out of his dressing-case, and opened the door. Right in front of him he saw, in the wan moonlight, an old man of terrible aspect. His eyes were as red burning coals; long grey hair fell over his shoulders in matted coils; his garments, which were of antique cut, were soiled and ragged, and from his wrists and ankles hung heavy manacles and rusty gyves.

'My dear sir,' said Mr. Otis, 'I really must insist on your oiling those chains, and have brought you for that purpose a small bottle of the Tammany Rising Sun Lubricator. It is said to be completely efficacious upon one application, and there are several testimonials to that effect on the wrapper from some of our most eminent native divines. I shall leave it here for you by the bedroom candles, and will be happy to supply you with more should you require it.' With these words the United States Minister laid the bottle down on a marble table, and, closing his door, retired to rest.

For a moment the Canterville ghost stood quite motionless in natural indignation; then, dashing the bottle violently upon the polished floor, he fled down the corridor, uttering hollow groans, and emitting a ghastly green light. Just, however, as he reached the top of the great oak staircase, a door was flung open, two little white-robed figures appeared, and a large pillow whizzed past his head! There was evidently no time to be lost, so, hastily adopting the Fourth Dimension of Space as a means of escape, he vanished through the wainscoting, and the house became quite quiet.

On reaching a small secret chamber in the left wing, he leaned up against a moonbeam to recover his breath, and began to try and realise his position. Never, in a brilliant and uninterrupted career of three hundred years, had he been so grossly insulted. He thought of the Dowager Duchess, whom he had frightened into a fit as she stood before the glass in her lace and diamonds; of the four housemaids, who had gone off into hysterics when he merely grinned at them through the curtains of one of the spare bedrooms; of the rector of the parish, whose candle he had blown out as he was coming late one night from the library, and who had been under the care of Sir William Gull ever since, a perfect martyr to nervous disorders; and of old Madame de Tremouillac, who, having wakened up one morning early and seen a skeleton seated in an arm-chair by the fire reading her diary, had been confined to her bed for six weeks with an attack of brain fever, and, on her recovery, had become reconciled to the Church, and broken off her connection with that notorious sceptic Monsieur de Voltaire. He remembered the terrible night when the wicked Lord Canterville was found choking in his dressing-room, with the knave of diamonds half-way down his throat, and confessed, just before he died, that he had cheated Charles James Fox out of 50,000 pounds at Crockford's by means of that very card, and swore that the ghost had made him swallow it. All his great achievements came back to him again, from the butler who had shot himself in the pantry because he had seen a green hand tapping at the window pane, to the beautiful Lady Stutfield, who was always obliged to wear a black velvet band round her throat to hide the mark of five fingers burnt upon her white skin, and who drowned herself at last in the carp-pond at the end of the King's Walk. With the enthusiastic egotism of the true artist he went over his most celebrated performances, and smiled bitterly to himself as he recalled to mind his last appearance as 'Red Ruben, or the Strangled Babe,' his debut as 'Gaunt Gibeon, the Blood-sucker of Bexley Moor,' and the furore he had excited one lovely June evening by merely playing ninepins with his own bones upon the lawn-tennis ground. And after all this, some wretched modern Americans were to come and offer him the Rising Sun Lubricator, and throw pillows at his head! It was quite unbearable. Besides, no ghosts in history had ever been treated in this manner. Accordingly, he determined to have vengeance, and remained till daylight in an attitude of deep thought.

# 3

The next morning when the Otis family met at breakfast, they discussed the ghost at some length. The United States Minister was naturally a little annoyed to find that his present had not been accepted. 'I have no wish,' he said, 'to do the ghost any personal injury, and I must say that, considering the length of time he has been in the house, I don't think it is at all polite to throw pillows at him'— a very just remark, at which, I am sorry to say, the twins burst into shouts of laughter. 'Upon the other hand,' he continued, 'if he really declines to use the Rising Sun Lubricator, we shall have to take his chains from him. It would be quite impossible to sleep, with such a noise going on outside the bedrooms.'

For the rest of the week, however, they were undisturbed, the only thing that excited any attention being the continual renewal of the blood-stain on the library floor. This certainly was very strange, as the door was always locked at night by Mr. Otis, and the windows kept closely barred. The chameleon-like colour, also, of the stain excited a good deal of comment. Some mornings it was a dull (almost Indian) red, then it would be vermilion, then a rich purple, and once when they came down for family prayers, according to the simple rites of the Free American Reformed Episcopalian Church, they found it a bright emerald-green. These kaleidoscopic changes naturally amused the party very much, and bets on the subject were freely made every evening. The only person who did not enter into the joke was little Virginia, who, for some unexplained reason, was always a good deal distressed at the sight of the blood-stain, and very nearly cried the morning it was emerald-green.

The second appearance of the ghost was on Sunday night. Shortly after they had gone to bed they were suddenly alarmed by a fearful crash in the hall. Rushing downstairs, they found that a large suit of old armour had become detached from its stand, and had fallen on the stone floor, while, seated in a high-backed chair, was the Canterville ghost, rubbing his knees with an expression of acute agony on his face. The twins, having brought their pea-shooters with them, at once discharged two pellets on him, with that accuracy of aim which can only be attained by long and careful practice on a writing-master, while the United States Minister covered him with his revolver, and called upon him, in accordance with Californian etiquette, to hold up his hands! The ghost started up with a wild shriek of rage, and swept through them like a mist, extinguishing Washington Otis's candle as he passed, and so leaving them all in total darkness. On reaching the top of the staircase he recovered himself, and determined to give his celebrated peal of demoniac laughter. This he had on more than one occasion found extremely useful. It was said to have turned Lord Raker's wig grey in a single night, and had certainly made three of Lady Canterville's French governesses give warning before their month was up. He accordingly laughed his most horrible laugh, till the old vaulted roof rang and rang again, but hardly had the fearful echo died away when a door opened, and Mrs. Otis came out in a light blue dressing-gown. 'I am afraid you are far from well,' she said, 'and have brought you a bottle of Dr. Dobell's tincture. If it is indigestion, you will find it a most excellent remedy.' The ghost glared at her in fury, and began at once to make preparations for turning himself into a large black dog, an accomplishment for which he was justly renowned, and to which the family doctor always attributed the permanent idiocy of Lord Canterville's uncle, the Hon. Thomas Horton. The sound of approaching footsteps, however, made him hesitate in his fell purpose, so he contented himself with becoming faintly phosphorescent, and vanished with a deep churchyard groan, just as the twins had come up to him.

On reaching his room he entirely broke down, and became a prey to the most violent agitation. The vulgarity of the twins, and the gross materialism of Mrs. Otis, were naturally extremely annoying, but what really distressed him most was, that he had been unable to wear the suit of mail. He had hoped that even modern Americans would be thrilled by the sight of a Spectre In Armour, if for no more sensible reason, at least out of respect for their national poet Longfellow, over whose graceful and attractive poetry he himself had whiled away many a weary hour when the Cantervilles were up in town. Besides, it was his own suit. He had worn it with great success at the Kenilworth tournament, and had been highly complimented on it by no less a person than the Virgin Queen herself. Yet when he had put it on, he had been completely overpowered by the weight of the huge breastplate and steel casque, and had fallen heavily on the stone pavement, barking both his knees severely, and bruising the knuckles of his right hand.

For some days after this he was extremely ill, and hardly stirred out of his room at all, except to keep the blood-stain in proper repair. However, by taking great care of himself, he recovered, and resolved to make a third attempt to frighten the United States Minister and his family. He selected Friday, the 17th of August, for his appearance, and spent most of that day in looking over his wardrobe, ultimately deciding in favour of a large slouched hat with a red feather, a winding-sheet frilled at the wrists and neck, and a rusty dagger. Towards evening a violent storm of rain came on, and the wind was so high that all the windows and doors in the old house shook and rattled. In fact, it was just such weather as he loved. His plan of action was this. He was to make his way quietly to Washington Otis's room, gibber at him from the foot of the bed, and stab himself three times in the throat to the sound of slow music. He bore Washington a special grudge, being quite aware that it was he who was in the habit of removing the famous Canterville blood-stain, by means of Pinkerton's Paragon Detergent. Having reduced the reckless and foolhardy youth to a condition of abject terror, he was then to proceed to the room occupied by the United States Minister and his wife, and there to place a clammy hand on Mrs. Otis's forehead, while he hissed into her trembling husband's ear the awful secrets of the charnel-house. With regard to little Virginia, he had not quite made up his mind. She had never insulted him in any way, and was pretty and gentle. A few hollow groans from the wardrobe, he thought, would be more than sufficient, or, if that failed to wake her, he might grabble at the counterpane with palsy-twitching fingers. As for the twins, he was quite determined to teach them a lesson. The first thing to be done was, of course,

坎特維爾大宅之鬼　The Canterville Ghost

to sit upon their chests, so as to produce the stifling sensation of nightmare. Then, as their beds were quite close to each other, to stand between them in the form of a green, icy-cold corpse, till they became paralysed with fear, and finally, to throw off the winding-sheet, and crawl round the room, with white bleached bones and one rolling eye-ball, in the character of 'Dumb Daniel, or the Suicide's Skeleton,' a role in which he had on more than one occasion produced a great effect, and which he considered quite equal to his famous part of 'Martin the Maniac, or the Masked Mystery.'

At half-past ten he heard the family going to bed. For some time he was disturbed by wild shrieks of laughter from the twins, who, with the light-hearted gaiety of schoolboys, were evidently amusing themselves before they retired to rest, but at a quarter past eleven all was still, and, as midnight sounded, he sallied forth. The owl beat against the window panes, the raven croaked from the old yew-tree, and the wind wandered moaning round the house like a lost soul; but the Otis family slept unconscious of their doom, and high above the rain and storm he could hear the steady snoring of the Minister for the United States. He stepped stealthily out of the wainscoting, with an evil smile on his cruel, wrinkled mouth, and the moon hid her face in a cloud as he stole past the great oriel window, where his own arms and those of his murdered wife were blazoned in azure and gold. On and on he glided, like an evil shadow, the very darkness seeming to loathe him as he passed. Once he thought he heard something call, and stopped; but it was only the baying of a dog from the Red Farm, and he went on, muttering strange sixteenth-century curses, and ever and anon brandishing the rusty dagger in the midnight air. Finally he reached the corner of the passage that led to luckless Washington's room. For a moment he paused there, the wind blowing his long grey locks about his head, and twisting into grotesque and fantastic folds the nameless horror of the dead man's shroud. Then the clock struck the quarter, and he felt the time was come. He chuckled to himself, and turned the corner; but no sooner had he done so, than, with a piteous wail of terror, he fell back, and hid his blanched face in his long, bony hands. Right in front of him was standing a horrible spectre, motionless as a carven image, and monstrous as a madman's dream! Its head was bald and burnished; its face round, and fat, and white; and hideous laughter seemed to have writhed its features into an eternal grin. From the eyes streamed rays of scarlet light, the mouth was a wide well of fire, and a hideous garment, like to his own, swathed with its silent snows the Titan form. On its breast was a placard with strange writing in antique characters, some scroll of shame it seemed, some record of wild sins, some awful calendar of crime, and, with its right hand, it bore aloft a falchion of gleaming steel.

Never having seen a ghost before, he naturally was terribly frightened, and, after a second hasty glance at the awful phantom, he fled back to his room, tripping up in his long winding-sheet as he sped down the corridor, and finally dropping the rusty dagger into the Minister's jack-boots, where it was found in the morning by the butler. Once in the privacy of his own apartment, he flung himself down on a small pallet-bed, and hid his face under the clothes. After a time, however, the brave old Canterville spirit asserted itself, and he determined to go and speak to the other ghost as soon as it was daylight. Accordingly, just as the dawn was touching the hills with silver, he returned towards the spot where he had first laid eyes on the grisly phantom, feeling that, after all, two ghosts were better than one, and that, by the aid of his new friend, he might safely grapple with the twins. On reaching the spot, however, a terrible sight met his gaze. Something had evidently happened to the spectre, for the light had entirely faded from its hollow eyes, the gleaming falchion had fallen from its hand, and it was leaning up against the wall in a strained and uncomfortable attitude. He rushed forward and seized it in his arms, when, to his horror, the head slipped off and rolled on the floor, the body assumed a recumbent posture, and he found himself clasping a white dimity bed-curtain, with a sweeping-brush, a kitchen cleaver, and a hollow turnip lying at his feet! Unable to understand this curious transformation, he clutched the placard with feverish haste, and there, in the grey morning light, he read these fearful words:—

坎特維爾大宅之鬼 The Canterville Ghost

YE OLDE GHOSTE

Ye Onlie True and Originale Spook.

Beware of Ye Imitationes.

All others are Counterfeite.

The whole thing flashed across him. He had been tricked, foiled, and outwitted! The old Canterville look came into his eyes; he ground his toothless gums together; and, raising his withered hands high above his head, swore, according to the picturesque phraseology of the antique school, that when Chanticleer had sounded twice his merry horn, deeds of blood would be wrought, and Murder walk abroad with silent feet.

Hardly had he finished this awful oath when, from the red-tiled roof of a distant homestead, a cock crew. He laughed a long, low, bitter laugh, and waited. Hour after hour he waited, but the cock, for some strange reason, did not crow again. Finally, at half-past seven, the arrival of the housemaids made him give up his fearful vigil, and he stalked back to his room, thinking of his vain hope and baffled purpose. There he consulted several books of ancient chivalry, of which he was exceedingly fond, and found that, on every occasion on which his oath had been used, Chanticleer had always crowed a second time. 'Perdition seize the naughty fowl,' he muttered, 'I have seen the day when, with my stout spear, I would have run him through the gorge, and made him crow for me an 'twere in death!' He then retired to a comfortable lead coffin, and stayed there till evening.

4

The next day the ghost was very weak and tired. The terrible excitement of the last four weeks was beginning to have its effect. His nerves were completely shattered, and he started at the slightest noise. For five days he kept his room, and at last made up his mind to give up the point of the blood-stain on the library floor. If the Otis family did not want it, they clearly did not deserve it. They were evidently people on a low, material plane of existence, and quite incapable of appreciating the symbolic value of sensuous phenomena. The question of phantasmic apparitions, and the development of astral bodies, was of course quite a different matter, and really not under his control. It was his solemn duty to appear in the corridor once a week, and to gibber from the large oriel window on the first and third Wednesday in every month, and he did not see how he could honourably escape from his obligations. It is quite true that his life had been very evil, but, upon the other hand, he was most conscientious in all things connected with the supernatural. For the next three Saturdays, accordingly, he traversed the corridor as usual between midnight and three o'clock, taking every possible precaution against being either heard or seen. He removed his boots, trod as lightly as possible on the old worm-eaten boards, wore a large black velvet cloak, and was careful to use the Rising Sun Lubricator for oiling his chains. I am bound to acknowledge that it was with a good deal of difficulty that he brought himself to adopt this last mode of protection. However, one night, while the family were at dinner, he slipped into Mr. Otis's bedroom and carried off the bottle. He felt a little humiliated at first, but afterwards was sensible enough to see that there was a great deal to be said for the invention, and, to a certain degree, it served his purpose. Still, in spite of everything, he was not left unmolested. Strings were continually being stretched across the corridor, over which he tripped in the dark, and on one occasion, while dressed for the part of 'Black Isaac, or the Huntsman of Hogley Woods,' he met with a severe fall, through treading on a butter-slide, which the twins had constructed from the entrance of the Tapestry Chamber to the top of the oak staircase. This last insult so enraged him, that he resolved to make one final effort to assert his dignity and social position, and determined to visit the insolent young Etonians the next night in his celebrated character of 'Reckless Rupert, or the Headless Earl.'

He had not appeared in this disguise for more than seventy

坎特維爾大宅之鬼 The Canterville Ghost

years; in fact, not since he had so frightened pretty Lady Barbara Modish by means of it, that she suddenly broke off her engagement with the present Lord Canterville's grandfather, and ran away to Gretna Green with handsome Jack Castleton, declaring that nothing in the world would induce her to marry into a family that allowed such a horrible phantom to walk up and down the terrace at twilight. Poor Jack was afterwards shot in a duel by Lord Canterville on Wandsworth Common, and Lady Barbara died of a broken heart at Tunbridge Wells before the year was out, so, in every way, it had been a great success. It was, however, an extremely difficult 'make-up,' if I may use such a theatrical expression in connection with one of the greatest mysteries of the supernatural, or, to employ a more scientific term, the higher-natural world, and it took him fully three hours to make his preparations. At last everything was ready, and he was very pleased with his appearance. The big leather riding-boots that went with the dress were just a little too large for him, and he could only find one of the two horse-pistols, but, on the whole, he was quite satisfied, and at a quarter past one he glided out of the wainscoting and crept down the corridor. On reaching the room occupied by the twins, which I should mention was called the Blue Bed Chamber, on account of the colour of its hangings, he found the door just ajar. Wishing to make an effective entrance, he flung it wide open, when a heavy jug of water fell right down on him, wetting him to the skin, and just missing his left shoulder by a couple of inches. At the same moment he heard stifled shrieks of laughter proceeding from the four-post bed. The shock to his nervous system was so great that he fled back to his room as hard as he could go, and the next day he was laid up with a severe cold. The only thing that at all consoled him in the whole affair was the fact that he had not brought his head with him, for, had he done so, the consequences might have been very serious.

He now gave up all hope of ever frightening this rude American family, and contented himself, as a rule, with creeping about the passages in list slippers, with a thick red muffler round his throat for fear of draughts, and a small arquebuse, in case he should be attacked by the twins. The final blow he received occurred on the 19th of September. He had gone downstairs to the great entrance-hall, feeling sure that there, at any rate, he would be quite unmolested, and was amusing himself by making satirical remarks on the large Saroni photographs of the United States Minister and his wife, which had now taken the place of the Canterville family pictures. He was simply but neatly clad in a long shroud, spotted with churchyard mould, had tied up his jaw with a strip of yellow linen, and carried a small lantern and a sexton's spade. In fact, he was dressed for the character of 'Jonas the Graveless, or the Corpse-Snatcher of Chertsey Barn,' one of his most remarkable impersonations, and one which the Cantervilles had every reason to remember, as it was the real origin of their quarrel with their neighbour, Lord Rufford. It was about a quarter past two o'clock in the morning, and, as far as he could ascertain, no one was stirring. As he was strolling towards the library, however, to see if there were any traces left of the blood-stain, suddenly there leaped out on him from a dark corner two figures, who waved their arms wildly above their heads, and shrieked out 'BOO!' in his ear.

Seized with a panic, which, under the circumstances, was only natural, he rushed for the staircase, but found Washington Otis waiting for him there with the big garden-syringe; and being thus hemmed in by his enemies on every side, and driven almost to bay, he vanished into the great iron stove, which, fortunately for him, was not lit, and had to make his way home through the flues and chimneys, arriving at his own room in a terrible state of dirt, disorder, and despair.

After this he was not seen again on any nocturnal expedition. The twins lay in wait for him on several occasions, and strewed the passages with nutshells every night to the great annoyance of their parents and the servants, but it was of no avail. It was quite evident that his feelings were so wounded that he would not appear. Mr. Otis consequently resumed his great work on the history of the Democratic Party, on which he had been engaged for some years; Mrs. Otis organised a wonderful clam-bake, which amazed the whole county; the boys took to lacrosse, euchre, poker, and other American national games; and Virginia rode about the lanes on her pony, accompanied by the young Duke of Cheshire, who had come to spend the last week of his holidays at Canterville Chase. It was generally assumed that the ghost had gone away, and, in fact, Mr. Otis wrote a letter to that effect to Lord Canterville, who, in reply, expressed his great pleasure at the news, and sent his best congratulations to the Minister's worthy wife.

The Otises, however, were deceived, for the ghost was still in the house, and though now almost an invalid, was by no means ready to let matters rest, particularly as he heard that among the guests was the young Duke of Cheshire, whose grand-uncle, Lord Francis Stilton, had once bet a hundred guineas with Colonel Carbury that he would play dice with the Canterville ghost, and was found the next morning lying on the floor of the card-room in such a helpless paralytic state, that though he lived on to a great age, he was never able to say anything again but 'Double Sixes.' The story was well known at the time, though, of course, out of respect to the feelings of the two noble families, every attempt was made to hush it up; and a full account of all the circumstances connected with it will be found in the third volume of Lord Tattle's Recollections of the Prince Regent and his Friends. The ghost, then, was naturally very anxious to show that he had not lost his influence over the Stiltons, with whom, indeed, he was distantly connected, his own first cousin having been married en secondes noces to the Sieur de Bulkeley, from whom, as every one knows, the Dukes of Cheshire are lineally descended. Accordingly, he made arrangements for appearing to Virginia's little lover in his celebrated impersonation of 'The Vampire Monk, or, the Bloodless Benedictine,' a performance so horrible that when old Lady Startup saw it, which she did on one fatal New Year's Eve, in the year 1764, she went off into the most piercing shrieks, which culminated in violent apoplexy, and died in three days, after disinheriting the Cantervilles, who were her nearest relations, and leaving all her money to her London apothecary. At the last moment, however, his terror of the twins prevented his leaving his room, and the little Duke slept in peace under the great feathered canopy in the Royal Bedchamber, and dreamed of Virginia.

# 5

A few days after this, Virginia and her curly-haired cavalier went out riding on Brockley meadows, where she tore her habit so badly in getting through a hedge, that, on her return home, she made up her mind to go up by the back staircase so as not to be seen. As she was running past the Tapestry Chamber, the door of which happened to be open, she fancied she saw some one inside, and thinking it was her mother's maid, who sometimes used to bring her work there, looked in to ask her to mend her habit. To her immense surprise, however, it was the Canterville Ghost himself! He was sitting by the window, watching the ruined gold of the yellowing trees fly through the air, and the red leaves dancing madly down the long avenue. His head was leaning on his hand, and his whole attitude was one of extreme depression. Indeed, so forlorn, and so much out of repair did he look, that little Virginia, whose first idea had been to run away and lock herself in her room, was filled with pity, and determined to try and comfort him. So light was her footfall, and so deep his melancholy, that he was not aware of her presence till she spoke to him.

'I am so sorry for you,' she said, 'but my brothers are going back to Eton tomorrow, and then, if you behave yourself, no one will annoy you.'

'It is absurd asking me to behave myself,' he answered, looking round in astonishment at the pretty little girl who had ventured to address him, 'quite absurd. I must rattle my chains, and groan through keyholes, and walk about at night, if that is what you mean. It is my only reason for existing.'

'It is no reason at all for existing, and you know you have been very wicked. Mrs. Umney told us, the first day we arrived here, that you had killed your wife.'

'Well, I quite admit it,' said the Ghost petulantly, 'but it was a purely family matter, and concerned no one else.'

'It is very wrong to kill any one,' said Virginia, who at times had a sweet Puritan gravity, caught from some old New England ancestor.

'Oh, I hate the cheap severity of abstract ethics! My wife was very plain, never had my ruffs properly starched, and knew nothing about cookery. Why, there was a buck I had shot in Hogley Woods, a magnificent pricket, and do you know how she had it sent up to table? However, it is no matter now, for it is all over, and I don't think it was very nice of her brothers to starve me to death, though I did kill her.'

'Starve you to death? Oh, Mr. Ghost, I mean Sir Simon, are you hungry? I have a sandwich in my case. Would you like it?'

'No, thank you, I never eat anything now; but it is very kind of you, all the same, and you are much nicer than the rest of your horrid, rude, vulgar, dishonest family.'

'Stop!' cried Virginia, stamping her foot, 'it is you who are rude, and horrid, and vulgar, and as for dishonesty, you know you stole the paints out of my box to try and furbish up that ridiculous blood-stain in the library. First you took all my reds, including the vermilion, and I couldn't do any more sunsets, then you took the emerald-green and the chrome-yellow, and finally I had nothing left but indigo and Chinese white, and could only do moonlight scenes, which are always depressing to look at, and not at all easy to paint. I never told on you, though I was very much annoyed, and it was most ridiculous, the whole thing; for who ever heard of emerald-green blood?'

'Well, really,' said the Ghost, rather meekly, 'what was

I to do? It is a very difficult thing to get real blood nowadays, and, as your brother began it all with his Paragon Detergent, I certainly saw no reason why I should not have your paints. As for colour, that is always a matter of taste: the Cantervilles have blue blood, for instance, the very bluest in England; but I know you Americans don't care for things of this kind.'

'You know nothing about it, and the best thing you can do is to emigrate and improve your mind. My father will be only too happy to give you a free passage, and though there is a heavy duty on spirits of every kind, there will be no difficulty about the Custom House, as the officers are all Democrats. Once in New York, you are sure to be a great success. I know lots of people there who would give a hundred thousand dollars to have a grandfather, and much more than that to have a family Ghost.'

'I don't think I should like America.'

'I suppose because we have no ruins and no curiosities,' said Virginia satirically.

'No ruins! no curiosities!' answered the Ghost; 'you have your navy and your manners.'

'Good evening; I will go and ask papa to get the twins an extra week's holiday.'

'Please don't go, Miss Virginia,' he cried; 'I am so lonely and so unhappy, and I really don't know what to do. I want to go to sleep and I cannot.'

'That's quite absurd! You have merely to go to bed and blow out the candle. It is very difficult sometimes to keep awake, especially at church, but there is no difficulty at all about sleeping. Why, even babies know how to do that, and they are not very clever.'

'I have not slept for three hundred years,' he said sadly,

and Virginia's beautiful blue eyes opened in wonder; 'for three hundred years I have not slept, and I am so tired.'

Virginia grew quite grave, and her little lips trembled like rose-leaves. She came towards him, and kneeling down at his side, looked up into his old withered face.

'Poor, poor Ghost,' she murmured; 'have you no place where you can sleep?'

'Far away beyond the pine-woods,' he answered, in a low dreamy voice, 'there is a little garden. There the grass grows long and deep, there are the great white stars of the hemlock flower, there the nightingale sings all night long. All night long he sings, and the cold, crystal moon looks down, and the yew-tree spreads out its giant arms over the sleepers.'

Virginia's eyes grew dim with tears, and she hid her face in her hands.

'You mean the Garden of Death,' she whispered.

'Yes, Death. Death must be so beautiful. To lie in the soft brown earth, with the grasses waving above one's head, and listen to silence. To have no yesterday, and no tomorrow. To forget time, to forgive life, to be at peace. You can help me. You can open for me the portals of Death's house, for Love is always with you, and Love is stronger than Death is.'

Virginia trembled, a cold shudder ran through her, and for a few moments there was silence. She felt as if she was in a terrible dream.

Then the Ghost spoke again, and his voice sounded like the sighing of the wind.

'Have you ever read the old prophecy on the library window?'

'Oh, often,' cried the little girl, looking up; 'I know it quite well. It is painted in curious black letters, and it is difficult to read. There are only six lines:

When a golden girl can win

Prayer from out the lips of sin,

When the barren almond bears,

And a little child gives away its tears,

Then shall all the house be still

And peace come to Canterville.

But I don't know what they mean.'

'They mean,' he said sadly, 'that you must weep for me for my sins, because I have no tears, and pray with me for my soul, because I have no faith, and then, if you have always been sweet, and good, and gentle, the Angel of Death will have mercy on me. You will see fearful shapes in darkness, and wicked voices will whisper in your ear, but they will not harm you, for against the purity of a little child the powers of Hell cannot prevail.'

Virginia made no answer, and the Ghost wrung his hands in wild despair as he looked down at her bowed golden head. Suddenly she stood up, very pale, and with a strange light in her eyes. 'I am not afraid,' she said firmly, 'and I will ask the Angel to have mercy on you.'

He rose from his seat with a faint cry of joy, and taking her hand bent over it with old-fashioned grace and kissed it. His fingers were as cold as ice, and his lips burned like fire, but Virginia did not falter, as he led her across the dusky room. On the faded green tapestry were broidered little huntsmen. They blew their tasselled horns and with their tiny hands waved to her to go back. 'Go back! little Virginia,' they cried, 'go back!' but the Ghost clutched her hand more tightly, and she shut her eyes against them. Horrible animals with lizard tails, and goggle eyes, blinked at her from the carven chimney-piece, and murmured 'Beware! little Virginia, beware! we may never see you again,' but the Ghost glided on more swiftly, and Virginia did not listen. When they reached the end of the room he stopped, and muttered some words she could not understand. She opened her eyes, and saw the wall slowly fading away like a mist, and a great black cavern in front of her. A bitter cold wind swept round them, and she felt something pulling at her dress.

'Quick, quick,' cried the Ghost, 'or it will be too late,' and, in a moment, the wainscoting had closed behind them, and the Tapestry Chamber was empty.

# 6

About ten minutes later, the bell rang for tea, and, as Virginia did not come down, Mrs. Otis sent up one of the footmen to tell her. After a little time he returned and said that he could not find Miss Virginia anywhere. As she was in the habit of going out to the garden every evening to get flowers for the dinner-table, Mrs. Otis was not at all alarmed at first, but when six o'clock struck, and Virginia did not appear, she became really agitated, and sent the boys out to look for her, while she herself and Mr. Otis searched every room in the house. At half-past six the boys came back and said that they could find no trace of their sister anywhere. They were all now in the greatest state of excitement, and did not know what to do, when Mr. Otis suddenly remembered that, some few days before, he had given a band of gypsies permission to camp in the park. He accordingly at once set off for Blackfell Hollow, where he knew they were, accompanied by his eldest son and two of the farm-servants. The little Duke of Cheshire, who was perfectly frantic with anxiety, begged hard to be allowed to go too, but Mr. Otis would not allow him, as he was afraid there might be a scuffle. On arriving at the spot, however, he found that the gypsies had gone, and it was evident that their departure had been rather sudden, as the fire was still burning, and some plates were lying on the grass. Having sent off Washington and the two men to scour the district, he ran home, and despatched telegrams to all the police inspectors in the county, telling them to look out for a little girl who had been kidnapped by tramps or gypsies. He then ordered his horse to be brought round, and, after insisting on his wife and the three boys sitting down to dinner, rode off down the Ascot Road with a groom. He had hardly, however, gone a couple of miles when he heard somebody galloping after him, and, looking round, saw the little Duke coming up on his pony, with his face very flushed and no hat. 'I'm awfully sorry, Mr. Otis,' gasped out the boy, 'but I can't eat any dinner as long as Virginia is lost. Please, don't be angry with me; if you had let us be engaged last year, there would never have been all this trouble. You won't send me back, will you? I can't go! I won't go!'

The Minister could not help smiling at the handsome young scapegrace, and was a good deal touched at his devotion to Virginia, so leaning down from his horse, he patted him kindly on the shoulders, and said, 'Well, Cecil, if you won't go back I suppose you must come with me, but I must get you a hat at Ascot.'

'Oh, bother my hat! I want Virginia!' cried the little Duke, laughing, and they galloped on to the railway station. There Mr. Otis inquired of the station-master if any one answering the description of Virginia had been seen on the platform, but could get no news of her. The station-master, however, wired up and down the line, and assured him that a strict watch would be kept for her, and, after having bought a hat for the little Duke from a linen-draper, who was just putting up his shutters, Mr. Otis rode off to Bexley, a village about four miles away, which he was told was a well-known haunt of the gypsies, as there was a large common next to it. Here they roused up the rural policeman, but could get no information from him, and, after riding all over the common, they turned their horses' heads homewards, and reached the Chase about eleven o'clock, dead-tired and almost heart-broken. They found

坎特維爾大宅之鬼 The Canterville Ghost

Washington and the twins waiting for them at the gate-house with lanterns, as the avenue was very dark. Not the slightest trace of Virginia had been discovered. The gypsies had been caught on Brockley meadows, but she was not with them, and they had explained their sudden departure by saying that they had mistaken the date of Chorton Fair, and had gone off in a hurry for fear they might be late. Indeed, they had been quite distressed at hearing of Virginia's disappearance, as they were very grateful to Mr. Otis for having allowed them to camp in his park, and four of their number had stayed behind to help in the search. The carp-pond had been dragged, and the whole Chase thoroughly gone over, but without any result. It was evident that, for that night at any rate, Virginia was lost to them; and it was in a state of the deepest depression that Mr Otis and the boys walked up to the house, the groom following behind with the two horses and the pony. In the hall they found a group of frightened servants, and lying on a sofa in the library was poor Mrs. Otis, almost out of her mind with terror and anxiety, and having her forehead bathed with eau-decologne by the old housekeeper. Mr. Otis at once insisted on her having something to eat, and ordered up supper for the whole party. It was a melancholy meal, as hardly any one spoke, and even the twins were awestruck and subdued, as they were very fond of their sister. When they had finished, Mr. Otis, in spite of the entreaties of the little Duke, ordered them all to bed, saying that nothing more could be done that night, and that he would telegraph in the morning to Scotland Yard for some detectives to be sent down immediately. Just as they were passing out of the dining-room, midnight began to boom from the clock tower, and when the last stroke sounded they heard a crash and a sudden shrill cry; a dreadful peal of thunder shook the house, a strain of unearthly music floated through the air, a panel at the top of the staircase flew back with a loud noise, and out on the landing, looking very pale and white, with a little casket in her hand, stepped Virginia. In a moment they had all rushed up to her. Mrs. Otis clasped her passionately in her arms, the Duke smothered her with violent kisses, and the twins executed a wild war-dance round the group.

'Good heavens! child, where have you been?' said Mr. Otis, rather angrily, thinking that she had been playing some foolish trick on them. 'Cecil and I have been riding all over the country looking for you, and your mother has been frightened to death. You must never play these practical jokes any more.'

'Except on the Ghost! except on the Ghost!' shrieked the twins, as they capered about.

'My own darling, thank God you are found; you must never leave my side again,' murmured Mrs. Otis, as she kissed the trembling child, and smoothed the tangled gold of her hair.

'Papa,' said Virginia quietly, 'I have been with the Ghost. He is dead, and you must come and see him. He had been very wicked, but he was really sorry for all that he had done, and he gave me this box of beautiful jewels before he died.'

The whole family gazed at her in mute amazement, but she was quite grave and serious; and, turning round, she led them through the opening in the wainscoting down a narrow secret corridor, Washington following with a lighted candle, which he had caught up from the table. Finally, they came to a great oak door, studded with rusty nails. When Virginia touched it, it swung back on its heavy hinges, and they found themselves in a little low room, with a vaulted ceiling, and one tiny grated window. Imbedded in the wall was a huge iron ring, and chained to it was a gaunt skeleton, that was stretched out at full length on the stone floor, and seemed to be trying to grasp with its long fleshless fingers an old-fashioned trencher and ewer, that were placed just out of its reach. The jug had evidently been once filled with water, as it was covered inside with green mould. There was nothing on the trencher but a pile of dust. Virginia knelt down beside the skeleton, and, folding her little hands together, began to pray silently, while the rest of the party looked on in wonder at the terrible tragedy whose secret was now disclosed to them.

坎特維爾大宅之鬼 The Canterville Ghost

'Hallo!' suddenly exclaimed one of the twins, who had been looking out of the window to try and discover in what wing of the house the room was situated. 'Hallo! the old withered almond-tree has blossomed. I can see the flowers quite plainly in the moonlight.'

'God has forgiven him,' said Virginia gravely, as she rose to her feet, and a beautiful light seemed to illumine her face.

'What an angel you are!' cried the young Duke, and he put his arm round her neck and kissed her.

# 7

Four days after these curious incidents a funeral started from Canterville Chase at about eleven o'clock at night. The hearse was drawn by eight black horses, each of which carried on its head a great tuft of nodding ostrich-plumes, and the leaden coffin was covered by a rich purple pall, on which was embroidered in gold the Canterville coat-of-arms. By the side of the hearse and the coaches walked the servants with lighted torches, and the whole procession was wonderfully impressive. Lord Canterville was the chief mourner, having come up specially from Wales to attend the funeral, and sat in the first carriage along with little Virginia. Then came the United States Minister and his wife, then Washington and the three boys, and in the last carriage was Mrs. Umney. It was generally felt that, as she had been frightened by the ghost for more than fifty years of her life, she had a right to see the last of him. A deep grave had been dug in the corner of the churchyard, just under the old yew-tree, and the service was read in the most impressive manner by the Rev. Augustus Dampier. When the ceremony was over, the servants, according to an old custom observed in the Canterville family, extinguished their torches, and, as the coffin was being lowered into the grave, Virginia stepped forward and laid on it a large cross made of white and pink almond-blossoms. As she did so, the moon came out from behind a cloud, and flooded with its silent silver the little churchyard, and from a distant copse a nightingale began to sing. She thought of the ghost's description of the Garden of Death, her eyes became dim with tears, and she hardly spoke a word during the drive home.

The next morning, before Lord Canterville went up to town, Mr. Otis had an interview with him on the subject of the jewels the ghost had given to Virginia. They were perfectly magnificent, especially a certain ruby necklace with old Venetian setting, which was really a superb specimen of sixteenth-century work, and their value was so great that Mr. Otis felt considerable scruples about allowing his daughter to accept them.

'My lord,' he said, 'I know that in this country mortmain is held to apply to trinkets as well as to land, and it is quite clear to me that these jewels are, or should be, heirlooms in your family. I must beg you, accordingly, to take them to London with you, and to regard them simply as a portion of your property which has been restored to you under certain strange conditions. As for my daughter, she is merely a child, and has as yet, I am glad to say, but little interest in such appurtenances of idle luxury. I am also informed by Mrs. Otis, who, I may say, is no mean authority upon Art — having had the privilege of spending several winters in Boston when she was a girl — that these gems are of great monetary worth, and if offered for sale would fetch a tall price. Under these circumstances, Lord Canterville, I feel sure that you will recognise how impossible it would be for me to allow them to remain in the possession of any member of my family; and, indeed, all such vain gauds and toys, however suitable or necessary to the dignity of the British aristocracy, would be completely out of place among those who have been brought up on the severe, and I believe immortal, principles of republican simplicity. Perhaps I should mention that Virginia is very anxious that you should allow her to retain the box as a memento of your unfortunate but misguided ancestor. As it is extremely old, and consequently a good deal out of repair, you may perhaps think fit to comply with her request. For my own part, I confess I am a good deal surprised to find a child of mine expressing sympathy with mediaevalism in any form, and can only account for it by the fact that Virginia was born in one of your London suburbs shortly after Mrs. Otis had returned from a trip to Athens.'

Lord Canterville listened very gravely to the worthy Minister's speech, pulling his grey moustache now and then to hide an involuntary smile, and when Mr. Otis had ended, he shook him cordially by the hand, and said, 'My dear sir, your charming little daughter rendered my unlucky ancestor, Sir Simon, a very important service, and I and my family are much indebted to her for her marvellous courage and pluck. The jewels are clearly hers, and, egad, I believe that if I were heartless enough to take them from her, the wicked old fellow would be out of his grave in a fortnight, leading me the devil of a life. As for their being heirlooms, nothing is an heirloom that is not so mentioned in a will or legal document, and the existence of these jewels has been quite unknown. I assure you I have no more claim on them than your butler, and when Miss Virginia grows up I daresay she will be pleased to have pretty things to wear. Besides, you forget, Mr. Otis, that you took the furniture and the ghost at a valuation, and anything that belonged to the ghost passed at once into your possession, as, whatever activity Sir Simon may have shown in the corridor at night, in point of law he was really dead, and you acquired his property by purchase.'

Mr. Otis was a good deal distressed at Lord Canterville's refusal, and begged him to reconsider his decision, but the good-natured peer was quite firm, and finally induced the Minister to allow his daughter to retain the present the ghost had given her, and, when, in the spring of 1890, the young Duchess of Cheshire was presented at the Queen's first drawing-room on the occasion of her marriage, her jewels were the universal theme of admiration. For Virginia received the coronet, which is the reward of all good little American girls, and was married to her boy-lover as soon as he came of age. They were both so charming, and they loved each other so much, that every one was delighted at the match, except the old Marchioness of Dumbleton, who had tried to catch the Duke for one of her seven unmarried daughters, and had given no less than three expensive dinner-parties for that purpose, and, strange to say, Mr. Otis himself. Mr. Otis was extremely fond of the young Duke personally, but, theoretically, he objected to titles, and, to use his own words, 'was not without apprehension lest, amid the enervating influences of a pleasure-loving aristocracy, the true principles of republican simplicity should be forgotten.' His objections, however, were completely overruled, and I believe that when he walked up the aisle of St. George's, Hanover Square, with his daughter leaning on his arm, there was not a prouder man in the whole length and breadth of England.

The Duke and Duchess, after the honeymoon was over, went down to Canterville Chase, and on the day after their arrival they walked over in the afternoon to the lonely churchyard by the pine-woods. There had been a great deal of difficulty at first about the inscription on Sir Simon's tombstone, but finally it had been decided to engrave on it simply the initials of the old gentleman's name, and the verse from the library window. The Duchess had brought with her some lovely roses, which she strewed upon the grave, and after they had stood by it for some time they strolled into the ruined chancel of the old abbey. There the Duchess sat down on a fallen pillar, while her husband lay at her feet smoking a cigarette and looking up at her beautiful eyes. Suddenly he threw his cigarette away, took hold of her hand, and said to her, 'Virginia, a wife should have no secrets from her husband.'

'Dear Cecil! I have no secrets from you.'

'Yes, you have,' he answered, smiling, 'you have never told me what happened to you when you were locked up with the ghost.'

'I have never told any one, Cecil,' said Virginia gravely.

'I know that, but you might tell me.'

'Please don't ask me, Cecil, I cannot tell you. Poor Sir Simon! I owe him a great deal. Yes, don't laugh, Cecil, I really do. He made me see what Life is, and what Death signifies, and why Love is stronger than both.'

The Duke rose and kissed his wife lovingly.

'You can have your secret as long as I have your heart,' he murmured.

'You have always had that, Cecil.'

'And you will tell our children some day, won't you?'

Virginia blushed.

# 好樣百萬富翁

像他這樣的乞丐可不是每天都遇得到。
你總不會希望乞丐看起來很開心吧？
你口中的破衣服，我管它叫做浪漫色彩。
你眼中的貧窮，在我看來別具趣味。

除非有錢，否則就算魅力十足，也無濟於事。浪漫，是富人的特權，失業賦閒者不該如此大放厥詞。窮人就該平淡無奇地務實度日。擁有一份固定收入遠勝過個性迷人。

這些是現代生活的偉大真理，可惜休伊·厄斯金從來都不明白。可憐的休伊，我們必須承認，在智識上他並無特出之處——他一生從未說出一句令人讚嘆的妙語，甚至吐不出一句居心不良的惡毒話。可是話說回來，他長得非常好看，一頭俐落的棕髮，線條分明的輪廓，還有一雙灰色眼眸。他的同性緣和異性緣一樣好。他具備十八般武藝，可惜獨缺賺錢這一項。

休伊的父親留給他一把騎兵劍和一套十五冊的《拿破崙半島戰爭史》，他將前者掛在家中鏡子上方，把後者放上書架，塞進《洛夫賽馬指南》和《貝禮運動休閒雜誌》①之間，然後僅憑一位老姑媽供給他一年兩百英鎊的生活費過活。

他試過各種謀生的方法——去證券交易所工作了半年；可是，一隻蝴蝶混在公牛群和熊群之間能有什麼成就呢？他買賣茶葉的資歷則稍長一點，但很快就厭倦了什麼白毫與小種。接著又嘗試兜售雪莉酒，也不成，這一行實在太無趣。最終，他成了窩囊廢，一個討人喜歡卻不中用的年輕人，空有完美輪廓，卻找不到工作。

雪上加霜的是，他戀愛了。他鍾情的對象叫做蘿拉·莫頓，是一名退休上校的千金。這位上校派任印度時脾氣變得很大，胃口變得很差，此後便再也找不回好脾氣與健康。蘿拉愛慕休伊，而他也隨時願意親吻她的鞋帶。他們是全倫敦最登對出色的情侶，但兩人都是窮光蛋。上校非常喜歡休伊，卻不願聽到他提起訂婚的事。

「小子，等哪天你名下擁有一萬英鎊，咱們再來想這事吧。」上校總是這麼說。聽到這樣的回答，休伊就會有好一陣子非常消沉，不得不去找蘿拉討安慰。

有天早晨，休伊要去荷蘭公園找蘿拉，中途順道拜訪好友艾倫·崔佛。崔佛是個畫家——說真的，如今誰不是畫家呢？此外，他還是個藝術家，這就比較稀有了。我個人認為，他是個奇怪的莽夫，滿臉雀斑，赤髯如虯。話雖如此，當他拿起畫筆，卻是個貨真價實的大師，他的畫作廣受眾人熱切追捧。

他一直深受休伊的吸引——不容否認，起初完全是因為休伊的個人魅力。他總是說：「畫家唯一該認識的，就是那些美麗的蠢才。他們長得賞心悅目，而且跟他們聊天不必費心勞神。花花公子和嬌嬌女主宰著這世界，至少他們理應如此。」而等到他跟休伊變得更熟稔之後，更是欣賞休伊快活樂觀的態度和大方無畏的天性，因此答應休伊可以隨時進出他的工作室。

休伊走進畫室的時候，便發現崔佛正在為一幅真人大小

的乞丐畫像收尾。乞丐本人站在工作室角落一處墊高的臺座上——他是個乾瘦的老頭，臉龐像張皺巴巴的羊皮紙，神情十分可憐。他披著一件粗糙的棕色斗篷，上頭滿是破洞和裂口。他的厚靴七拼八湊，全是補丁。他用單手握住一根粗糙的棍棒，倚著它，同時伸出另一隻手，拿著舊帽子央人施捨。

「真是個出色的模特兒呀！」休伊和朋友握手致意時，低聲說道。

「出色的模特兒？」崔佛拔高了嗓門嚷道，「沒錯，我是該這麼想！像他這樣的乞丐可不是每天都遇得到。好兄弟，他可是個寶，活脫是委拉斯奎茲筆下的人物！哎呀，不知道林布蘭會將他做成怎樣的蝕刻版畫呢！②」

「可憐的老頭兒！」休伊說，「他看起來好悲慘哪！不過我想，對你們畫家來說，他的臉正是他的財富吧？」

「那當然，」崔佛答道，「你總不會希望乞丐看起來很開心吧？」

「當模特兒能賺多少錢？」休伊在一張無靠背的長沙發上，為自己找了個舒服的位置。

「每小時一先令。」崔佛答。

「艾倫，你賣掉一幅畫能賺進多少錢？」休伊又問？

「噢，這一幅我可以拿到兩千！」崔佛愉快地說。

「英鎊嗎？」休伊好奇。

「是基尼③。畫家、詩人和醫生拿到的報酬永遠是基尼。」崔佛解釋。

「噢，我認為這個模特兒應該分得其中一部分，」休伊笑著說，「畢竟他們跟你一樣拚命。」

「胡說八道，真是荒謬！你想想，光是一層層塗上顏料，還得在畫架前站一整天，有多辛苦呀！休伊，雖然你這麼說好像也有道理，可是我敢打包票，藝術的勞動有時也不輸體力活

兒的。你先別閒扯淡了，我現在很忙。你抽根菸，保持安靜，好嗎？」

過了一會兒，僕役走進來稟報，說裱框師傅想跟崔佛談一談。

「休伊，別走。」他邊走出房間邊說，「我去去就來。」

那個老叫化子趁機就著背後的木頭長椅坐下來歇息。他看起來是如此無依無靠、如此苦命，讓休伊不禁憐憫起他，便摸了摸口袋，確認自己身上有多少錢。結果只找到一枚金鎊④和少許銅板。「可憐的老大爺，」休伊心想，「他比我更需要這些錢，反正不過是兩個星期沒辦法搭馬車罷了。」他走到乞丐身邊，把那枚金鎊迅速塞進對方手中。

老人嚇得跳了起來，接著，一抹淡淡的微笑略過他憔悴的雙唇。「謝謝您，先生，」他說，「多謝。」

正好這時崔佛走了進來。休伊向他告辭，對自己剛才的作為感到有點羞赧。他和蘿拉一起度過了這一天，因為那揮霍而挨了她一頓迷人的責罵，最後還因沒錢坐馬車，只能走路回家。

那天晚上十一點左右，休伊漫步走進調色盤俱樂部，發現崔佛獨自一人坐在吸菸室喝著霍克酒和蘇打水。

「噢，艾倫，你順利完成那幅畫了嗎？」休伊一邊說，一邊點燃手上的香菸。

「嗯，不但完成了，連框都裱好了呢！」崔佛答道，「對了，你在畫室裡見過的那個老人很喜歡你，對你很有好感。我不得不把你的一切全告訴他——你是誰，住在哪裡，做哪一行，前景如何……」

「我親愛的艾倫啊，」休伊提高音量說道，「所以等我回到家，可能會發現他在門口等我，是吧。但顯然你只是尋我開心。可憐的老窮光蛋，我真希望自己能為他做點什麼。我覺得任何人淪落到那種悲慘境地都是很可怕的事。我家裡有很多舊衣服，你覺得他可能會想要嗎？欸，他那身破衣服都快解體

啦。」

「但他穿上那些破爛不堪的衣服，看起來可是很華麗耀眼哪，」崔佛說，「就算給我再高的報酬，我也不想畫他身穿長大衣的模樣。你口中的破衣服，我管它叫做浪漫色彩。你眼中的貧窮，在我看來別具趣味。不管如何，我會把你的提議轉告他。」

「艾倫，」休伊語氣嚴肅地說，「你們畫家可真是冷酷薄情。」

「藝術家的心就是他的腦，」崔佛回答，「更何況，我們這一行是如實表現眼中所見的世界，而不是改革我們所知的世界。不過是各司其事嘍。現在，跟我說說蘿拉近來可好？那個老模對她可是很感興趣呢。」

「你該不會跟他提起她吧？」休伊說。

「當然嘍。他知道了所有的一切，包括狠心的上校、可愛的蘿拉，還有一萬英鎊的約定。」

「什麼，你把我所有的私事全都跟那老乞丐說了？」休伊氣得大叫，整張臉脹得通紅。

「兄弟啊，」崔佛面帶微笑地說，「你口中的那個老乞丐，是全歐洲最富有的人。就算明天買下整個倫敦，他的戶頭也不會透支。他在歐洲各國首都都有房子，吃飯時用純金盤子裝盛菜餚。如果他願意，還能阻止俄國發動戰爭呢。」

「你到底在說什麼？」休伊驚呼道。

「我是說，」崔佛說，「今天你在工作室看見的那個老頭是郝思柏格男爵。他是我的摯友，買下我所有的畫作和其他創作。一個月前，他委託我把他畫成一個叫化子。他想做什麼？不就是完成他百萬富翁的幻想！我得承認，他穿上他那套襤褸破衣還真是有模有樣，不，應該說是我的破舊衣服，因為那是我在西班牙買來的。」

「郝思柏格男爵！」休伊高喊道，「天哪，我還塞給他一枚金鎊！」說完，沮喪地跌坐在扶手椅上。

「你給他一枚金鎊！」崔佛大叫，接著爆出一陣哈哈大笑，「兄弟，那真是肉包子打狗啊——他的事業，就是管理別人的錢。」

「艾倫，你該早點告訴我，」休伊繃起臉埋怨道，「別讓我把自己弄得像個傻瓜似的。」

「哎喲，休伊，」崔佛說，「首先，我從來沒想過你會對乞丐這麼大方。如果你偷親一個漂亮的模特兒，我可以了解。可是你把一枚金鎊送給一個容貌醜陋的模特兒——噢，我怎麼也想不透！再說，今天的狀況讓我有點綁手綁腳。當你走進工作室的時候，我並不確定郝思柏格願不願意讓我說破他的身分。你知道他當時的衣著並不正式，也不得體。」

「他一定認為我是個蠢才！」休伊說。

「不見得吧。在你離開後，他變得精神煥發，不斷得意地嘻嘻輕笑，還不停搓摩那雙滿是皺紋的老手。當時我搞不懂他為什麼那麼想知道有關你的一切，但現在我明白了——他會代你投資那一金鎊，每半年付你一次利息，然後把這事當成閒聊話題。」

「我真是倒楣，」休伊哀嘆道，「這會兒我能做的事就是上床睡覺。對了，我親愛的艾倫，你可千萬別告訴任何人這件事，否則我就沒膽在我家那條街露臉了。」

「胡說！休伊，這件事無疑是對你善良天性的最高讚揚。別走，再抽根菸，你可以大談特談蘿拉的事呀。」

可是休伊不願多待，他悶悶不樂地步行回家，留下艾倫・崔佛自己一人在那兒笑個不停。

第二天早上，休伊正在吃早餐時，僕役送上一張卡片，上頭寫著——「古斯塔夫・努達先生　代表郝思柏格男爵來訪。」

休伊心想：「他肯定是來要求我道歉的。」便吩咐僕役帶客人進來。

一名戴著金框眼鏡、滿頭華髮的老先生走進房間，並開口說道：「我有這榮幸跟厄斯金先生說話嗎？」他的口音帶著些微的法國腔調。

休伊欠身行禮。

「我代表郝思柏格男爵前來，」老先生接著說，「男爵……」

「先生，勞煩您代我向男爵致上最誠摯的歉意。」休伊結結巴巴地說。

「男爵大人，」老先生面帶微笑地說，「交代我送這封信給您。」接著，呈上一只密封的信封。

信封上寫著──「給休伊‧厄斯金與蘿拉‧莫頓的結婚賀禮 老叫化子敬贈」，裡頭是一張面額一萬英鎊的支票！

休伊和蘿拉結婚時，艾倫‧崔佛是伴郎，男爵則在婚宴上致詞祝賀新人。

「百萬富翁當模特兒，」艾倫評論道，「已經夠稀有的了。但老天哪，百萬富翁做好榜樣更是罕見哪！」


譯註

① 《洛夫賽馬指南》（*Ruff's Guide to the Turf*）和《貝禮運動休閒雜誌》（*Bailey's Magazine of Sports and Pastimes*），是當時的運動競技刊物。

② 委拉斯奎茲（Diego Velázquez，1599～1660），文藝復興後期的現實主義畫家。其肖像畫栩栩如生，往往予人彷彿畫中人物就要走出畫外的感受。

林布蘭（Rembrandt, 1606～1669），十七世紀荷蘭畫家，素有光影魔術師之稱。

③ 基尼，是英國的舊貨幣單位，一基尼相當於二十一先令。
（先令已於一九七一年廢止），亦等於一點〇五英鎊，比一
英鎊面額稍高。

④ 金鎊（又名沙弗林），指英國舊時面值一英鎊的金幣。

# The Model Millionaire

Unless one is wealthy there is no use in being a charming fellow. Romance is the privilege of the rich, not the profession of the unemployed. The poor should be practical and prosaic. It is better to have a permanent income than to be fascinating. These are the great truths of modern life which Hughie Erskine never realised. Poor Hughie! Intellectually, we must admit, he was not of much importance. He never said a brilliant or even an ill-natured thing in his life. But then he was wonderfully good-looking, with his crisp brown hair, his clear-cut profile, and his grey eyes. He was as popular with men as he was with women and he had every accomplishment except that of making money. His father had bequeathed him his cavalry sword and a History of the Peninsular War in fifteen volumes. Hughie hung the first over his looking-glass, put the second on a shelf between Ruff's Guide and Bailey's Magazine, and lived on two hundred a year that an old aunt allowed him. He had tried everything. He had gone on the Stock Exchange for six months; but what was a butterfly to do among bulls and bears? He had been a tea-merchant for a little longer, but had soon tired of pekoe and souchong. Then he had tried selling dry sherry. That did not answer; the sherry was a little too dry. Ultimately he became nothing, a delightful, ineffectual young man with a perfect profile and no profession.

To make matters worse, he was in love. The girl he loved was Laura Merton, the daughter of a retired Colonel who had lost his temper and his digestion in India, and had never found either of them again. Laura adored him, and he was ready to kiss her shoe-strings. They were the handsomest couple in London, and had not a penny-piece between them. The Colonel was very fond of Hughie, but would not hear of any engagement.

'Come to me, my boy, when you have got ten thousand pounds of your own, and we will see about it,' he used to say; and Hughie looked very glum in those days, and had to go to Laura for consolation.

One morning, as he was on his way to Holland Park, where the Mertons lived, he dropped in to see a great friend of his, Alan Trevor. Trevor was a painter. Indeed, few people escape that nowadays. But he was also an artist, and artists are rather rare. Personally he was a strange rough fellow, with a freckled face and a red ragged beard. However, when he took up the brush he was a real master, and his pictures were eagerly sought after. He had been very much attracted by Hughie at first, it must be acknowledged, entirely on account of his personal charm. 'The only people a painter should know,' he used to say, 'are people who are bete and beautiful, people who are an artistic pleasure to look at and an intellectual repose to talk to. Men who are dandies and women who are darlings rule the world, at least they should do so.' However, after he got to know Hughie better, he liked him quite as much for his bright, buoyant spirits and his generous, reckless nature, and had given him the permanent entree to his studio.

When Hughie came in he found Trevor putting the finishing

touches to a wonderful life-size picture of a beggar-man. The beggar himself was standing on a raised platform in a corner of the studio. He was a wizened old man, with a face like wrinkled parchment, and a most piteous expression. Over his shoulders was flung a coarse brown cloak, all tears and tatters; his thick boots were patched and cobbled, and with one hand he leant on a rough stick, while with the other he held out his battered hat for alms.

'What an amazing model!' whispered Hughie, as he shook hands with his friend.

'An amazing model?' shouted Trevor at the top of his voice; 'I should think so! Such beggars as he are not to be met with every day. A trouvaille, mon cher; a living Velasquez! My stars! what an etching Rembrandt would have made of him!'

'Poor old chap!' said Hughie, 'how miserable he looks! But I suppose, to you painters, his face is his fortune?'

'Certainly,' replied Trevor, 'you don't want a beggar to look happy, do you?'

'How much does a model get for sitting?' asked Hughie, as he found himself a comfortable seat on a divan.

'A shilling an hour.'

'And how much do you get for your picture, Alan?'

'Oh, for this I get two thousand!'

'Pounds?'

'Guineas. Painters, poets, and physicians always get guineas.'

'Well, I think the model should have a percentage,' cried Hughie, laughing; 'they work quite as hard as you do.'

'Nonsense, nonsense! Why, look at the trouble of laying on the paint alone, and standing all day long at one's easel! It's all very well, Hughie, for you to talk, but I assure you that there are moments when Art almost attains to the dignity of manual labour. But you mustn't chatter; I'm very busy. Smoke a cigarette, and keep quiet.'

After some time the servant came in, and told Trevor that the framemaker wanted to speak to him.

'Don't run away, Hughie,' he said, as he went out, 'I will be back in a moment.'

The old beggar-man took advantage of Trevor's absence to rest for a moment on a wooden bench that was behind him. He looked so forlorn and wretched that Hughie could not help pitying him, and felt in his pockets to see what money he had. All he could find was a sovereign and some coppers. 'Poor old fellow,' he thought to himself, 'he wants it more than I do, but it means no hansoms for a fortnight'; and he walked across the studio and slipped the sovereign into the beggar's hand.

The old man started, and a faint smile flitted across his withered lips. 'Thank you, sir,' he said, 'thank you.'

Then Trevor arrived, and Hughie took his leave, blushing a little at what he had done. He spent the day with Laura, got a charming scolding for his extravagance, and had to walk home.

That night he strolled into the Palette Club about eleven o'clock, and found Trevor sitting by himself in the smoking-room drinking hock and seltzer.

'Well, Alan, did you get the picture finished all right?' he said, as he lit his cigarette.

'Finished and framed, my boy!' answered Trevor; 'and, by the bye, you have made a conquest. That old model you saw is quite devoted to you. I had to tell him all about you — who you are, where you live, what your income is, what prospects you have —'

'My dear Alan,' cried Hughie, 'I shall probably find him waiting for me when I go home. But of course you are only joking. Poor old wretch! I wish I could do something for him. I think it is dreadful that any one should be so miserable. I have got heaps of old clothes at home — do you think he would care for any of them? Why, his rags were falling to bits.'

'But he looks splendid in them,' said Trevor. 'I wouldn't paint him in a frock coat for anything. What you call rags I call romance. What seems poverty to you is picturesqueness to me. However, I'll tell him of your offer.'

'Alan,' said Hughie seriously, 'you painters are a heartless lot.'

'An artist's heart is his head,' replied Trevor; 'and besides, our business is to realise the world as we see it, not to reform it as we know it. A chacun son metier. And now tell me how Laura is. The old model was quite interested in her.'

'You don't mean to say you talked to him about her?' said Hughie.

'Certainly I did. He knows all about the relentless colonel, the lovely Laura, and the 10,000 pounds.'

'You told that old beggar all my private affairs?' cried Hughie, looking very red and angry.

'My dear boy,' said Trevor, smiling, 'that old beggar, as you call him, is one of the richest men in Europe. He could buy all London tomorrow without overdrawing his account. He has a house in every capital, dines off gold plate, and can prevent Russia going to war when he chooses.'

'What on earth do you mean?' exclaimed Hughie.

'What I say,' said Trevor. 'The old man you saw today in the studio was Baron Hausberg. He is a great friend of mine, buys all my pictures and that sort of thing, and gave me a commission a month ago to paint him as a beggar. Que voulez-vous? La fantaisie d'un millionnaire! And I must say he made a magnificent figure in his rags, or perhaps I should say in my rags; they are an old suit I got in Spain.'

'Baron Hausberg!' cried Hughie. 'Good heavens! I gave him a sovereign!' and he sank into an armchair the picture of dismay.

'Gave him a sovereign!' shouted Trevor, and he burst into a roar of laughter. 'My dear boy, you'll never see it again. Son affaire c'est l'argent des autres.'

'I think you might have told me, Alan,' said Hughie sulkily, 'and not have let me make such a fool of myself.'

'Well, to begin with, Hughie,' said Trevor, 'it never entered my mind that you went about distributing alms in that reckless way. I can understand your kissing a pretty model, but your giving a sovereign to an ugly one — by Jove, no! Besides, the fact is that I really was not at home today to any one; and when you came in I didn't know whether Hausberg would like his name mentioned. You know he wasn't in full dress.'

'What a duffer he must think me!' said Hughie.

'Not at all. He was in the highest spirits after you left; kept chuckling to himself and rubbing his old wrinkled hands together. I couldn't make out why he was so interested to know all about you; but I see it all now. He'll invest your sovereign for you, Hughie, pay you the interest every six months, and have a capital story to tell after dinner.'

'I am an unlucky devil,' growled Hughie. 'The best thing I can do is to go to bed; and, my dear Alan, you mustn't tell any one. I shouldn't dare show my face in the Row.'

'Nonsense! It reflects the highest credit on your philanthropic spirit, Hughie. And don't run away. Have another cigarette, and you can talk about Laura as much as you like.'

However, Hughie wouldn't stop, but walked home, feeling very unhappy, and leaving Alan Trevor in fits of laughter.

The next morning, as he was at breakfast, the servant brought him up a card on which was written, 'Monsieur Gustave Naudin, de la part de M. le Baron Hausberg.' 'I suppose he has come for an apology,' said Hughie to himself; and he told the servant to show the visitor up.

An old gentleman with gold spectacles and grey hair came into the room, and said, in a slight French accent, 'Have I the honour of addressing Monsieur Erskine?'

Hughie bowed.

'I have come from Baron Hausberg,' he continued. 'The Baron —'

'I beg, sir, that you will offer him my sincerest apologies,' stammered Hughie.

'The Baron,' said the old gentleman with a smile, 'has commissioned me to bring you this letter'; and he extended a sealed envelope.

On the outside was written, 'A wedding present to Hugh Erskine and Laura Merton, from an old beggar,' and inside was a cheque for 10,000 pounds.

When they were married Alan Trevor was the best man, and the Baron made a speech at the wedding breakfast.

'Millionaire models,' remarked Alan, 'are rare enough; but, by Jove, model millionaires are rarer still!'

# 亞瑟勛爵的罪行

黎明的嬌貴美好中，

藏著讓他覺得無法形容的可憐，

他想著燦爛破曉但風雨入夜的所有日子。

一個擺脫夜之罪孽與日之煙霧的倫敦，

一座毫無血色、鬼魅般的城市！

## 1

　　這是溫德米爾夫人在復活節前舉行的最後一次宴會，班亭克大宅的人氣因此顯得比平日更旺。六名內閣大臣佩著星星和綬帶從下議院趕來，所有漂亮女子全都穿上最時髦的服裝；站在畫廊盡頭的，是卡爾思魯厄的蘇菲亞公主，一名韃靼人容貌的魁梧女子，黑色小眼睛，戴著出色的祖母綠寶石，用最大音量說著蹩腳的法語，而且只要有人跟她說任何事，她就毫無節制地放聲大笑。

　　這肯定是個絕妙的賓客組合——雍容華貴的貴婦人與狂熱的激進分子親切地交談；受歡迎的牧師槓上了著名的懷疑論者；一整群主教緊緊尾隨一名身形粗壯的歌劇女主角，從這個

房間跟到那個房間；樓梯上站著好幾名偽裝成藝術家的皇家院士；有人說，當天，晚餐室在同一時間擠滿了天才。事實上，那是溫德米爾夫人最風光的一夜。

蘇菲亞公主待到將近十一點半才離開。等公主一離開，溫德米爾夫人便回到畫廊，有個知名的政治經濟學家一本正經地向一位憤怒的匈牙利著名演奏家解釋音樂的科學理論，溫德米爾夫人則開始和裴斯利公爵夫人攀談起來。

公爵夫人的美貌絕世無雙——粉頸、勿忘我藍的杏眼、濃密的金色鬢髮。這頭金髮是純金色的，不是如今妄尊金色優雅名號的淡麥稈色，而是彷若織入日光或隱藏在奇特琥珀中的那種金黃；它們賦予了她的臉某種聖潔的光輝輪廓，毫無「罪」人的魅力。

公爵夫人是個引人好奇的心理學研究對象。她從很年輕時便發現，沒有什麼比不檢點看起來更清白的了——藉著一連串不計後果、但約半數相當無害的胡作非為，讓她從此享有這種品格帶來的任何特權。她不只一次改換結婚對象，《英國貴族名人錄》便記載她曾有過三段婚姻；但由於從未換過情人，這世界早就停止議論她的醜聞。如今她年滿四十，膝下猶虛，因沉溺於尋歡作樂而依舊保持著青春風采。

突然間，溫德米爾夫人熱切地環顧房間四周，用清晰的女低音說：「我的手相師在哪兒？」

「你的什麼，葛拉狄絲？」公爵夫人不由自主地脫口驚呼。

「公爵夫人，我的手相師；如今，我的生活不能沒有他。」

「親愛的葛拉狄絲，你總是這麼獨樹一格！」公爵夫人一邊低聲讚嘆，一邊設法回想手相師究竟是做什麼的，並暗自希望它跟足部按摩師是不一樣的。

「他每週固定兩次來看我的手，」溫德米爾夫人接著 道，「而且他對人的手最感興趣了。」

「天哪！」公爵夫人自言自語，「他果然是某種手足按摩師。這可真討厭。無論如何我都希望他是個外國人，那樣的話，情況就還不算太糟。」

「我一定要把他介紹給你認識。」

「介紹他！」公爵夫人慌亂地喊道，「你的意思該不會是說他人就在這裡吧？」同時開始尋找她的龜殼小扇和那條破舊的蕾絲披巾，以做好準備。

「他當然就在這裡，我做夢也無法想像宴客少了他該怎麼辦才好。他跟我說，我的手相顯示我擁有一顆純淨的心靈，假設大拇指稍微短一點點，我就會是個徹底的悲觀主義者，早已進入修道院苦修。」

「噢，我懂了！」公爵夫人感覺如釋重負，說：「我想，他可以預言幸運事，對吧？」

「也可以推測不幸災難的降臨，」溫德米爾夫人應道，「不管厄運是大或小。比方，明年我在陸地與海上都會遭逢大難，所以得住在熱氣球上，每天傍晚再將裝有晚餐的竹籃拉上來。這全都寫在我小小的手指，還是我的手掌上……我忘了是哪一個。」

「但葛拉狄絲，那樣做豈不是玩命嗎？」

「我親愛的公爵夫人，到這種時候不冒點險怎麼成。我認為，每個人每個月都該看一次手相，這樣才能知道什麼事不該做。當然，人還是會照常行事，但能事先得到警告讓人覺得很快活。現在，要是沒有人願意馬上幫我找到包覺思先生，我只好自己來了。」

「溫德米爾夫人，讓我來。」一名高大英俊的年輕人自告奮勇。剛才他就站在旁邊，帶著開心的笑容聆聽這整段對話。

「亞瑟勛爵，非常謝謝你，不過我怕你認不出他。」

「溫德米爾夫人，假設他正如您所說的那樣出色，我絕不想

錯過他。告訴我，他長得什麼模樣，我立刻把他帶到您眼前。」

「好，他長得一點都不像個手相師。我是說，他的外貌並不特別神祕、高深莫測，或浪漫好看。他的個頭矮小粗壯，頂著一顆滑稽的光頭，戴著一副大金框眼鏡，模樣介於家庭醫師和鄉下律師之間。這樣形容他讓我覺得很抱歉，可是這不是我的錯，這些人就是如此令人惱火——我所有的鋼琴師看起來就像詩人，而我所有的詩人看起來就像鋼琴師。

「我還記得，上一季曾邀請一位非常厲害的陰謀家來吃晚餐。他曾經炸死過很多人，永遠穿著一件鎖子甲，同時在襯衫袖子上佩帶著一把匕首。可是你知道嗎，他來赴宴的時候，看起來活像個善良的老牧師，整個晚上不停地講笑話；當然，他很風趣，沒別的了，這讓我非常失望。我問起他的鎖子甲，他只是一笑置之，說在英格蘭穿那個太寒冷了。啊，包覺思先生來了！

「好了，包覺思先生，我希望你能幫裴斯利公爵夫人看手相。公爵夫人，您得把手套脫下來呀。不，不是左手，另一隻手。」

「親愛的葛拉狄絲，我覺得這麼做真的不太恰當。」公爵夫人雖然這麼說，卻還是順從地解開一隻略顯髒汙的小山羊皮手套。

「有趣的事向來不太恰當，」溫德米爾夫人說，「那就是這世界運行的方式。可是我必須為你們倆引介彼此。公爵夫人，這是包覺思先生，我最喜愛的手相師。包覺思先生，這是裴斯利公爵夫人，如果你膽敢說她的月丘比我的大，以後我就再也不相信你了。」

「葛拉狄絲，我相信我手上沒有什麼月丘的。」公爵夫人認真地說。

「夫人所言不差，」包覺思先生看了一眼那隻胖胖的小

手和短而方的手指頭，說：「月丘尚未發育。不過，生命線倒是長得好極了。請翻轉一下您的手腕，謝謝。有三條非常明顯的線！公爵夫人，您會活到很大的歲數，而且非常幸福。事業心——不太強烈，智慧線不是特別誇張，感情線……」

「好啦，包覺思先生，不必講得那麼慎重。」溫德米爾夫人大喊道。

「沒有什麼比幫人看手相能帶給我更大的快樂。」包覺思先生欠身致意，說，「假如公爵夫人曾有過輕率的歲月，我很遺憾地說，我看到了天長地久的情感，並且結合了強烈的責任感。」

「包覺思先生，請繼續。」公爵夫人神情相當愉快地表示。

「節約是您的美德。」包覺思先生接著說。

溫德米爾夫人突然爆出陣陣大笑。

「節約是非常棒的事，」公爵夫人得意地評論著，「當初我嫁給裴斯利時，他名下有十一座城堡，卻沒有半間房子適合居住。」

「而今他有十二間房子，沒有半座城堡。」溫德米爾夫人嚷道。

「沒錯，親愛的，」公爵夫人說，「因為我喜歡……」

「住得舒適，」包覺思先生說，「以及現代化裝修，讓每間臥房都有熱水可用。夫人的見解非常正確。舒適，是文明唯一能帶給我們的事。」

「包覺思先生，你把公爵夫人的性格說得令人好生欽佩，接下來你一定要看看符羅拉小姐的手相。」溫德米爾夫人興致十分高昂。

為了回應女主人笑容滿面地朝自己點頭示意，有個人高馬大、淺棕色髮、肩胛骨高聳的女孩，從沙發後方彆扭地走了過來，伸出一隻細長骨感的手，指頭呈湯匙形狀。

「啊，一個鋼琴家！我明白了，」包覺思先生說，「一個

出色的鋼琴家，但也許成不了音樂家。非常沉默寡言，為人無比正直，還熱愛動物。」

「好準哪！」公爵夫人轉向溫德米爾夫人，驚呼道，「完全正確耶！符羅拉在麥洛斯基養了兩打可麗牧羊犬。如果她父親同意，她還打算把我們在城裡的房子變成動物園呢！」

「噢，那正是每週四晚上我使用自家房子的方式哪！」溫德米爾夫人笑著說，「只不過我喜歡獅子，遠勝過可麗牧羊犬。」

「溫德米爾夫人，這您可就失算了。」包覺思先生行了一個浮誇的鞠躬後。

「假如一個女人犯的錯不夠迷人，充其量只是個雌性動物，算不上是女人。」這是溫德米爾夫人的回答，接著又說，「可是你一定得為我們多看幾個人的手相。來嘛，湯瑪斯爵士，把你的手秀給包覺思先生看。」

一名穿著白色西裝背心，模樣很友善的老者走上前來，伸出一隻強健厚實的手，中指非常長。

「生性冒險犯難；過去曾參與四趟漫長的旅途，並且即將動身前往下一趟旅程。曾遭遇三次船難，不，目前只有兩次，但您的下一趟旅程會發生沉船的海難危險。堅定的保守黨黨員，非常守時，熱中蒐羅各種珍奇之物。十六至十八歲間曾生過一場大病。約莫三十歲時得到一大筆遺產。對貓和激進分子極為反感。」

「了不起！」湯瑪斯爵士讚嘆道，「你務必看看我妻子的手相。」

「是您第二任妻子的手相，」包覺思先生平靜地說，手中仍握著湯瑪斯爵士的手。「您第二任妻子的手相，我應該會深受吸引。」可惜，頂著一頭棕髮，雙眼頻送秋波，愁容滿面的馬謀夫人完全拒絕揭露她的過去或未來。

此外，儘管溫德米爾夫人竭盡了全力，也無法說服俄國大使狄柯洛夫先生脫下他的手套。事實上，許多人似乎害怕面對這個古怪的矮小男子和他公式化的笑容、金邊眼鏡，以及炯炯有神的銳利目光。因此，在他當著眾人的面告訴可憐的佛莫夫人，說她壓根兒不在乎音樂，只是很喜歡與音樂家為伍時，大家普遍認為手相術是一種最危險的學問，除非是兩人私下密談，否則實在不該鼓勵他人在公開場合為之。

然而，亞瑟・薩佛勛爵並不清楚有關佛莫夫人的不幸傳聞，只是興致勃勃地在旁觀看包覺思先生為人看相，他很好奇自己的手相能透露出什麼訊息，又有點羞於自告奮勇，便橫越房間走到溫德米爾夫人的座位，羞紅著臉問，包覺思先生會不會介意他的唐突。

「當然不會，他不會在意的，」溫德米爾夫人說，「那就是他在這裡的理由。亞瑟勛爵，我所有的獅子全都表現得像獅子，只要我下令，他們就會跳過火圈。不過醜話得說在前頭，我可是會把所有的事一五一十說給西碧兒聽喔。她明天會來和我共進午餐，討論軟帽的事，假如包覺思先生發現你脾氣壞，有可能會得痛風，或是有個妻子住在貝斯沃特，我肯定會讓她知道這一切。」

亞瑟勛爵笑著搖頭，答道：「我不怕。西碧兒對我的了解和我對她的認識一樣深。」

「啊，聽你這麼說讓我覺得有點遺憾，因為婚姻的基礎正是建立在彼此的誤解上。不，我並不是憤世嫉俗，只是有過經驗，不過兩者其實大同小異。」溫德米爾夫人介紹道，「包覺思先生，亞瑟・薩佛勛爵十分希望你幫他看看手相。可千萬別說他訂婚的對象是倫敦最美的女孩，因為那消息早在一個月前就出現在《晨間郵報》囉。」

「親愛的溫德米爾夫人，」杰德布拉侯爵小姐嚷道，「請

讓包覺思先生在這裡待久一點。他方才說我應該走上舞臺，而我對這建議很感興趣呢。」

「杰德布拉小姐，如果他真那麼說，那我非把他帶走不可。包覺思先生，馬上過來這邊看亞瑟勛爵的手相。」

「好吧，」杰德布拉小姐從沙發站起身時扮了個鬼臉，說道，「假如我不被允許站上舞臺，好歹也可以當個觀眾吧。」

「當然，我們全都是觀眾。」溫德米爾夫人說，「現在，包覺思先生，務必告訴我們讓人開心的事。亞瑟勛爵可是我特別鍾愛的客人呢。」

可是，當包覺思先生端詳過亞瑟勛爵的手相後，臉色卻變得出奇蒼白，不發一語。一陣戰慄穿過他全身，兩道濃眉以一種令人煩躁的古怪方式痙攣抽動——每當他迷惑困擾時，就會出現這種反應。接著，他發黃的額頭開始冒出斗大的汗珠，彷彿有毒的露珠，短胖的手指變得又濕又冷。

亞瑟勛爵將這些奇怪的焦躁跡象全看在眼裡，因此，他人生頭一遭感覺到了恐懼。他心中湧起一股想要逃出這房間的衝動，但仍設法把持住自己。與其提心吊膽、處於這種駭人的不確定感中，不如先知道最壞的狀況，無論那指的是什麼。

「包覺思先生，我在等呢！」他說。

「我們全都等著呢！」溫德米爾夫人不耐煩地急急嚷叫，可是手相師默不作聲，並不回應。

「我相信亞瑟就要站上舞臺了，」杰德布拉小姐說，「只不過，經歷你剛才的責罵，包覺思先生這下不敢對亞瑟這麼說了。」

突然間，包覺思先生放下亞瑟勛爵的右手，改抓住他的左手，彎著腰仔細研究；由於湊得太近，包覺思先生的金邊眼鏡幾乎快碰到他的手掌了。有那麼片刻，這位手相師的臉活像戴了張驚恐的白色面具，不過很快就恢復鎮定，抬起頭看著溫德

米爾夫人，露出勉強的微笑，說：「這是迷人青年的手。」

「那當然！」溫德米爾夫人應道，「但他會是個瀟灑風流的丈夫嗎？那才是我想知道的。」

「每個風度翩翩的年輕男子都會是。」包覺思先生說。

「我可不覺得丈夫太有魅力是件好事，」杰德布拉小姐心事重重咕噥著說，「那樣太危險了。」

「我親愛的孩子，做丈夫的，是絕不可能太有魅力的。」溫德米爾夫人大聲說，「可是我想知道細節，詳細的內容才是真正有趣之處。未來會有什麼事發生在亞瑟勛爵身上呢？」

「這個嘛，在接下來的幾個月內，亞瑟勛爵將會展開長途旅行……」

「那當然，度蜜月嘛！」溫德米爾夫人會意。

「他將痛失一位親人。」

「但願不是他姊姊，是她嗎？」杰德布拉小姐以哀憐的語調說道。

「當然不是，」包覺思先生揮了揮手，否定了這個猜測，並且補充說道，「只是個遠房親戚。」

「噢，我真是太失望了。」溫德米爾夫人說，「這下子，我明天我根本沒有事情可以說給西碧兒聽。如今誰會在乎遠房親戚，他們多年前就落伍啦。話說回來，我想她最好先備妥一套黑色綢緞衣裳，你知道的，那永遠適合穿去教堂。現在我們去吃點宵夜吧，他們肯定早就把菜餚全吃光了，但我們也許還能找到一些熱湯喝。弗朗索瓦曾經很擅長烹煮美味的湯品，但眼下只要談到政治，他就變得無比激動，那是我一直不大明白的事。我真心期望布朗熱將軍①能低調些。公爵夫人，我想你累了吧？」

「親愛的，我沒事，」公爵夫人蹣跚走向門口，一邊應道：「今晚很愉快，那位手足按摩師，噢，我是指那位手相師

非常有意思。符羅拉，你知道我的龜殼扇在哪兒嗎？噢，湯瑪斯爵士，非常謝謝你。符羅拉，我的蕾絲披巾呢？噢，湯瑪斯爵士，謝謝，你人真好。」她總算順利下了樓，幸好香水瓶沒再落下第三次。

在這段時間裡，亞瑟・薩佛勛爵一直站在壁爐旁，恐懼感控制了他的心思，這和即將降臨的災難同樣令人厭惡。當姊姊挽著普利姆戴爾勛爵的手臂掠過他身旁時，亞瑟勛爵也只能朝她苦笑──身穿粉紅色織錦緞、戴著珍珠項鍊的她，看起來很迷人。他幾乎沒聽見溫德米爾夫人大聲喊他過去的聲音。他想起了西碧兒・莫頓，以及可能從中作梗、阻撓他倆幸福的災厄，不禁濕了眼眶。

看看他此刻的模樣，別人可能會說──都得怪復仇女神偷了雅典娜的盾，讓他瞧見盾上蛇髮女妖的頭，害他化作石像！他意志消沉，表情像大理石一樣冷。過去由於出身富貴，他一直過著錦衣玉食的生活，不必為俗事煩心，日子過得無憂無慮。而今，他第一次意識到「命運」的神祕莫測和「劫數」的可怕意涵。

整件事如此瘋狂，如此殘忍！那寫在他手上，用他無從辨識但另一個人能解讀的符號，會是某種罪孽的駭人祕密、某種犯行的血紅跡象嗎，難道沒有逃脫的可能？難道我們跟棋子一樣，聽憑某種看不見的力量擺布，或像陶匠手中的花瓶，聽憑搓揉捏塑，不是成就榮耀便是迎來羞辱嗎？

他的理智反抗這樣的想法，然而他感覺自己籠罩在某種不幸當中，如此突然地被要求挑起那難以忍受的重擔。演員何其幸運，他們可以選擇演悲劇或喜劇，受苦或作樂，垂淚或歡笑。可是在真實生活中，完全不是這麼回事。絕大多數的男男女女被迫扮演他們無法勝任的角色。現實中，眾多的紀登斯騰為我們扮演哈姆雷特，而眾多的哈姆雷特卻得像哈爾王子那樣

打諢說笑②。世界是一座舞臺，可惜戲劇的選角卻很差勁。

　　沒想到，包覺思先生走進了房間。當他看見亞瑟勛爵，不禁大吃一驚，那張肥胖而粗俗的臉瞬間發青。兩人四目相覷，沉默了好一會兒。

　　「亞瑟勛爵，公爵夫人不小心把一隻手套掉在這裡，吩咐我來拿，」最後還是包覺思先生先開口，「啊，它在沙發上！那麼，晚安。」

　　「包覺思先生，我堅持，針對以下我要問你的問題，你一定要給我一個直言不諱的答案。」

　　「改天好嗎，亞瑟勛爵，公爵夫人急著想取回她的手套。抱歉，我得快點送過去才行。」

　　「你不能走。公爵夫人並不趕時間。」

　　「亞瑟勛爵，我們不該讓女士枯等，」包覺思先生露出令人不快的笑容，「婦道人家往往沒什麼耐性。」

　　亞瑟勛爵稜角分明的唇高高翹起，透露出任性的輕蔑。在那一刻，可憐的公爵夫人於他似乎一點也不重要。他穿過房間，走到包覺思先生站立的地方，伸出手。「告訴我，你在那裡看見了什麼。告訴我真相，我必須知道。我不是小孩。」

　　包覺思先生的雙眼在金邊眼鏡後方眨個不停，同時不安地將身體重心從這腳換到那腳，手指還神經質地不斷撥弄華麗的錶鍊。

　　「亞瑟勛爵，是什麼讓你覺得，我在你手上看見的，不只是我告訴你的那些而已？」

　　「我就是知道，而且我堅決要求你必須毫無保留地實話實說。我願意付錢，我會開一張一百英鎊的支票給你。」

　　包覺思那對綠色的眼眸頓時發亮，隨即又變得暗淡無光。「一百基尼③可以嗎？」最後，包覺思先生低聲說。

　　「沒問題。明天我派人把支票送過去。你隸屬於哪家俱樂

部？」

「我沒參加任何俱樂部，目前暫時沒有。我的住址是——讓我給你一張我的名片。」包覺思先生從西裝背心口袋掏出一張邊緣鍍金的名片，哈腰遞給亞瑟勛爵，勛爵細讀著上頭的資訊——

**塞普提墨斯・R・包覺思**
**專業手相師，月西街１０３ａ號**

「我的服務時間是早上十點到下午四點，」包覺思先生公式化地小聲說道，「家族服務另有折扣優惠。」

亞瑟勛爵臉色非常蒼白，伸出手命令道：「快點。」

包覺思先生緊張地環顧四周，將厚重的門簾拉上：「亞瑟勛爵，這會費點時間，您最好能先坐下。」

「先生，請你動作快點。」亞瑟勛爵再次出聲催促，氣急敗壞地在光滑地板上踩腳。

包覺思先生露出微笑，從胸前的口袋取出一只小型放大鏡，並且用自己的手帕仔細拂拭。

「我完全準備好了。」手相師說。

## 2

十分鐘後，亞瑟・薩佛勛爵衝出班亭克大宅，臉色因恐懼而發白，眼神因悲傷而狂亂，他在一大群聚在大型條紋遮雨篷下、身穿毛皮外套的僕從之間，擠出了一條路，彷彿看不見、也聽不到周遭的一切。

這一夜氣溫嚴寒，街心廣場周圍的煤氣燈在刺骨寒風中搖曳閃爍；可是他的手熱得發燙，他的額頭灼熱得像著了火。他不斷地往前走，腳步跟蹌，彷若醉漢。有個警察好奇地看著他

走過身邊；一名乞丐從拱廊無精打采地走過來想求他施捨，卻看見這人比自己還淒慘，不禁心生畏懼。亞瑟勛爵一度在路燈下停下腳步，凝視著自己的雙手。他心想，他能察覺到它們已經沾染了血跡，一聲微弱的吶喊從他顫抖的雙唇冒了出來。

謀殺！——那就是手相師在他手上看見的事物。謀殺！——夜晚孤獨淒涼的風在他耳中怒吼著那個字眼。街道的漆黑角落全都充滿了它，它從房子的屋頂朝自己齜牙咧嘴。

他來到海德公園，裡頭灰暗的林地似乎使他著迷。他疲憊地斜倚在欄杆上，用濕冷的金屬冷卻自己的額頭，並聆聽群樹顫抖的沉默。「謀殺！謀殺！」他不斷反覆唸著，彷彿重複地唸就能減弱這個詞的恐怖程度。自己的嗓音令他不寒而慄，然而他幾乎希望「回聲」能聽見他的話，並將沉睡的城市從夢中喚醒。他感受到一股瘋狂的欲望，想隨便叫住某個路人，向對方和盤托出。

接著他跨越牛津街，隨意走進不怎麼體面的狹窄巷弄。兩名塗脂抹粉的女子在他經過時嘲弄他。一處黑暗的庭院傳來發誓與重擊的聲音，緊接著是淒厲的慘叫聲。然後，他看見一個又窮又老的駝子蜷縮在一戶人家潮濕的大門石階上。他突然感受到一陣奇異的憐憫。莫非這些深受罪孽與苦難折磨的人也跟他一樣，他們的命運早就注定了嗎？他們是否跟他一樣，不過是一場殘忍表演的傀儡？

然而，給他重重一擊的並不是神祕的命運，而是受苦的鬧劇，它一點意義也沒有，它的存在非常荒謬；一切都顯得如此矛盾，如此不和諧！白天膚淺的樂觀和生命的實相之間竟如此不協調，讓他好生吃驚。他還那麼年輕呀！

後來，他發現自己來到馬里朋教堂前。寧靜的道路看起來像是一條熠熠發亮的銀色長絲帶，搖動暗影的渦捲線狀圖案在這裡和那裡灑下斑塊。遠處，閃爍的煤氣燈線條彎曲，一棟有

圍牆的屋子外停著一輛有篷雙輪馬車，馬夫在裡頭熟睡。

他匆匆朝波特蘭廣場的方向走去，不時四下張望，彷彿害怕被人跟蹤。兩個男人站在瑞奇街的轉角，讀著告示板上的一張小布告，一股奇異的好奇心促使他橫越過街。當他走近，以黑色字體印刷的「謀殺」二字映入他眼簾，他嚇得跳了起來，臉頰漲得通紅。那是一張懸賞告示，凡提供資訊、協助緝拿要犯者，有賞。犯人是個中等身材男子，年約三、四十歲，戴圓頂高帽，著黑色外套與格紋長褲，右頰有一道疤。他反覆閱讀這張布告，揣想這個不幸的男子是否會被逮到，此人的精神將如何飽受磨難。也許有一天，他自己的名字也會被張貼在倫敦街頭，也許有一天，他的項上人頭也會被標上價格。

這個念頭讓他很害怕。他急忙掉頭，匆匆走入夜色中。

他不太清楚自己到過哪些地方，只隱約記得自己穿過許多髒亂房子組成的迷宮，還在灰暗街道構成的巨大羅網中迷失了方向；當他發現自己最後來到皮卡底里廣場時，已是破曉時分。他朝貝爾格雷夫廣場的方向走回家，遇見了正要駛往柯芬園的大型四輪運貨馬車車隊。

身穿白色罩衫、皮膚曬得黝黑的運貨馬車夫，頂著討人喜歡的臉孔與滿頭粗糙鬈髮，強健地邁步前行，他們甩著響鞭，不時彼此吆喝。一匹高大的灰馬領著一支叮噹作響的隊伍，牠背上坐著一個胖嘟嘟的小男孩，頭上破舊的帽簷別著一束報春花，男孩的小手緊抓住馬鬃，笑得很燦爛。在清晨天空的襯托下，堆積如山的蔬菜看起來像是許多玉石；在嬌豔玫瑰的粉紅花瓣陪襯下，則像極了綠翡翠。

目睹此情此景，亞瑟勛爵深受感動，卻說不清是為什麼。黎明的嬌貴美好中，藏著讓他覺得無法形容的可憐，他想起燦爛破曉但風雨入夜的所有日子。這些莊稼漢也是如此，他們開朗粗啞的聲音，安之若素的行事風格，他們看見的是何等奇怪

的倫敦——一個擺脫夜之罪孽與日之煙霧的倫敦，一座毫無血色、鬼魅般的城市，一處荒涼的墓群！

他想知道他們怎麼看待它，他們是否知道它的輝煌與羞恥，它強烈激昂的歡樂與駭人的渴望，它從白天到黑夜的種種創造與破壞。也許對他們來說，這只是一處可以販售自家水果的市場，最多只在這兒逗留幾個小時，最終留下依舊寧靜的街道、仍然沉睡的屋舍。

觀看他們經過自己身邊帶給他很大的樂趣。他們是如此粗壯強健，穿著鞋底釘有平頭釘的沉重鞋靴，步態笨拙，身上的錢不多。他感覺他們與大自然同在，而大自然讓他們明白什麼是平靜。他羨慕他們，但他們並不知情。

待他抵達貝爾格雷夫廣場時，天空呈現淡藍色，鳥兒開始在花園中嘰嘰喳喳。

# 3

亞瑟勛爵醒來時，已是中午十二點，正午的陽光透過象牙色的絲質窗簾照射進他的房間。他起床，望向窗外。蒸騰的熱氣高懸在這座偉大城市的上空，房屋的屋頂像上了一層霧銀色。樓下，幾個孩子像白色蝴蝶般，在廣場的綠意擺動間穿梭嬉戲，人行道上熱鬧擁擠的人群正朝海德公園前行。對他來說，生命從未顯得如此討人喜愛，那些邪惡事物發生的機率從未顯得如此微小。

他的貼身男僕用托盤送來一杯巧克力。喝完後，他拉開一道厚重的蜜桃色長毛絨門簾，走進浴室。陽光穿過透光的縞瑪瑙薄板，從上方輕柔灑下，大理石浴缸的水像月光石般發出微光。他迫不及待跳入水中，直到冷涼的水波觸及喉嚨與頭髮；接著，他把頭潛入水底下，彷彿這麼做能抹去一些不光彩的記憶汙點；當他跨出浴缸時，幾乎恢復了心平氣和。此刻，精緻

的物質享受讓他暫時忘卻煩惱——這種情形其實經常發生在天性纖細的人身上，因為感官享受就像火，可以毀滅人心，也能淨化人心。

吃過早餐後，他靠在一張貴妃椅上抽菸。壁爐架上立著一張西碧兒・莫頓的大尺寸照片，邊框飾以精緻的老金線織花錦緞，如同他第一次在諾爾夫人家的舞會上看見她的模樣。那小巧、形狀美好的頭顱略略垂向一側，纖細似蘆葦的頸項彷彿快撐不住那麼多的美；她的雙唇微啟，似乎就要唱出美妙的樂音；女孩的深情單純，從那雙懷有夢想的明眸驚奇地向外張望。柔軟貼身的廣東縐紗洋裝和大型葉狀扇子，讓她看起來就像那些在塔納格拉附近橄欖樹林中、被人發現的纖細優美小陶俑——姿勢和神情永遠帶有一抹希臘式的優雅。然而，她並不嬌小，只是比例很完美——在許多女子經常自我膨脹或根本毫不起眼的這個年代，是很稀有的。

此刻，亞瑟勛爵看著她，心中滿是由愛而生的深刻遺憾。他認為，在謀殺的劫數高懸於頂之際，娶她為妻就像猶大的背叛那樣，是一種比博吉亞家族④任何成員可能想到的罪孽，還要更深重的罪惡。當他隨時都可能應命運召喚，執行寫在他手上的預言，他倆怎能有幸福可言？當命運的天秤上仍存在這項可怕的運數，他倆又將會有什麼樣的生活方式？無論如何，這椿婚事必得延後；對於這一點，他已下定決心。

儘管他愛這個女孩愛得轟轟烈烈，當他們並肩而坐，光是碰到她的手指，就能讓他身體的每條神經因強烈歡喜而激動不已，但他仍清楚意識到自己的責任所在，也完全明白除非他已犯下謀殺，否則無權結婚的這個事實。

只要完成那件事，他就能與西碧兒・莫頓站在教堂聖壇前，將他的人生交付在她手中，無須害怕自己會為非作歹。只要完成那件事，他就能讓她挽著自己的手臂，心裡清楚她永遠

無須為他臉紅，永遠無須因羞愧而抬不起頭。但是它必須先被完成；對他們兩人來說，愈快愈好。

面對他的處境，許多人寧可尋歡作樂，也不願面對責任的峭崖；可是亞瑟勛爵為人太勤懇，無法將逸樂置於原則之上。他的愛，不光是激情；西碧兒之於他，是良善與清高的化身。有那麼片刻，他對自己被要求去做的事油然生出一種反感，但隨即煙消雲散。他的心告訴他，那不是罪行，而是犧牲；他的理智提醒他，沒有其他活路可選。他必須在為自己而活與為他人而活之間二選一，儘管擺在眼前的任務確實艱困，但他明白為了愛情，絕不能自私。

我們遲早都得就同樣的議題做出抉擇，我們全都得面對同樣的問題。對亞瑟勛爵來說，這抉擇來得早了些，發生在他的心因邁入中年的算計挖苦而變質之前，或被當今膚淺時髦的自負給腐蝕之前；正因如此，他對履行自己的責任無半點遲疑。同等幸運的是，他不是個不切實際的人，也不是個袖手旁觀的半調子。倘若他是那種人，就會像哈姆雷特那樣猶豫不決，任憑優柔寡斷破壞自己的目標。但他是個很務實的人，對他來說，人生意謂著行動，而不是思想。此外，他還擁有非常罕見的物事——常識。

此時此刻，前一晚那種思緒紊亂的狂野感覺已完全消失無蹤，回顧昨晚四處瘋狂游蕩的行徑和強烈的痛苦煩惱，他心中不禁湧出一種羞愧感——那些真情流露的痛苦折磨對現在的他來說，似乎不大真實。他想知道自己怎麼會如此愚蠢，竟朝無法避免的事怒不可遏地大聲叫嚷。

如今唯一困擾他的問題是——該殺死誰；他心裡明白，正如異教徒世界裡的各種宗教必定有神職人員，謀殺也必定得有受害者。但他顯然沒有敵人，況且他認為此刻不是滿足個人宿怨或嫌惡的時機，他所要執行的是一樁偉大且莊重嚴肅的任

務哪！

　　他在一張便條紙上列出所有親戚和朋友的名字，經過審慎考慮，決定優先選擇克萊姆提納・畢歐強普夫人為目標。這名可愛的老婦人住在柯岑街，是他母親這邊的親戚，她和亞瑟勛爵是五等親的關係。他一直都很喜歡克萊姆夫人（大家都這麼稱呼她），此外，由於他本身非常富有（等到達法定年齡，便可繼承拉格比勛爵的所有財產），她的死亡並無可能為他帶來任何庸俗的金錢利益。事實上，他愈是仔細考慮這件事，就益發覺得她是再恰當不過的人選。由於他認為任何延遲對西碧兒都是不公平的，便決定立刻著手安排相關事宜。

　　第一件要辦的事，當然是付清該給手相師的錢。於是他在窗戶邊一張謝拉頓⑤風格的小型寫字檯前坐下，開了張面額一〇五鎊的支票，領款人為塞普提墨斯・包覺思先生，然後將支票放進一只信封，吩咐貼身男僕送到月西街。接下來，他打電話到馬廄讓他們準備馬車，自己則換上外出服裝。正要離開房間時，他回頭看了看西碧兒・莫頓的照片，他發誓不管發生什麼事，絕不會讓她知道，他為了她做了些什麼，而將這自我犧牲的祕密永遠深藏在心中。

　　前往白金漢俱樂部的路上，他在花店選了一籃漂亮的水仙花（娟秀的白色花瓣和那總盯著人瞧的雉雞眼刹是美麗），讓店家送去給西碧兒。一抵達俱樂部，他便直奔圖書室，搖鈴吩咐侍者為他準備一杯檸檬蘇打水，還有一本毒物學的書。他最後決定，毒藥是進行這件棘手事的最佳手段。

　　人身傷害之類的舉動令他十分反感，再說，他很不希望謀殺克萊姆提納夫人這件事引來眾人注目，因為他可不想在溫德米爾夫人家被當成名人對待，或是看見自己的名字出現在社會版新聞上。他也考慮到西碧兒的雙親，他們是相當老派的人，倘若發生醜聞，可能會反對這樁婚事；雖說他敢肯定，如

果據實說出事情始末，他們必定是第一個能理解其動機的人。因此，他有充分的理由優先選擇毒藥，它安全、可靠、寂靜無聲，排除了各種惱人不快的場景——他跟大多數英國人一樣，對此深惡痛絕。

儘管如此，他對於毒藥這門學問一無所知，而且俱樂部侍者除了《洛夫賽馬指南》和《貝禮運動休閒雜誌》，似乎怎麼也找不著圖書室裡的任何書籍。他決定自個兒檢視書架，最後找到一冊裝訂氣派的《藥典》，以及一本由皇家內科醫學院院長馬修·李德爵爺編纂的《厄斯金毒物學》。李德爵爺是白金漢俱樂部最資深的會員之一，被誤以為是別人而當選了醫學院院長；這件不幸的尷尬使校務委員會極為憤怒，因此當正牌人物出現時，他們全體一致投下了反對票。

亞瑟勛爵實在搞不懂兩本書中的大量術語，很後悔以前在牛津大學沒有對古典語言下更多功夫。他在《厄斯金毒物學》第二冊中，找到一段非常有趣且完整說明烏頭鹼特性的敘述，文字以非常淺白的英文寫成，這似乎正是他想要的那種毒藥。若以膠囊（這是馬修爵爺推薦的作法）而非其他不可口的形式服用，它的藥效十分迅速（幾乎是即時），完全無痛。

他在襯衫袖口記下致命所需的劑量，將書本放回原位，步行前往聖詹姆士街的「沛索與漢貝大藥房」。總是親自接待貴族的沛索先生看到藥方嚇了一大跳，但還是很恭敬地低聲說名這必須有處方箋才行。然而，一聽亞瑟勛爵說這是要給一條大型挪威獒犬吃的，因為牠出現了初期狂犬病跡象，而且已經咬了馬車夫的小腿兩次，這才不得不取牠性命，沛索先生轉而改口表示自己很滿意這個說法，並稱讚亞瑟勛爵的毒物學知識很豐富，立即完成配藥。

亞瑟勛爵把膠囊放進一只小巧可愛的銀製糖果盒中，那是他在龐德街一家商店櫥窗看見的戰利品；然後扔掉藥房給的醜

陌藥丸盒子後，立刻驅車前往克萊姆提納夫人的家。

當他一走進房間，老婦人即高聲說道：「噢，小淘氣先生，怎麼這麼久都沒來看我呀？」

「親愛的姨媽，我最近很忙，身不由己呀！」亞瑟勛爵笑著說。

「我想你是指自己成天和西碧兒・莫頓小姐卿卿我我，逛街買漂亮衣服，說些言不及義的事吧？我實在不懂大家為什麼會為了結婚而如此大費周章。我們那個年代啊，從沒想過要在公共場合或私底下接吻擁抱，談情說愛。」

「姨媽，我向您保證，我整整二十四個小時沒見到西碧兒了。據我了解，她現在都跟她的女帽訂製商待在一起。」

「我懂，所以你才會來探望像我這樣醜陋的老女人。我想你們男人是學不乖的。看看我，過去也曾揮霍金錢裝扮自己，而今卻只是個患有風濕的可憐老骨頭，戴著假髮，有副壞脾氣。唔，要不是親愛的簡森夫人送來了她所能找到最難看的法國小說，我還真不知要怎麼打發時間。除了從病患身上掏錢，醫生根本一無用處，他們連我的胃灼熱都治不好。」

「姨媽，我今天為您帶來了治療它的新藥。」亞瑟勛爵鄭重地說。「它很神奇，是美國人發明的。」

「亞瑟，我不覺得我會喜歡美國的發明。我很確定我不愛。最近我讀了幾部美國小說，它們全都又蠢又荒謬。」

「噢，姨媽，但這顆藥丸可不含糊！我向您保證，它可是最佳良方。答應我，您一定要試試！」亞瑟勛爵從口袋取出那只小盒子，呈給克萊姆夫人。

「哎呀，亞瑟，這盒子還真漂亮。這真的是禮物嗎？你真是非常貼心。這就是你說的神奇藥物嗎？看起來就像糖果。我現在就吃。」

「天哪！姨媽，」亞瑟勛爵提高音量，抓著她的手，說，

「您千萬別這麼做。它是一種順勢療法藥物，如果您在沒有症狀的時候服用，就沒辦法發揮作用了。等到您感覺胃灼熱發作，那時再吃才有效。它的效果肯定會讓您吃驚的。」

「哎呀，我真想現在就服用它。」克萊姆提納夫人捏住那顆透明小膠囊對著光線瞧，裡頭液態烏頭鹼⑥帶有浮動的泡沫。「我敢肯定它一定很美味。說實話，雖然我討厭醫生，可是我愛吃藥。不過，我會把它保留到下一次胃灼熱來襲時再吃。」

「那大概會是什麼時候？」亞瑟勛爵熱切地追問，「會很快嗎？」

「我希望一個星期內不會再發生。昨天早上，它害我難受得要命。可是誰也不知道下一次會是什麼時候。」

「姨媽，您能確定月底之前會發生嗎？」

「恐怕會吧。不過，亞瑟，你今天怎麼特別有同情心啊？看來西碧兒確實帶給你很好的影響。好啦，現在你該離開了，晚一點我要和幾個非常無趣的人一起吃飯，他們不道人是非，也不談論八卦，我現在如果不先小睡片刻，吃晚飯的時候絕對無法保持清醒。再見了，亞瑟，代我問候西碧兒，非常謝謝你帶給我的美國藥。」

亞瑟勛爵從座位站起身，說：「姨媽，您不會忘了吃藥吧？」

「你這傻孩子，我怎麼會忘了。謝謝你想到我，如果我還想再多吃這種藥，我會寫信告訴你的。」

亞瑟勛爵懷著大好的心情離開那間房子，感覺如釋重負。

那天晚上他去見了西碧兒·莫頓，說自己突然被指派出任一個非常困難的職務，而無論從榮譽或責任角度來看，都不容他退縮。他告訴她，婚宴的事必須暫緩，因為除非他能擺脫那些可怕的障礙，否則他無法當個隨心所欲的自由人。他懇求她相信他，無須對他們的未來有任何懷疑，一切都會順順利利，

只不過，耐心是必要的。

這番談話發生在莫頓先生家的溫室中。亞瑟勛爵一如往常來到這座位於公園道的宅第，和莫頓一家人共進晚餐。西碧兒從未顯得如此快樂，有那麼片刻，亞瑟勛爵很想當個懦夫，寫信給克萊姆提納夫人，向她坦承藥丸的事，同時讓婚事繼續進行，彷彿這世上並沒有包覺思先生這號人物。然而，出於善良的天性，他很快便堅持照原定計畫行事，就算西碧兒哭著投入他的懷抱，他也沒有動搖。這位擾亂他理智的美女更是觸動了他的良心；他相信，因為不想犧牲這短短幾個月的快樂，而毀了這樣一條美麗的生命，是錯誤的作為。

他陪著西碧兒，直到午夜將近。他安撫她，也接受她的撫慰。翌日一大早，他寫了封有男子氣概、態度堅定的信給莫頓先生，說明婚事必須延後的理由，接著便動身前往威尼斯。

# 4

他在威尼斯巧遇兄長瑟比頓勛爵，他正巧駕著遊艇從希臘科府島此。兩名年輕男子於是結伴同行，度過了愉快的兩個星期。上午，他們在利多海濱浴場騎馬，或搭乘自家的黑色長鳳尾船穿梭在綠色運河中；下午，他們通常在遊艇上招待賓客；夜晚，他們在弗洛里安咖啡館用餐，然後在廣場上抽很多香菸，數量多得數也數不清。

然而不知怎麼地，亞瑟勛爵就是快樂不起來。他每天都會仔細閱讀《泰晤士報》訃告欄，期待看見克萊姆提納夫人喪亡的訊息，但每天都落空。他開始擔心她發生了什麼意外，還經常懊悔那時她急著想嘗試烏頭鹼的藥效時，自己為什麼要阻止她服藥。西碧兒的來信也是如此，儘管內容充滿愛意、信任與溫柔，但字裡行間經常透露出傷心欲絕的情緒，有時令他感覺自己是否得永遠與她分離。

十四天後，瑟比頓勛爵已厭倦威尼斯，決定沿著海岸線往下航行到拉維耶納，他聽說有場絕妙的射公雞大賽將在那裡的松柏園舉行。起初亞瑟勛爵完全不肯去，但出於敬愛自己的哥哥，最終還是被瑟比頓說服，因為瑟比頓說，假如亞瑟獨自留在達涅利旅館，他肯定會抑鬱而終。

他們在第十五日的清晨啟程，當天吹的是東北風，白浪掀天，波濤洶湧。比賽很精彩，這種無拘無束的露天生活讓亞瑟勛爵的臉頰恢復了紅潤，可惜到了第二十二天前後，他又掛念起克萊姆提納夫人，因而不顧瑟比頓反對仍執意搭火車回威尼斯。

當他踏出鳳尾船、登上旅館臺階時，旅館老闆帶著一捆電報迎上前來。亞瑟勛爵從他手中搶過那些電報，撕開它們——成功了！克萊姆夫人非常突然地在第十七個夜晚溘然長逝！

他第一個想到的就是西碧兒，他發電報宣告他將立刻返回倫敦。接著命令貼身男僕打包他的物品，交由夜間郵務列車運回，並支付鳳尾船船夫約莫平常五倍收費的報酬，然後踩著輕盈的腳步，懷著快樂自信的心情跑上樓，回到他的起居室。他發現那兒有三封信等著他。一封來自西碧兒，信中滿是同情與慰問；另外兩封分別來自他母親，以及克萊姆提納夫人的律師。

看來那天晚上，老太太和公爵夫人共進晚餐，她幽默風趣的言辭和生氣勃勃的精神逗得在場每個人都很開心，後來她抱怨胃灼熱，身體不太舒服，便提早回家歇息。次日清晨，她被人發現死在床上，顯然沒受什麼苦就走了。儘管立刻派人請來馬修‧李德爵爺，但其實早已回天乏術。

她在第二十二天下葬在畢歐強普家族墓地。過世前幾天，她才剛立妥遺囑，將柯岑街的小房子，所有家具、私人物品和畫作留給亞瑟勛爵；小型畫作收藏則留給自己的姊姊瑪格麗特‧拉佛德夫人；她的紫水晶項鍊贈予西碧兒‧莫頓。那棟房

子的價值並不高，可是律師曼斯菲爾德先生焦急萬分，希望亞瑟勛爵如果方便，能即刻返回倫敦，因為有許多帳單待付，但克萊姆提納夫人的帳記得不太好。

亞瑟勛爵非常感動，沒想到克萊姆提納夫人會記得他，同時認為包覺思先生必須為此事負起很大的責任。然而，他對西碧兒的愛遠超過其他任何情感，他已經完成自己責任的想法帶給他平靜與安慰。當他抵達查令十字時，覺得非常開心。

莫頓一家人非常親切地接待他。西碧兒要他承諾，絕不會再讓任何事妨礙他倆，同時婚期就定在六月七日。他的人生似乎又再度恢復了光明與美麗，往日的歡樂又重回他身邊。

然而有一天，他陪伴克萊姆提納夫人的律師和西碧兒，前往柯岑街那棟房子燒毀褪色的舊信件、清空抽屜裡奇奇怪怪的垃圾時，突然間，女孩發出一聲開心的驚呼。

「西碧兒，你找到什麼了？」亞瑟勛爵從手邊的工作抬起頭，面帶笑容地說。

「亞瑟，你看這可愛的銀色小糖果盒。不覺得它很精巧、又帶點荷蘭風嗎？請把它送給我！我想得年過八十，紫水晶才會適合我。」

那正是裝有烏頭鹼的盒子。

亞瑟勛爵大吃一驚，淡淡的紅暈爬上了他的臉頰。他幾乎完全忘了自己曾做過什麼事，在他看來，這是個奇異的巧合，因為西碧兒正是他經歷那一切可怕焦慮的理由，沒想到第一個提醒他這件事的，居然是她。

「西碧兒，你當然可以保有它，那是我送給姨媽的禮物。」

「噢，亞瑟，謝謝你！我也可以保留那顆糖果嗎？我不知道原來克萊姆提納夫人喜歡甜食。畢竟她那麼有學問，怎麼會愛吃糖。」

亞瑟勛爵的臉色變得慘白，有個可怕的想法掠過他腦海。

「糖果？西碧兒，你在說什麼？」他用沙啞沉悶的聲音問道。

「盒子裡頭有一顆糖果，沒別的了。那糖果看起來好古舊，顏色灰灰的，我完全不打算吃它。亞瑟，你怎麼了？你的臉色好蒼白！」

亞瑟勳爵衝過房間，用力抓住那只盒子，裡頭裝著那顆帶有毒泡泡的琥珀色膠囊。到頭來，克萊姆提納夫人竟是壽終正寢！

這項發現帶來的衝擊讓他幾乎承受不住。他用力將膠囊扔進火焰中，頹喪地倒在沙發上，發出絕望的叫喊。

## 5

莫頓先生對婚期第二次推遲感到十分不安，而早就訂製好婚宴禮服的茱莉亞女士則用盡全力向西碧兒施壓，要她解除婚約。儘管西碧兒非常愛母親，但她已將自己的人生託付給亞瑟勳爵，不管茱莉亞女士怎麼說，都無法動搖她的信念。

至於亞瑟勳爵，他花了好幾天時間才從心灰意冷中打起精神，還一度神經衰弱。幸好，他傑出的常識很快便重新堅持自己的主張，而他健全務實的心智也未任憑他對接下來該怎麼做一直猶豫不決。毒藥作法已被證明徹底失敗，而炸藥或其他形式的爆裂物顯然值得一試。

因此，他再度檢視親友名單，經過仔細考慮後，決定炸死自己的舅舅，卻奇斯特教區的教長。這位教長是個飽學之士，非常喜愛鐘錶，珍藏了一批巧奪天工的計時器，從十五世紀到當代的作品均囊括其中。亞瑟勳爵似乎認為，這位善良教長的嗜好給了自己一個執行陰謀的絕佳機會。

至於上哪兒取得爆炸裝置，則是另一回事。倫敦電話簿無法就這一點提供他任何訊息，同時他感覺去蘇格蘭警場打聽這件事可能也沒什麼用，因為警方似乎總是無法在爆炸案發生前掌握爆炸攻擊者的動向，甚至在爆炸發生後也一樣茫無頭緒。

突然間，他想起盧洛夫，這名懷有強烈革命傾向的年輕俄國朋友，他倆在冬天於溫德米爾夫人的住所相識。盧洛夫伯爵本來想寫彼得大帝的傳記，他來英格蘭的目的，是研究沙皇當年以造船木工身分住在這個國家的檔案資料，不過，大家普遍懷疑他是個無政府主義者；毫無疑問，俄國大使館並不樂見他出現在倫敦。亞瑟勛爵認為他正是自己需要的那個人，於是某天早上駕車前往盧洛夫在布盧姆茨伯里寄宿的地方，尋求建議與協助。

　　當亞瑟勛爵告訴盧洛夫伯爵，自己執行這項任務的目標對象是誰時，盧洛夫驚訝地問：「所以，你對政治是認真的嗎？」可是亞瑟勛爵討厭自吹自擂，同時覺得有必要向對方坦誠自己對社會問題毫無興趣，之所以想弄到爆炸機關，純粹是為了處理只有自己、沒有別人會關心的家務事。

　　盧洛夫伯爵訝異地瞅著他好一會兒，發現他是認真的，便在紙上寫了個地址，簽上自己姓名的首字母，越過桌子遞給他：「我親愛的同伴，為了掌握這個地址，蘇格蘭警場會願意付出很大代價的。」

　　「他們不會拿到它的。」亞瑟勛爵笑著說。與這名俄國青年熱情握手後，他跑下樓，仔細研究那張紙，接著吩咐馬車夫駛往蘇活廣場。

　　他在那裡將馬車夫打發走，然後沿著希臘街往下走，直到抵達一個叫做貝歐坊的地方。他穿過拱廊，赫然發現自己置身在一條古怪的死巷中，它顯然被某家法式洗衣店占據了，因為晾滿衣服的曬衣繩所構成的完美網絡從這戶人家延伸到那戶人家，白色亞麻布在早晨的空氣中飄蕩翻飛。

　　他逕直走到巷底，敲了敲一棟綠色小屋的大門。等了一會兒才有人來應門；等待時，庭院裡的每扇窗前都擠滿了看熱鬧的面孔。來開門的是個橫眉豎目的外國人，操著非常蹩腳的

英語問他有何貴幹。亞瑟勛爵把盧洛夫伯爵給的那張紙遞給對方。那人見了，立刻躬身致意，邀請亞瑟勛爵進入一樓前方的一間寒酸客廳。幾分鐘後，有位在英格蘭被稱為溫科考夫先生的男子闖入房間裡，脖子圍著一條布滿酒漬的餐巾，左手還握著一把叉子。

「盧洛夫伯爵介紹我來找您，」亞瑟勛爵一邊鞠躬一邊說，「我急著想與您簡短會面，商談一件委託案。我的名字是史密斯，羅伯特・史密斯先生，希望您為我打造一座會爆炸的時鐘。」

「很榮幸能見到您，亞瑟勛爵。」這名身材短小的德國人親切地笑著說，「您別那麼驚恐，認識每個人是我的本分，而我記得某天晚上曾在溫德米爾夫人家見過您。我希望夫人一切安好。您介意坐著等我吃完早餐嗎？這個肉派很棒。我的朋友很客氣地說，我的萊茵河葡萄酒比他們在德國大使館喝過的更美味。」

還沒從被人認出的吃驚情狀恢復過來，亞瑟勛爵已被帶到後面的房間坐下，用一只印有皇室花押字的淺黃色霍克杯，啜飲無比美味的萊茵河流域白葡萄酒，與著名的陰謀家以最友善的方式閒聊。

「會爆炸的時鐘，」溫科考夫先生說，「不太適合輸出到國外，因為就算它們能順利通過海關，火車的運轉狀況也常有變化，它們往往會在抵達適當的目的地前就先行爆炸。不過，如果是在國內使用，我可以提供您一個出色的物件，同時保證您一定會對結果感到滿意。我可以請教您的目標對象是誰嗎？假如是對付警方，或者用在跟蘇格蘭警場有關的任何人身上，請恕我無法協助您。英國警探實在是我們最棒的盟友，我一直認為，多虧了他們的愚蠢，我們才能為所欲為。我不願將他們任何一個讓給別人。」

「我向您保證，」亞瑟勛爵回答，「這件事跟警方毫無瓜葛。事實上，時鐘是為卻奇斯特教區教長準備的。」

「天哪！亞瑟勛爵，我不知道您對宗教有那麼強烈的主張。如今很少有年輕人在乎了。」

「溫科考夫先生，您太高估我了，」亞瑟勛爵羞紅了臉，說，「其實，我對神學一無所知。」

「所以只是單純的私人恩怨嗎？」

「沒錯。」

溫科考夫先生聳聳肩，走了出去，幾分鐘後再回來時，拿著一塊一便士大小的炸藥圓餅，還有一座漂亮的小型法式時鐘，頂端站著一尊鍍金的自由女神像，其腳底踩著代表專制暴政的九頭蛇。

亞瑟勛爵看見它的時候，整張臉都亮了起來。「那正是我想要的，」他高聲叫道，「現在請告訴我如何啟動它，讓它爆炸。」

「啊！那是我的祕密。」溫科考夫先生帶著理直氣壯的自豪神情，凝視著自己的創作，回應道：「告訴我，您希望它何時爆炸，我來設定它的引爆時間。」

「唔，今天是星期二，如果您能立刻將它送出……」

「那是不可能的。我手邊有很多莫斯科朋友委託的重要工作正在進行。不過，明天我也許能將它寄出。」

「噢，如果能在明天晚上或星期四上午寄出，時間都還很充裕！」亞瑟勛爵客氣地表示，「至於引爆時間，就定在星期五正午時分吧。教區教長那時都會在家。」

「星期五，正午。」溫科考夫先生複誦著，並在壁爐旁大辦公桌上的一本大型登記簿寫下約定內容。

「現在，」亞瑟勛爵從座椅站起身，說，「請問我該付您多少錢呢？」

「亞瑟勛爵，這不過是舉手之勞，我不在乎有沒有收費。炸藥本身是七先令六便士，時鐘三鎊十先令，運費大約五先令。光是能幫上盧洛夫伯爵朋友的忙，就讓我夠開心的了。」

「溫科考夫先生，那讓您費心勞神的製作費用呢？」

「噢，那沒什麼！那對我而言是樂事。我不為錢而工作，我的生命完全奉獻給我的藝術。」

亞瑟勛爵在桌上留下四鎊二先令六便士，感謝這名小個子德國人的付出，並成功回絕在接下來的星期六，與這些無政府主義者在傍晚茶點時會面，而後便離開了那間房子，前往海德公園。

接下來兩天，他一直處於很興奮的狀態。星期五那天的中午十二點，他駕車來到白金漢俱樂部等消息。整個下午，神情淡漠的門房忙著張貼來自全國各地的電報，內容包括賽馬結果、離婚訴訟判決、天氣狀況等等，自動收報機的紙帶則不斷吐出下議院通宵開會的無聊細節，以及股票交易市場的一場小恐慌。

下午四點，晚報送來了。亞瑟勛爵帶著《波茂時事報》、《聖詹姆士報》、《環球晚報》和《回聲報》鑽進圖書室，這舉動引起古柴德上校的不滿，因為他想閱讀報紙對他當天早上在市長官邸發表演說的報導，演說主題包括南非宣教活動；在每個省份均設有黑人教長是否明智，以及基於某種原因對《晚間新聞報》懷有強烈偏見而不願讀它。

然而，沒有任何一份晚報提到卻奇斯特教區教長，就連最輕微的暗示也沒有，亞瑟勛爵因而認為這次的行動必定失敗了。這對他是個沉重的打擊，讓他一度相當氣餒。

第二天他去找溫科考夫先生，這位德國人向他致歉連連，並允諾免費給他另一座時鐘，或以成本價提供他一盒硝化甘油炸彈。可是他對炸藥已完全失去信心，而且溫科考夫先生自己

也承認，當今攙偽造假如此盛行，就連炸藥也很難拿到純的。

　　儘管這個小個子德國人承認那機關必定哪裡出了差錯，但他依然抱持希望，相信那時鐘仍舊會爆炸。他舉了個實例，以前曾經寄一支氣壓計給敖德薩的都督，原本設定十天後會爆炸，結果三個月後才真的爆炸。沒錯，當爆炸發生時，它只成功地將一名女傭炸得粉身碎骨，都督早在六週前就出城了，但至少它證明炸藥做為一種毀滅力量，在機械裝置的控制下，儘管不夠準時，卻是一種威力強大的媒介。

　　這段說明讓亞瑟勛爵略感安慰，不過就連這一點，他也注定要失望。因為兩天後，當他上樓時，公爵夫人把他叫進自己的閨房，讓他看她剛收到教長宅邸寄來的信。

　　「珍的信寫得真好，」公爵夫人說，「你一定要看看這封信的最後一段。它跟穆迪⑤寄給我們的小說，同樣精彩呢！」亞瑟勛爵從她手中搶過那封信。內容如下──

教長宅邸，卻奇斯特
五月二十七日

親愛的姨媽：

　　非常謝謝您為多加慈善會捐獻法蘭絨布，也謝謝您提供格紋棉布。我很贊同您的看法，那些貧民想穿漂亮的衣物實在荒謬，可是如今每個人都很激進、又不敬神，想要讓他們明白自己不該努力穿得像上流階級是很困難的事。我真不知道我們來這兒為的是什麼。就像爸爸常在講道時說的，我們活在一個不信上帝的年代。

　　上週四有個不知名的仰慕者送爸爸一座時鐘，它逗得我們好開心。它裝在一個木盒子裡，從倫敦送出，運費已付。爸爸認為，必定是讀了他〈放縱等同於自由嗎？〉這篇不平

凡佈道文的讀者寄來的，因爲那座時鐘頂端有個女子雕像，爸爸說她頭上戴的是自由帽⑥。我個人並不覺得這座鐘有何特別的魅力，可是爸爸說它具有歷史意義，所以我想就這樣吧。帕克打開包裹取出它，接著爸爸將它放在書房的壁爐臺上。週五上午我們全都坐在書房中，當那座鐘敲了第十二響之後，我們聽見一陣嘶嘶聲，一陣煙從雕像的臺座冒出來，那尊自由女神竟然摔下來，在壁爐前的圍欄上撞破了鼻子！瑪麗亞相當驚慌，可是它看起來如此滑稽，害詹姆士和我笑得停不下來，就連爸爸也被逗樂了。後來我們仔細檢查它，發現那是一種鬧鈴時鐘，只要你把它設定在某個時間，在鐘鎚下方放一點紙包火藥，它就能在你希望的時間爆炸。爸爸說它不能繼續放在書房，因爲它會製造噪音，所以瑞吉把它拿去教室放，它沒別的招數，就是整天製造小型爆炸。您覺得亞瑟會想要一個當作結婚禮物嗎？我猜，這類時鐘在倫敦可能挺時髦的。爸爸說它們對世人非常有益，因爲它們表明自由無法恆久遠，遲早注定要垮臺。爸爸說，自由是法國大革命時虛構的東西。它看起來真可怕！

　　現在我得去多加慈善會服務了。我會將您非常富有教育意義的信唸給他們聽。親愛的姨媽，您的見解再正確不過，就他們的身分地位來說，他們想穿的服裝並不得體。我必須說，考慮到這一世和下輩子還有更多重要的事，不禁讓人覺得他們對於衣著的渴望實在荒謬。我很開心您的印花府綢穿起來如此令人滿意，而且蕾絲都沒有破損呢。週三那天，我打算穿您好意送我的黃色綢緞上主教家，我想它看起來肯定會挺不錯的。換作是您，會不會佩戴蝴蝶結呢？珍寧絲說，現在人人都戴蝴蝶結，而且襯裙得有褶邊才行。瑞吉剛剛遇上了另一次爆炸，爸爸吩咐他將那座時鐘移到馬廄去。我認爲，雖然爸爸覺得很榮幸能收到這樣一件漂亮又精巧的玩

具，但他不像起初那樣喜歡它了，儘管它確實表明大眾閱讀他的佈道文，並從中獲益。

爸爸要我問候您，詹姆士、瑞吉與瑪麗亞和我全都希望賽索姨丈的痛風比較舒緩了些。相信我，親愛的姨媽，最愛您的外甥女，

珍・裴西

另，請務必告訴我蝴蝶結的事。珍寧絲堅持那是最時尚的東西。

亞瑟勛爵對這封信露出非常不開心的嚴肅表情，令公爵夫人為之噗哧一笑。「親愛的亞瑟，」她大聲說道，「我再也不會拿年輕女孩的信給你看了！但是對於那座時鐘，我該怎麼說才好呢？我想它是首都的新發明，我自己也很想擁有一個。」

「我不太喜歡那些玩意兒。」亞瑟勛爵露出悲傷的笑容說。親吻了母親後，隨即離開這個房間。上樓後，他整個人倒在沙發上，眼中滿是淚水。他已竭盡全力想讓這樁謀殺罪行成立，但兩次都失敗了，而且錯不在他。他努力履行自己的義務，但命運女神似乎背叛了他。他深深覺得好心沒好報，努力行善全是徒勞。

也許，徹底解除婚約會是比較好的選擇。西碧兒會因而受苦，確實如此，但受苦並不會真正玷污她高貴的天性。至於他自己，那又有什麼關係呢？總有戰爭可以讓男人戰死沙場，總有理由可以讓男人捐棄生命，既然人生對他而言已無樂趣，死又何足懼。就讓命運帶來死亡，他不願再幫忙她了。

晚間七點半，他起身著衣，前往俱樂部。瑟比頓和一幫小夥子在那裡聚會，他不得不和他們共進晚餐。他們瑣碎的談話和無聊的玩笑引不起他的興趣，一等到咖啡端上桌，他就虛構

了個約會，以求順利脫身。正要離開俱樂部之際，門房交給他一封信。信是溫科考夫先生寄的，邀請他翌日傍晚過去一趟，看一支會爆炸的傘，只要一打開傘，就會立刻引爆。它是最新的發明，剛從日內瓦送來。他把信撕成碎片，並已下定決心，不再嘗試任何實驗。

接著他漫步來到泰晤士河堤岸，在河岸邊坐了好幾個小時。月娘從一片長而濃密的黃褐色雲層間張望塵世，彷若獅子的一隻眼睛；數不清的星辰在無垠蒼穹中閃閃發亮，像金粉灑在紫色圓頂上。

偶爾，一艘大平底船掉頭，駛入渾濁的河水中，順著潮水漸行漸遠，而鐵路信號則在火車呼嘯過橋時從綠色轉為深紅色。不久之後，西敏寺的高塔響起午夜十二點的鐘聲，宏亮的鐘聲聲聲撼動著黑夜。接著，鐵路沿線的燈全熄滅了，獨留一盞孤燈發出微弱的光線，像巨大桅杆上的一顆大紅寶石，城市的喧囂沉寂了下來。

深夜兩點，他站起身，朝布萊克弗萊爾的方向躂步走去。這一切顯得如此不真實，多麼像一場奇怪的惡夢！河岸對面的房子彷彿建築在黑暗之外；有人會說，銀色和陰影讓這世界煥然一新。聖保羅大教堂的巨大圓頂隱約可見，像一顆穿越昏暗夜空的氣泡。

接近克麗歐佩特拉方尖碑時，他看見一個男人斜倚在護牆上，等他走得更近些，對方抬起頭，煤油燈光照亮了那人的臉。

沒想到是包覺思先生，那個手相師！沒有人會認錯那張肥胖鬆垮的臉，那副金邊眼鏡，令人厭惡的軟弱笑容，肥厚的嘴。

亞瑟勛爵停下腳步。一個絕妙的主意閃過他腦海，他靜靜地尾隨在後。他瞬間抓住包覺思先生的雙腿，用力將他扔進泰晤士河。先是響起粗俗的咒罵、大量的拍打水面聲響，接著，一切歸於寂靜。

亞瑟勛爵焦急地四下張望，但除了一頂大禮帽在月色下的河水中急急打轉，到處都看不見手相師的蹤影。過了一會兒，那頂帽子也沉入水中，找不到包覺思先生的蛛絲馬跡。有一度，他以為自己瞥見那身形醜陋的龐大人影奮力朝橋墩旁的樓梯游去，他忽然感到一陣毛骨悚然的失敗感，結果那只是一個倒影，等到月亮從雲朵背後發出光芒，它便消失了。最後，他似乎終於領悟了命運的安排，如釋重負地深深嘆了口氣，嘴裡不禁唸著西碧兒的名字。

「先生，您掉了什麼東西嗎？」一個聲音突然在他背後響起。

他轉身，看見一名警察提著一盞牛眼燈。

「警官，不是什麼重要的東西。」他笑著回答，招了一輛路過的載客馬車。上車後，吩咐車夫前往貝爾格雷夫廣場。

接下來的幾天，他一直在希望與恐懼之間擺盪。有些時候，他幾乎以為包覺思先生就要走進房間內，然而其他時候又覺得命運不會待他如此不公。他曾兩度前往手相師位在月西街的住所，但就是無法按下門鈴——他渴求確定，卻又害怕一翻兩瞪眼。

終於，結果出爐。當侍者拿著晚報走進來的時候，他正坐在俱樂部的吸菸室喝茶，不耐煩地聽著瑟比頓訴說歡樂劇場最新的滑稽歌曲。他拿起《聖詹姆士報》，無精打采地翻閱每一版，這時，一則奇怪的標題擄獲了他的目光——「手相師自殺」。他臉色發白但內心興奮，開始往下閱讀。這則新聞的內容如下——

昨日清晨七點，著名手相師塞普提墨斯・R・包覺思的遺體被沖上格林威治的河岸，正好停在船艦旅館前方。這名不幸男子失蹤多日，手相圈莫不為他的安危感到擔憂。據推測，自殺原因可能是工作太過勞累，導致他產生暫時性精神錯亂，驗

屍官陪審團已於今日下午裁定為自殺。包覺思先生剛剛完成一部以人類手相為題的詳盡專著，近期內便會出版問世，屆時必能吸引眾人的重視。死者享壽六十又五，似乎沒有留下任何遺族。

　　亞瑟勛爵手上拽著報紙，衝出了俱樂部，門房見狀無比驚愕，試圖阻止卻徒勞。他隨即驅車前往公園道。西碧兒從窗戶瞧見他，直覺告訴她，未婚夫帶來的是好消息。她跑下樓迎接，她一看見他，就知道一切都將雨過天青。

　　「我親愛的西碧兒，」亞瑟勛爵開心嚷道，「我們明天就結婚吧！」

　　「你這傻瓜，結婚蛋糕都還沒訂呢！」西碧兒又哭又笑地說。

## 6

　　婚禮在三週後舉行，聖彼得大教堂擠滿一群漂亮時髦的人。婚禮儀式由卻奇斯特教區教長以最令人印象深刻的方式主持，眾人一致同意這對璧人是最登對的新娘與新郎；而且他們不只登對，還很幸福。亞瑟勛爵不曾有片刻後悔自己為西碧兒嘗盡了苦頭，西碧兒則給了亞瑟無限的崇拜、柔情與愛，那是女人所能給予男人最棒的東西。他們的浪漫戀情沒有被現實扼殺，他們的心境永保年輕。

　　多年後，他們生了一雙漂亮的孩子，溫德米爾夫人前來艾爾頓修道院探望他們——艾爾頓修道院是棟漂亮的老房子，是公爵送給兒子的結婚禮物。有天下午，溫德米爾夫人與亞瑟夫人一起坐在庭院的菩提樹下，看著小男孩與小女孩在玫瑰花棚下到處嬉戲玩耍，像極了跳動閃耀的陽光。溫德米爾夫人突然握住女主人的手，說：「西碧兒，你幸福嗎？」

「親愛的溫德米爾夫人，我當然很幸福啊。難道您不是嗎？」

「西碧兒，我沒時間感受幸福。我總是見一個愛一個，偏偏，認識對方的那一刻，通常也就是我厭倦對方的開端。」

「您的那些雄獅無法滿足您嗎？」

「噢，親愛的，當然不能！雄獅的魅力只能維持一季。一旦他們的鬃毛被剪下，就成了眼下最無趣的生物。更何況，如果你對他們很好，他們反而會很不聽話。你還記得那個可惡的包覺思先生嗎？他是個糟糕的騙子。當然，我根本不在乎，就算他想跟我借錢，我也能原諒他，但我不能忍受的是，他向我示愛。他真的讓我恨透了手相術。我現在改做心電感應，這有趣多了。」

「溫德米爾夫人，您千萬別在我家說您反對手相術，這是亞瑟唯一不喜歡別人拿它開玩笑的事。我向您保證，他對這件事可是很認真的。」

「西碧兒，你的意思是說他相信手相術嗎？」

「溫德米爾夫人，您自個兒問他吧，他來了。」亞瑟勛爵手裡捧著一大束黃玫瑰現身在庭園中，兩個孩子繞著他手舞足蹈。

「亞瑟勛爵？」

「是，溫德米爾夫人。」

「你該不會真的相信手相術吧？」

「我當然相信。」亞瑟勛爵笑著說。

「為什麼呢？」

「因為我人生的幸福全都得歸功於它，」他低聲說道，一屁股坐進籐椅中。

「我親愛的亞瑟勛爵，你認為什麼該歸功於它？」

「西碧兒。」他一邊說，一邊把玫瑰送給妻子，還深情凝視著她紫羅蘭色的雙眸。

「胡說八道！」溫德米爾夫人大聲嚷道，「我這輩子從未聽過這麼荒謬的事。」

譯注

① 布朗熱將軍（Georges Ernest Boulanger，1837～1891），法國陸軍部長，後來離開軍隊，投身政壇。在法蘭西第三共和時期欲發起軍事政變，卻以失敗收場，只得逃亡比利時，最終自殺身亡。

② 紀登斯騰（Guildensterns）是《哈姆雷特》中的配角；魯莽的哈爾王子（Prince Hal）後來在《亨利五世》中繼位，成為亨利五世。意喻命運和際遇半點不由人。

③ 一基尼為一點〇五鎊，一百基尼則是一百〇五鎊；這是一宗抬價成功的交易。

④ 來自西班牙瓦倫西亞的博吉亞家族（House of Borgia）於十五、十六世紀，透過聯姻與政治結盟而權傾天下。博吉亞家族出了兩位教宗，但家族成員也涉及許多不名譽的醜聞，如通姦、買賣聖職、賄賂、偷竊、下毒暗殺等等。後人常將裙帶關係、背信忘義、享樂主義、毒殺，與博吉亞家族畫上等號。

⑤ 謝拉頓（Thomas Sheraton，1751～1806），十八世紀英國家具設計三巨頭之一，其作品線條優美，裝飾精緻，結構簡潔。

⑥ 烏頭鹼，是由毛茛科植物「烏頭」的葉和根，所提煉出的一種生物鹼，具強烈毒性。口服約零點二毫克便會中毒，攝食三～五毫克即致命。烏頭，是常見中藥材。

⑦ 穆迪，是指英國書商查理・愛德華・穆迪（Charles Edward Mudie，1818～1890）。由於當時（維多利亞時代）的大多數中產階級，無法獨力負擔購買小說的金錢，因此類似穆迪經營的租書店，對出版商和作者來說具有強大的影響力。

穆迪的小說租賃事業十分成功，直到一九三○年代公共圖書館的數量增多後，才逐漸式微。

⑧ 一種無沿的錐形軟帽。原為古羅馬時代被釋放奴隸所戴的帽子，後來在十八世紀法國大革命時期被用以象徵自由。

# Lord Arthur Savile's Crime

## 1

It was Lady Windermere's last reception before Easter, and Bentinck House was even more crowded than usual. Six Cabinet Ministers had come on from the Speaker's Levee in their stars and ribands, all the pretty women wore their smartest dresses, and at the end of the picture-gallery stood the Princess Sophia of Carlsruhe, a heavy Tartar-looking lady, with tiny black eyes and wonderful emeralds, talking bad French at the top of her voice, and laughing immoderately at everything that was said to her. It was certainly a wonderful medley of people. Gorgeous peeresses chatted affably to violent Radicals, popular preachers brushed coat-tails with eminent sceptics, a perfect bevy of bishops kept following a stout prima-donna from room to room, on the staircase stood several Royal Academicians, disguised as artists, and it was said that at one time the supper-room was absolutely crammed with geniuses. In fact, it was one of Lady Windermere's best nights, and the Princess stayed till nearly half-past eleven.

As soon as she had gone, Lady Windermere returned to the picture-gallery, where a celebrated political economist was solemnly explaining the scientific theory of music to an indignant virtuoso from Hungary, and began to talk to the Duchess of Paisley. She looked wonderfully beautiful with her grand ivory throat, her large blue forget-me-not eyes, and her heavy coils of golden hair. Or pur they were — not that pale straw colour that nowadays usurps the gracious name of gold, but such gold as is woven into sunbeams or hidden in strange amber; and they gave to her face something of the frame of a saint, with not a little of the fascination of a sinner. She was a curious psychological study. Early in life she had discovered the important truth that nothing looks so like innocence as an indiscretion; and by a series of reckless escapades, half of them quite harmless, she had acquired all the privileges of a personality. She had more than once changed her husband; indeed, Debrett credits her with three marriages; but as she had never changed her lover, the world had long ago ceased to talk scandal about her. She was now forty years of age, childless, and with that inordinate passion for pleasure which is the secret of remaining young.

Suddenly she looked eagerly round the room, and said, in her clear contralto voice, 'Where is my cheiromantist?'

'Your what, Gladys?' exclaimed the Duchess, giving an involuntary start.

'My cheiromantist, Duchess; I can't live without him at present.'

'Dear Gladys! you are always so original,' murmured the Duchess, trying to remember what a cheiromantist really was, and hoping it was not the same as a cheiropodist.

'He comes to see my hand twice a week regularly,'

continued Lady Windermere, 'and is most interesting about it.'

'Good heavens!' said the Duchess to herself, 'he is a sort of cheiropodist after all. How very dreadful. I hope he is a foreigner at any rate. It wouldn't be quite so bad then.'

'I must certainly introduce him to you.'

'Introduce him!' cried the Duchess; 'you don't mean to say he is here?' and she began looking about for a small tortoise-shell fan and a very tattered lace shawl, so as to be ready to go at a moment's notice.

'Of course he is here; I would not dream of giving a party without him. He tells me I have a pure psychic hand, and that if my thumb had been the least little bit shorter, I should have been a confirmed pessimist, and gone into a convent.'

'Oh, I see!' said the Duchess, feeling very much relieved; 'he tells fortunes, I suppose?'

'And misfortunes, too,' answered Lady Windermere, 'any amount of them. Next year, for instance, I am in great danger, both by land and sea, so I am going to live in a balloon, and draw up my dinner in a basket every evening. It is all written down on my little finger, or on the palm of my hand, I forget which.'

'But surely that is tempting Providence, Gladys.'

'My dear Duchess, surely Providence can resist temptation by this time. I think every one should have their hands told once a month, so as to know what not to do. Of course, one does it all the same, but it is so pleasant to be warned. Now if some one doesn't go and fetch Mr. Podgers at once, I shall have to go myself.'

'Let me go, Lady Windermere,' said a tall handsome

young man, who was standing by, listening to the conversation with an amused smile.

'Thanks so much, Lord Arthur; but I am afraid you wouldn't recognise him.'

'If he is as wonderful as you say, Lady Windermere, I couldn't well miss him. Tell me what he is like, and I'll bring him to you at once.'

'Well, he is not a bit like a cheiromantist. I mean he is not mysterious, or esoteric, or romantic-looking. He is a little, stout man, with a funny, bald head, and great gold-rimmed spectacles; something between a family doctor and a country attorney. I'm really very sorry, but it is not my fault. People are so annoying. All my pianists look exactly like poets, and all my poets look exactly like pianists; and I remember last season asking a most dreadful conspirator to dinner, a man who had blown up ever so many people, and always wore a coat of mail, and carried a dagger up his shirt-sleeve; and do you know that when he came he looked just like a nice old clergyman, and cracked jokes all the evening? Of course, he was very amusing, and all that, but I was awfully disappointed; and when I asked him about the coat of mail, he only laughed, and said it was far too cold to wear in England. Ah, here is Mr. Podgers! Now, Mr. Podgers, I want you to tell the Duchess of Paisley's hand. Duchess, you must take your glove off. No, not the left hand, the other.'

'Dear Gladys, I really don't think it is quite right,' said the Duchess, feebly unbuttoning a rather soiled kid glove.

'Nothing interesting ever is,' said Lady Windermere: 'on a fait le monde ainsi. But I must introduce you. Duchess, this is Mr. Podgers, my pet cheiromantist. Mr. Podgers, this is the Duchess of Paisley, and if you say that she has a larger mountain of the moon than I have, I will never believe in you again.'

'I am sure, Gladys, there is nothing of the kind in my

hand,' said the Duchess gravely.

'Your Grace is quite right,' said Mr. Podgers, glancing at the little fat hand with its short square fingers, 'the mountain of the moon is not developed. The line of life, however, is excellent. Kindly bend the wrist. Thank you. Three distinct lines on the rascette! You will live to a great age, Duchess, and be extremely happy. Ambition — very moderate, line of intellect not exaggerated, line of heart —'

'Now, do be indiscreet, Mr. Podgers,' cried Lady Windermere.

'Nothing would give me greater pleasure,' said Mr. Podgers, bowing, 'if the Duchess ever had been, but I am sorry to say that I see great permanence of affection, combined with a strong sense of duty.'

'Pray go on, Mr. Podgers,' said the Duchess, looking quite pleased.

'Economy is not the least of your Grace's virtues,' continued Mr. Podgers, and Lady Windermere went off into fits of laughter.

'Economy is a very good thing,' remarked the Duchess complacently; 'when I married Paisley he had eleven castles, and not a single house fit to live in.'

'And now he has twelve houses, and not a single castle,' cried Lady Windermere.

'Well, my dear,' said the Duchess, 'I like —'

'Comfort,' said Mr. Podgers, 'and modern improvements, and hot water laid on in every bedroom. Your Grace is quite right. Comfort is the only thing our civilisation can give us.

'You have told the Duchess's character admirably, Mr. Podgers, and now you must tell Lady Flora's'; and in answer to a nod from the smiling hostess, a tall girl, with sandy Scotch hair, and high shoulder-blades, stepped awkwardly from behind the sofa, and held out a long, bony hand with spatulate fingers.

'Ah, a pianist! I see,' said Mr. Podgers, 'an excellent pianist, but perhaps hardly a musician. Very reserved, very honest, and with a great love of animals.'

'Quite true!' exclaimed the Duchess, turning to Lady Windermere, 'absolutely true! Flora keeps two dozen collie dogs at Macloskie, and would turn our town house into a menagerie if her father would let her.'

'Well, that is just what I do with my house every Thursday evening,' cried Lady Windermere, laughing, 'only I like lions better than collie dogs.'

'Your one mistake, Lady Windermere,' said Mr. Podgers, with a pompous bow.

'If a woman can't make her mistakes charming, she is only a female,' was the answer. 'But you must read some more hands for us. Come, Sir Thomas, show Mr. Podgers yours'; and a genial-looking old gentleman, in a white waistcoat, came forward, and held out a thick rugged hand, with a very long third finger.

'An adventurous nature; four long voyages in the past, and one to come. Been ship-wrecked three times. No, only twice, but in danger of a shipwreck your next journey. A strong Conservative, very punctual, and with a passion for collecting curiosities. Had a severe illness between the ages sixteen and eighteen. Was left a fortune when about thirty. Great aversion to cats and Radicals.'

'Extraordinary!' exclaimed Sir Thomas; 'you must really tell my wife's hand, too.'

'Your second wife's,' said Mr. Podgers quietly, still keeping Sir Thomas's hand in his. 'Your second wife's. I shall be charmed'; but Lady Marvel, a melancholy-looking woman, with brown hair and sentimental eyelashes, entirely declined to have her past or her future exposed; and nothing that Lady Windermere could do would induce Monsieur de Koloff, the Russian Ambassador, even to take his gloves off. In fact, many people seemed afraid to face the odd little man with his stereotyped smile, his gold spectacles, and his bright, beady eyes; and when he told poor Lady Fermor, right out before every one, that she did not care a bit for music, but was extremely fond of musicians, it was generally felt that cheiromancy was a most dangerous science, and one that ought not to be encouraged, except in a tete-a-tete.

Lord Arthur Savile, however, who did not know anything about Lady Fermor's unfortunate story, and who had been watching Mr. Podgers with a great deal of interest, was filled with an immense curiosity to have his own hand read, and feeling somewhat shy about putting himself forward, crossed over the room to where Lady Windermere was sitting, and, with a charming blush, asked her if she thought Mr. Podgers would mind.

'Of course, he won't mind,' said Lady Windermere, 'that is what he is here for. All my lions, Lord Arthur, are performing lions, and jump through hoops whenever I ask them. But I must warn you beforehand that I shall tell Sybil everything. She is coming to lunch with me tomorrow, to talk about bonnets, and if Mr. Podgers finds out that you have a bad temper, or a tendency to gout, or a wife living in Bayswater, I shall certainly let her know all about it.'

Lord Arthur smiled, and shook his head. 'I am not afraid,' he answered. 'Sybil knows me as well as I know her.'

'Ah! I am a little sorry to hear you say that. The proper basis for marriage is a mutual misunderstanding. No, I am not at all cynical, I have merely got experience, which, however, is very much the same thing. Mr. Podgers, Lord Arthur Savile is dying to have his hand read. Don't tell him that he is engaged to one of the most beautiful girls in London, because that appeared in the Morning Post a month ago.

'Dear Lady Windermere,' cried the Marchioness of Jedburgh, 'do let Mr. Podgers stay here a little longer. He has just told me I should go on the stage, and I am so interested.'

'If he has told you that, Lady Jedburgh, I shall certainly take him away. Come over at once, Mr. Podgers, and read Lord Arthur's hand.'

'Well,' said Lady Jedburgh, making a little moue as she rose from the sofa, 'if I am not to be allowed to go on the stage, I must be allowed to be part of the audience at any rate.'

'Of course; we are all going to be part of the audience,' said Lady Windermere; 'and now, Mr. Podgers, be sure and tell us something nice. Lord Arthur is one of my special favourites.'

But when Mr. Podgers saw Lord Arthur's hand he grew curiously pale, and said nothing. A shudder seemed to pass through him, and his great bushy eyebrows twitched convulsively, in an odd, irritating way they had when he was puzzled. Then some huge beads of perspiration broke out on his yellow forehead, like a poisonous dew, and his fat fingers grew cold and clammy.

Lord Arthur did not fail to notice these strange signs of agitation, and, for the first time in his life, he himself felt fear. His impulse was to rush from the room, but he restrained himself. It was better to know the worst, whatever it was, than to be left in this hideous uncertainty.

'I am waiting, Mr. Podgers,' he said.

'We are all waiting,' cried Lady Windermere, in her quick, impatient manner, but the cheiromantist made no reply.

'I believe Arthur is going on the stage,' said Lady Jedburgh, 'and that, after your scolding, Mr. Podgers is afraid to tell him so.'

Suddenly Mr. Podgers dropped Lord Arthur's right hand, and seized hold of his left, bending down so low to examine it that the gold rims of his spectacles seemed almost to touch the palm. For a moment his face became a white mask of horror, but he soon recovered his sang-froid, and looking up at Lady Windermere, said with a forced smile, 'It is the hand of a charming young man.

'Of course it is!' answered Lady Windermere, 'but will he be a charming husband? That is what I want to know.'

'All charming young men are,' said Mr. Podgers.

'I don't think a husband should be too fascinating,' murmured Lady Jedburgh pensively, 'it is so dangerous.'

'My dear child, they never are too fascinating,' cried Lady Windermere. 'But what I want are details. Details are the only things that interest. What is going to happen to Lord Arthur?'

'Well, within the next few months Lord Arthur will go a voyage —'

'Oh yes, his honeymoon, of course!'

'And lose a relative.'

'Not his sister, I hope?' said Lady Jedburgh, in a piteous tone of voice.

'Certainly not his sister,' answered Mr. Podgers, with a deprecating wave of the hand, 'a distant relative merely.'

'Well, I am dreadfully disappointed,' said Lady Windermere. 'I have absolutely nothing to tell Sybil tomorrow.

No one cares about distant relatives nowadays. They went out of fashion years ago. However, I suppose she had better have a black silk by her; it always does for church, you know. And now let us go to supper. They are sure to have eaten everything up, but we may find some hot soup. Francois used to make excellent soup once, but he is so agitated about politics at present, that I never feel quite certain about him. I do wish General Boulanger would keep quiet. Duchess, I am sure you are tired?'

'Not at all, dear Gladys,' answered the Duchess, waddling towards the door. 'I have enjoyed myself immensely, and the cheiropodist, I mean the cheiromantist, is most interesting. Flora, where can my tortoise-shell fan be? Oh, thank you, Sir Thomas, so much. And my lace shawl, Flora? Oh, thank you, Sir Thomas, very kind, I'm sure'; and the worthy creature finally managed to get downstairs without dropping her scent-bottle more than twice.

All this time Lord Arthur Savile had remained standing by the fireplace, with the same feeling of dread over him, the same sickening sense of coming evil. He smiled sadly at his sister, as she swept past him on Lord Plymdale's arm, looking lovely in her pink brocade and pearls, and he hardly heard Lady Windermere when she called to him to follow her. He thought of Sybil Merton, and the idea that anything could come between them made his eyes dim with tears.

Looking at him, one would have said that Nemesis had stolen the shield of Pallas, and shown him the Gorgon's head. He seemed turned to stone, and his face was like marble in its melancholy. He had lived the delicate and luxurious life of a young man of birth and fortune, a life exquisite in its freedom from sordid care, its beautiful boyish insouciance; and now for the first time he became conscious of the terrible mystery of Destiny, of the awful meaning of Doom.

How mad and monstrous it all seemed! Could it be that written on his hand, in characters that he could not read himself, but that another could decipher, was some fearful secret of sin, some blood-red sign of crime? Was there no escape possible? Were we no better than chessmen, moved by an unseen power, vessels the potter fashions at his fancy, for honour or for shame? His reason revolted against it, and yet he felt that some tragedy was hanging over him, and that he had been suddenly called upon to bear an intolerable burden. Actors are so fortunate. They can choose whether they will appear in tragedy or in comedy, whether they will suffer or make merry, laugh or shed tears. But in real life it is different. Most men and women are forced to perform parts for which they have no qualifications. Our Guildensterns play Hamlet for us, and our Hamlets have to jest like Prince Hal. The world is a stage, but the play is badly cast.

Suddenly Mr. Podgers entered the room. When he saw Lord Arthur he started, and his coarse, fat face became a sort of greenish-yellow colour. The two men's eyes met, and for a moment there was silence.

'The Duchess has left one of her gloves here, Lord Arthur, and has asked me to bring it to her,' said Mr. Podgers finally. 'Ah, I see it on the sofa! Good evening.'

'Mr. Podgers, I must insist on your giving me a straightforward answer to a question I am going to put to you.'

'Another time, Lord Arthur, but the Duchess is anxious. I am afraid I must go.'

'You shall not go. The Duchess is in no hurry.'

'Ladies should not be kept waiting, Lord Arthur,' said Mr. Podgers, with his sickly smile. 'The fair sex is apt to be impatient.'

Lord Arthur's finely-chiselled lips curled in petulant disdain. The poor Duchess seemed to him of very little importance at that moment. He walked across the room to where Mr. Podgers was standing, and held his hand out.

'Tell me what you saw there,' he said. 'Tell me the truth. I must know it. I am not a child.'

Mr. Podgers's eyes blinked behind his gold-rimmed spectacles, and he moved uneasily from one foot to the other, while his fingers played nervously with a flash watch-chain.

'What makes you think that I saw anything in your hand, Lord Arthur, more than I told you?'

'I know you did, and I insist on your telling me what it was. I will pay you. I will give you a cheque for a hundred pounds.'

The green eyes flashed for a moment, and then became dull again.

'Guineas?' said Mr. Podgers at last, in a low voice.

'Certainly. I will send you a cheque tomorrow. What is your club?'

'I have no club. That is to say, not just at present. My address is — but allow me to give you my card'; and producing a bit of gilt-edge pasteboard from his waistcoat pocket, Mr. Podgers handed it, with a low bow, to Lord Arthur, who read on it,

Mr. SEPTIMUS R. PODGERS

Professional Cheiromantist 103a West Moon Street

'My hours are from ten to four,' murmured Mr. Podgers mechanically, 'and I make a reduction for families.'

'Be quick,' cried Lord Arthur, looking very pale, and holding his hand out.

Mr. Podgers glanced nervously round, and drew the heavy portiere across the door.

'It will take a little time, Lord Arthur, you had better sit down.'

'Be quick, sir,' cried Lord Arthur again, stamping his foot angrily on the polished floor.

Mr. Podgers smiled, drew from his breast-pocket a small magnifying glass, and wiped it carefully with his handkerchief

'I am quite ready,' he said.

# 2

Ten minutes later, with face blanched by terror, and eyes wild with grief, Lord Arthur Savile rushed from Bentinck House, crushing his way through the crowd of fur-coated footmen that stood round the large striped awning, and seeming not to see or hear anything. The night was bitter cold, and the gas-lamps round the square flared and flickered in the keen wind; but his hands were hot with fever, and his forehead burned like fire. On and on he went, almost with the gait of a drunken man. A policeman looked curiously at him as he passed, and a beggar, who slouched from an archway to ask for alms, grew frightened, seeing misery greater than his own. Once he stopped under a lamp, and looked at his hands. He thought he could detect the stain of blood already upon them, and a faint cry broke from his trembling lips.

Murder! that is what the cheiromantist had seen there. Murder! The very night seemed to know it, and the desolate wind to howl it in his ear. The dark corners of the streets were full of it. It grinned at him from the roofs of the houses.

First he came to the Park, whose sombre woodland seemed to fascinate him. He leaned wearily up against the railings, cooling his brow against the wet metal, and listening to the tremulous silence of the trees. 'Murder! murder!' he kept repeating, as though iteration could dim the horror of the word. The sound of his own voice made him shudder, yet he almost hoped that Echo might hear him, and wake the slumbering city from its dreams. He felt a mad desire to stop the casual passer-by, and tell him everything.

Then he wandered across Oxford Street into narrow, shameful alleys. Two women with painted faces mocked at him as he went by. From a dark courtyard came a sound of oaths and blows, followed by shrill screams, and, huddled upon a damp door-step, he saw the crook-backed forms of poverty and eld. A strange pity came over him. Were these children of sin and misery predestined to their end, as he to his? Were they, like him, merely the puppets of a monstrous show?

And yet it was not the mystery, but the comedy of suffering that struck him; its absolute uselessness, its grotesque want of meaning. How incoherent everything seemed! How lacking in all harmony! He was amazed at the discord between the shallow optimism of the day, and the real facts of existence. He was still very young.

After a time he found himself in front of Marylebone Church. The silent roadway looked like a long riband of polished silver, flecked here and there by the dark arabesques of waving shadows. Far into the distance curved the line of flickering gas-lamps, and outside a little walled-in house stood a solitary hansom, the driver asleep inside. He walked hastily in the direction of Portland Place, now and then looking round, as though he feared that he was being followed. At the corner of Rich Street stood two men, reading a small bill upon a hoarding. An odd feeling of curiosity stirred him, and he crossed over. As he came near, the word 'Murder,' printed in black letters, met his eye. He started, and a deep flush came into his cheek. It was an advertisement offering a reward for any information leading to the arrest of a man of medium height, between thirty and forty years of age, wearing a billy-cock hat, a black coat, and check trousers, and with a scar upon his right cheek. He read it over and over again, and wondered if the wretched man would be caught, and how he had been scarred. Perhaps, some day, his own name might be placarded on the walls of London. Some day, perhaps, a price would be set on his head also.

The thought made him sick with horror. He turned on his heel, and hurried on into the night.

Where he went he hardly knew. He had a dim memory of wandering through a labyrinth of sordid houses, of being lost in a giant web of sombre streets, and it was bright dawn when he found himself at last in Piccadilly Circus. As he strolled home towards Belgrave Square, he met the great waggons on their way to Covent Garden. The white-smocked carters, with their pleasant sunburnt faces and coarse curly hair, strode sturdily on, cracking their whips, and calling out now and then to each other; on the back of a huge grey horse, the leader of a jangling team, sat a chubby boy, with a bunch of primroses in his battered hat, keeping tight hold of the mane with his little hands, and laughing; and the great piles of vegetables looked like masses of jade against the morning sky, like masses of green jade against the pink petals of some marvellous rose. Lord Arthur felt curiously affected, he could not tell why. There was something in the dawn's delicate loveliness that seemed to him inexpressibly pathetic, and he thought of all the days that break in beauty, and that set in storm. These rustics, too, with their rough, good-humoured voices, and their nonchalant ways, what a strange London they saw! A London free from the sin of night and the smoke of day, a pallid, ghost-like city, a desolate town of tombs! He wondered what they thought of it, and whether they knew anything of its splendour and its shame, of its fierce, fiery-coloured joys, and its horrible hunger, of all it makes and mars from morn to eve. Probably it was to them merely a mart where they brought their fruits to sell, and where they tarried for a few hours at most, leaving the streets still silent, the houses still asleep. It gave him pleasure to watch them as they went by. Rude as they were, with their heavy, hob-nailed shoes, and their awkward gait, they brought a little of a ready with them. He felt that they had lived with Nature, and that she had taught them peace. He envied them all that they did not know.

By the time he had reached Belgrave Square the sky was a faint blue, and the birds were beginning to twitter in the gardens.

# 3

When Lord Arthur woke it was twelve o'clock, and the midday sun was streaming through the ivory-silk curtains of his room. He got up and looked out of the window. A dim haze of heat was hanging over the great city, and the roofs of the houses were like dull silver. In the flickering green of the square below some children were flitting about like white butterflies, and the pavement was crowded with people on their way to the Park. Never had life seemed lovelier to him, never had the things of evil seemed more remote.

Then his valet brought him a cup of chocolate on a tray. After he had drunk it, he drew aside a heavy portiere of peach-coloured plush, and passed into the bathroom. The light stole softly from above, through thin slabs of transparent onyx, and the water in the marble tank glimmered like a moonstone. He plunged hastily in, till the cool ripples touched throat and hair, and then dipped his head right under, as though he would have wiped away the stain of some shameful memory. When he stepped out he felt almost at peace. The exquisite physical conditions of the moment had dominated him, as indeed often happens in the case of very finely-wrought natures, for the senses, like fire, can purify as well as destroy.

After breakfast, he flung himself down on a divan, and lit a cigarette. On the mantel-shelf, framed in dainty old brocade, stood a large photograph of Sybil Merton, as he had seen her first at Lady Noel's ball. The small, exquisitely-shaped head drooped slightly to one side, as though the thin, reed-like throat could hardly bear the burden of so much beauty; the lips were slightly parted, and seemed made for sweet music; and all the tender purity of girlhood looked out in wonder from the dreaming eyes. With her soft, clinging dress of crepe-dechine, and her large leaf-shaped fan, she looked like one of those delicate little figures men find in the olive-woods near Tanagra; and there was a touch of Greek grace in her pose and attitude. Yet she was not petite. She was simply perfectly proportioned — a rare thing in an age when so many women are either over life-size or insignificant.

Now as Lord Arthur looked at her, he was filled with the terrible pity that is born of love. He felt that to marry her, with the doom of murder hanging over his head, would be a betrayal like that of Judas, a sin worse than any the Borgia had ever dreamed of. What happiness could there be for them, when at any moment he might be called upon to carry out the awful prophecy written in his hand? What manner of life would be theirs while Fate still held this fearful fortune in the scales? The marriage must be postponed, at all costs. Of this he was quite resolved. Ardently though he loved the girl, and the mere touch of her fingers, when they sat together, made each nerve of his body thrill with exquisite joy, he recognised none the less clearly where his duty lay, and was fully conscious of the fact that he had no right to marry until he had committed the murder. This done, he could stand before the altar with Sybil Merton, and give his life into her hands without terror of wrongdoing. This done, he could take her to his arms, knowing that she would never have to blush for him, never have to hang her head in shame. But done it must be first; and the sooner the better for both.

Many men in his position would have preferred the primrose path of dalliance to the steep heights of duty; but Lord Arthur was too conscientious to set pleasure above principle. There was more than mere passion in his love; and Sybil was to him a symbol of all that is good and noble. For a moment he had a natural repugnance against what he was asked to do, but it soon passed away. His heart told him that it was not a sin, but a sacrifice; his reason reminded him that there was no other course open. He had to choose between living for himself and living for others, and terrible though the task laid upon him undoubtedly was, yet he knew that he must not suffer selfishness to triumph over love. Sooner or later we are all called upon to decide on the same issue — of us all, the same question is asked. To Lord Arthur it came early in life — before his nature had been spoiled by the calculating cynicism of middle-age, or his heart corroded by the shallow, fashionable egotism of our day, and he felt no hesitation about doing his duty. Fortunately also, for him, he was no mere dreamer, or idle dilettante. Had he been so, he would have hesitated, like Hamlet, and let irresolution mar his purpose. But he was essentially practical. Life to him meant action, rather than thought. He had that rarest of all things, common sense.

The wild, turbid feelings of the previous night had by this time completely passed away, and it was almost with a sense of shame that he looked back upon his mad wanderings from street to street, his fierce emotional agony. The very sincerity of his sufferings made them seem unreal to him now. He wondered how he could have been so foolish as to rant and rave about the inevitable. The only question that seemed to trouble him was, whom to make away with; for he was not blind to the fact that murder, like the religions of the Pagan world, requires a victim as well as a priest. Not being a genius, he had no enemies, and indeed he felt that this was not the time for the gratification of any personal pique or dislike, the mission in which he was engaged being one of great and grave solemnity. He accordingly made out a list of his friends and relatives on a sheet of notepaper, and after careful consideration, decided in favour of Lady Clementina Beauchamp, a dear old lady who lived in Curzon Street, and was his own second cousin by his mother's side. He had always been very fond of Lady Clem, as every one called her, and as he was very wealthy himself, having come into all Lord Rugby's property when he came of age, there was no possibility of his deriving any vulgar monetary advantage by her death. In fact, the more he thought over the matter, the more she seemed to him to be just the right person, and, feeling that any delay would be unfair to Sybil, he determined to make his arrangements at once.

The first thing to be done was, of course, to settle with the cheiromantist; so he sat down at a small Sheraton writing-table that stood near the window, drew a cheque for 105 pounds, payable to the order of Mr. Septimus Podgers, and, enclosing it in an envelope, told his valet to take it to West Moon Street. He then telephoned to the stables for his hansom, and dressed to go out. As he was leaving the room he looked back at Sybil Merton's photograph, and swore that, come what may, he would never let her know what he was doing for her sake, but would keep the secret of his self-sacrifice hidden always in his heart.

On his way to the Buckingham, he stopped at a florist's, and sent Sybil a beautiful basket of narcissus, with lovely white petals and staring pheasants' eyes, and on arriving at the club, went straight to the library, rang the bell, and ordered the waiter to bring him a lemon-and-soda, and a book on Toxicology. He had fully decided that poison was the best means to adopt in this troublesome business. Anything like personal violence was extremely distasteful to him, and besides, he was very anxious not to murder Lady Clementina in any way that might attract public attention, as he hated the idea of being lionised at Lady Windermere's, or seeing his name figuring in the paragraphs of vulgar society — newspapers. He had also to think of Sybil's father and mother, who were rather old-fashioned people, and might possibly object to the marriage if there was anything like a scandal, though he felt certain that if he told them the whole facts of the case they would be the very first to appreciate the motives that had actuated him. He had every reason, then, to decide in favour of poison. It was safe, sure, and quiet, and did away with any necessity for painful scenes, to which, like most Englishmen, he had a rooted objection.

Of the science of poisons, however, he knew absolutely nothing, and as the waiter seemed quite unable to find anything in the library but Ruff's Guide and Bailey's Magazine, he examined the book-shelves himself, and finally came across a handsomely-bound edition of the Pharmacopoeia, and a copy of Erskine's Toxicology, edited by Sir Mathew Reid, the President of the Royal College of Physicians, and one of the oldest members of the Buckingham, having been elected in mistake for somebody else; a contretemps that so enraged the Committee, that when the real man came up they black-balled him unanimously. Lord Arthur was a good deal puzzled at the technical terms used in both books, and had begun to regret that he had not paid more attention to his classics at Oxford, when in the second volume of Erskine, he found a very interesting and complete account of the properties of aconitine, written in fairly clear English. It seemed to him to be exactly the poison he wanted. It was swift — indeed, almost immediate, in its effect — perfectly painless, and when taken in the form of a gelatine capsule, the mode recommended by Sir Mathew, not by any means unpalatable. He accordingly made a note, upon his shirt-cuff, of the amount necessary for a fatal dose, put the books back in their places, and strolled up St. James's Street, to Pestle and Humbey's, the great chemists. Mr. Pestle, who always attended personally on the aristocracy, was a good deal surprised at the order, and in a very deferential manner murmured something about a medical certificate being necessary. However, as soon as Lord Arthur explained to him that it was for a large Norwegian mastiff that he was obliged to get rid of, as it showed signs of incipient rabies, and had already bitten the coachman twice in the calf of the leg, he expressed himself as being perfectly satisfied, complimented Lord Arthur on his wonderful knowledge of Toxicology, and had the prescription made up immediately.

Lord Arthur put the capsule into a pretty little silver bonbonniere that he saw in a shop window in Bond Street, threw away Pestle and Hambey's ugly pill-box, and drove off at once to Lady Clementina's.

'Well, monsieur le mauvais sujet,' cried the old lady, as he entered the room, 'why haven't you been to see me all this time?'

'My dear Lady Clem, I never have a moment to myself,' said Lord Arthur, smiling.

'I suppose you mean that you go about all day long with Miss Sybil Merton, buying chiffons and talking nonsense? I cannot understand why people make such a fuss about being married. In my day we never dreamed of billing and cooing in public, or in private for that matter.'

'I assure you I have not seen Sybil for twenty-four hours, Lady Clem. As far as I can make out, she belongs entirely to her milliners.'

'Of course; that is the only reason you come to see an ugly old woman like myself. I wonder you men don't take warning. On a fait des folies pour moi, and here I am, a poor rheumatic creature, with a false front and a bad temper. Why, if it were not for dear Lady Jansen, who sends me all the worst French novels she can find, I don't think I could get through the day. Doctors are no use at all, except to get fees out of one. They can't even cure my heartburn.'

'I have brought you a cure for that, Lady Clem,' said Lord Arthur gravely.  'It is a wonderful thing, invented by an American.'

'I don't think I like American inventions, Arthur. I am quite sure I don't. I read some American novels lately, and they were quite nonsensical.'

'Oh, but there is no nonsense at all about this, Lady Clem! I assure you it is a perfect cure. You must promise to try it'; and Lord Arthur brought the little box out of his pocket, and handed it to her.

'Well, the box is charming, Arthur. Is it really a present? That is very sweet of you. And is this the wonderful medicine? It looks like a bonbon. I'll take it at once.'

'Good heavens! Lady Clem,' cried Lord Arthur, catching hold of her hand, 'you mustn't do anything of the kind. It is a homoeopathic medicine, and if you take it without having heartburn, it might do you no end of harm. Wait till you have an attack, and take it then. You will be astonished at the result.'

'I should like to take it now,' said Lady Clementina, holding up to the light the little transparent capsule, with its floating bubble of liquid aconitine. I am sure it is delicious. The fact is that, though I hate doctors, I love medicines. However, I'll keep it till my next attack.'

'And when will that be?' asked Lord Arthur eagerly. 'Will it be soon?'

'I hope not for a week. I had a very bad time yesterday morning with it. But one never knows.'

'You are sure to have one before the end of the month then, Lady Clem?'

'I am afraid so. But how sympathetic you are today, Arthur! Really, Sybil has done you a great deal of good. And now you must run away, for I am dining with some very dull people, who won't talk scandal, and I know that if I don't get my sleep now I shall never be able to keep awake during dinner. Good-bye, Arthur, give my love to Sybil, and thank you so much for the American medicine.'

'You won't forget to take it, Lady Clem, will you?' said Lord Arthur, rising from his seat.

'Of course I won't, you silly boy. I think it is most kind of you to think of me, and I shall write and tell you if I want any more.'

Lord Arthur left the house in high spirits, and with a feeling of immense relief.

That night he had an interview with Sybil Merton. He told her how he had been suddenly placed in a position of terrible difficulty, from which neither honour nor duty would allow him to recede. He told her that the marriage must be put off for the present, as until he had got rid of his fearful entanglements, he was not a free man. He implored her to trust him, and not to have any doubts about the future. Everything would come right, but patience was necessary.

The scene took place in the conservatory of Mr. Merton's house, in Park Lane, where Lord Arthur had dined as usual. Sybil had never seemed more happy, and for a moment Lord Arthur had been tempted to play the coward's part, to write to Lady Clementina for the pill, and to let the marriage go on as if there was no such person as Mr. Podgers in the world. His better nature, however, soon asserted itself, and even when Sybil flung herself weeping into his arms, he did not falter. The beauty that stirred his senses had touched his conscience also. He felt that to wreck so fair a life for the sake of a few months' pleasure would be a wrong thing to do.

He stayed with Sybil till nearly midnight, comforting her and being comforted in turn, and early the next morning he left for Venice, after writing a manly, firm letter to Mr. Merton about the necessary postponement of the marriage.

# 4

In Venice he met his brother, Lord Surbiton, who happened to have come over from Corfu in his yacht. The two young men spent a delightful fortnight together. In the morning they rode on the Lido, or glided up and down the green canals in their long black gondola; in the afternoon they usually entertained visitors on the yacht; and in the evening they dined at Florian's, and smoked innumerable cigarettes on the Piazza. Yet somehow Lord Arthur was not happy. Every day he studied the obituary column in the Times, expecting to see a notice of Lady Clementina's death, but every day he was disappointed. He began to be afraid that some accident had happened to her, and often regretted that he had prevented her taking the aconitine when she had been so anxious to try its effect. Sybil's letters, too, though full of love, and trust, and tenderness, were often very sad in their tone, and sometimes he used to think that he was parted from her for ever.

After a fortnight Lord Surbiton got bored with Venice, and determined to run down the coast to Ravenna, as he heard that there was some capital cock-shooting in the Pinetum. Lord Arthur at first refused absolutely to come, but Surbiton, of whom he was extremely fond, finally persuaded him that if he stayed at Danieli's by himself he would be moped to death, and on the morning of the 15th they started, with a strong nor'-east wind blowing, and a rather choppy sea. The sport was excellent, and the free, open-air life brought the colour back to Lord Arthur's cheek, but about the 22nd he became anxious about Lady Clementina, and, in spite of Surbiton's remonstrances, came back to Venice by train.

As he stepped out of his gondola on to the hotel steps, the proprietor came forward to meet him with a sheaf of telegrams. Lord Arthur snatched them out of his hand, and tore them open. Everything had been successful. Lady Clementina had died quite suddenly on the night of the 17th!

His first thought was for Sybil, and he sent her off a telegram announcing his immediate return to London. He then ordered his valet to pack his things for the night mail, sent his gondoliers about five times their proper fare, and ran up to his sitting-room with a light step and a buoyant heart. There he found three letters waiting for him. One was from Sybil herself, full of sympathy and condolence. The others were from his mother, and from Lady Clementina's solicitor. It seemed that the old lady had dined with the Duchess that very night, had delighted every one by her wit and esprit, but had gone home somewhat early, complaining of heartburn. In the morning she was found dead in her bed, having apparently suffered no pain. Sir Mathew Reid had been sent for at once, but, of course, there was nothing to be done, and she was to be buried on the 22nd at Beauchamp Chalcote. A few days before she died she had made her will, and left Lord Arthur her little house in Curzon Street, and all her furniture, personal effects, and pictures, with the exception of her collection of miniatures, which was to go to her sister, Lady Margaret Rufford, and her amethyst necklace, which Sybil Merton was to have. The property was not of much value; but Mr. Mansfield, the solicitor, was extremely anxious for Lord Arthur to return at once, if possible, as there were a great many bills to be paid, and Lady Clementina had never kept any regular accounts.

Lord Arthur was very much touched by Lady Clementina's kind remembrance of him, and felt that Mr. Podgers had a great deal to answer for. His love of Sybil, however, dominated every other emotion, and the consciousness that he had done his duty gave him peace and comfort. When he arrived at Charing Cross, he felt perfectly happy.

The Mertons received him very kindly. Sybil made him promise that he would never again allow anything to come between them, and the marriage was fixed for the 7th June. Life seemed to him once more bright and beautiful, and all his old gladness came back to him again.

One day, however, as he was going over the house in Curzon Street, in company with Lady Clementina's solicitor and Sybil herself, burning packages of faded letters, and turning out drawers of odd rubbish, the young girl suddenly gave a little cry of delight.

'What have you found, Sybil?' said Lord Arthur, looking up from his work, and smiling.

'This lovely little silver bonbonniere, Arthur. Isn't it quaint and Dutch? Do give it to me! I know amethysts won't become me till I am over eighty.'

It was the box that had held the aconitine.

Lord Arthur started, and a faint blush came into his cheek. He had almost entirely forgotten what he had done, and it seemed to him a curious coincidence that Sybil, for whose sake he had gone through all that terrible anxiety, should have been the first to remind him of it.

'Of course you can have it, Sybil. I gave it to poor Lady Clem myself.'

'Oh! thank you, Arthur; and may I have the bonbon too? I had no notion that Lady Clementina liked sweets. I thought she was far too intellectual.'

Lord Arthur grew deadly pale, and a horrible idea crossed his mind.

'Bonbon, Sybil? What do you mean?' he said in a slow, hoarse voice.

'There is one in it, that is all. It looks quite old and dusty, and I have not the slightest intention of eating it. What is the matter, Arthur? How white you look!'

Lord Arthur rushed across the room, and seized the box. Inside it was the amber-coloured capsule, with its poison-bubble. Lady Clementina had died a natural death after all!

The shock of the discovery was almost too much for him. He flung the capsule into the fire, and sank on the sofa with a cry of despair.

# 5

Mr. Merton was a good deal distressed at the second postponement of the marriage, and Lady Julia, who had already ordered her dress for the wedding, did all in her power to make Sybil break off the match. Dearly, however, as Sybil loved her mother, she had given her whole life into Lord Arthur's hands, and nothing that Lady Julia could say could make her waver in her faith. As for Lord Arthur himself, it took him days to get over his terrible disappointment, and for a time his nerves were completely unstrung. His excellent common sense, however, soon asserted itself, and his sound, practical mind did not leave him long in doubt about what to do. Poison having proved a complete failure, dynamite, or some other form of explosive, was obviously the proper thing to try.

He accordingly looked again over the list of his friends and relatives, and, after careful consideration, determined to blow up his uncle, the Dean of Chichester. The Dean, who was a man of great culture and learning, was extremely fond of clocks, and had a wonderful collection of timepieces, ranging from the fifteenth century to the present day, and it seemed to Lord Arthur that this hobby of the good Dean's offered him an excellent opportunity for carrying out his scheme. Where to procure an explosive machine was, of course, quite another matter. The London Directory gave him no information on the point, and he felt that there was very little use in going to Scotland Yard about it, as they never seemed to know anything about the movements of the dynamite faction till after an explosion had taken place, and not much even then.

Suddenly he thought of his friend Rouvaloff, a young Russian of very revolutionary tendencies, whom he had met at Lady Windermere's in the winter. Count Rouvaloff was supposed to be writing a life of Peter the Great, and to have come over to England for the purpose of studying the documents relating to that Tsar's residence in this country as a ship carpenter; but it was generally suspected that he was a Nihilist agent, and there was no doubt that the Russian Embassy did not look with any favour upon his presence in London. Lord Arthur felt that he was just the man for his purpose, and drove down one morning to his lodgings in Bloomsbury, to ask his advice and assistance.

'So you are taking up politics seriously?' said Count Rouvaloff, when Lord Arthur had told him the object of his mission; but Lord Arthur, who hated swagger of any kind, felt bound to admit to him that he had not the slightest interest in social questions, and simply wanted the explosive machine for a purely family matter, in which no one was concerned but himself.

Count Rouvaloff looked at him for some moments in amazement, and then seeing that he was quite serious, wrote an address on a piece of paper, initialled it, and handed it to him across the table.

'Scotland Yard would give a good deal to know this address, my dear fellow.'

'They shan't have it,' cried Lord Arthur, laughing; and after shaking the young Russian warmly by the hand he ran downstairs, examined the paper, and told the coachman to drive to Soho Square.

There he dismissed him, and strolled down Greek Street, till he came to a place called Bayle's Court. He passed under the archway, and found himself in a curious cul-desac, that was apparently occupied by a French Laundry, as a perfect network of clothes-lines was stretched across from house to house, and there was a flutter of white linen in the morning air. He walked right to the end, and knocked at a little green house. After some delay, during which every window in the court became a blurred mass of peering faces, the door was opened by a rather rough-looking foreigner, who asked him in very bad English what his business was. Lord Arthur handed him the paper Count Rouvaloff had given him. When the man saw it he bowed, and invited Lord Arthur into a very shabby front parlour on the ground floor, and in a few moments Herr Winckelkopf, as he was called in England, bustled into the room, with a very wine-stained napkin round his neck, and a fork in his left hand.

'Count Rouvaloff has given me an introduction to you,' said Lord Arthur, bowing, 'and I am anxious to have a short interview with you on a matter of business. My name is

Smith, Mr. Robert Smith, and I want you to supply me with an explosive clock.'

'Charmed to meet you, Lord Arthur,' said the genial little German, laughing. 'Don't look so alarmed, it is my duty to know everybody, and I remember seeing you one evening at Lady Windermere's. I hope her ladyship is quite well. Do you mind sitting with me while I finish my breakfast? There is an excellent pate, and my friends are kind enough to say that my Rhine wine is better than any they get at the German Embassy,' and before Lord Arthur had got over his surprise at being recognised, he found himself seated in the back-room, sipping the most delicious Marcobrunner out of a pale yellow hock-glass marked with the Imperial monogram, and chatting in the friendliest manner possible to the famous conspirator.

'Explosive clocks,' said Herr Winckelkopf, 'are not very good things for foreign exportation, as, even if they succeed in passing the Custom House, the train service is so irregular, that they usually go off before they have reached their proper destination. If, however, you want one for home use, I can supply you with an excellent article, and guarantee that you will he satisfied with the result. May I ask for whom it is intended? If it is for the police, or for any one connected with Scotland Yard, I am afraid I cannot do anything for you. The English detectives are really our best friends, and I have always found that by relying on their stupidity, we can do exactly what we like. I could not spare one of them.'

'I assure you,' said Lord Arthur, 'that it has nothing to do with the police at all. In fact, the clock is intended for the Dean of Chichester.'

'Dear me! I had no idea that you felt so strongly about religion, Lord Arthur. Few young men do nowadays.'

'I am afraid you overrate me, Herr Winckelkopf,' said Lord Arthur, blushing. 'The fact is, I really know nothing about theology.'

'It is a purely private matter then?'

'Purely private.'

Herr Winckelkopf shrugged his shoulders, and left the room, returning in a few minutes with a round cake of dynamite about the size of a penny, and a pretty little French clock, surmounted by an ormolu figure of Liberty trampling on the hydra of Despotism.

Lord Arthur's face brightened up when he saw it. 'That is just what I want,' he cried, 'and now tell me how it goes off.'

'Ah! there is my secret,' answered Herr Winckelkopf, contemplating his invention with a justifiable look of pride; 'let me know when you wish it to explode, and I will set the machine to the moment.'

'Well, today is Tuesday, and if you could send it off at once —'

'That is impossible; I have a great deal of important work on hand for some friends of mine in Moscow. Still, I might send it off tomorrow.'

'Oh, it will be quite time enough!' said Lord Arthur politely, 'if it is delivered tomorrow night or Thursday morning. For the moment of the explosion, say Friday at noon exactly. The Dean is always at home at that hour.'

'Friday, at noon,' repeated Herr Winckelkopf, and he made a note to that effect in a large ledger that was lying on a bureau near the fireplace.

'And now,' said Lord Arthur, rising from his seat, 'pray let me know how much I am in your debt.'

'It is such a small matter, Lord Arthur, that I do not care to make any charge. The dynamite comes to seven and sixpence, the clock will be three pounds ten, and the carriage about five shillings. I am only too pleased to oblige any friend of Count Rouvaloff's.'

'But your trouble, Herr Winckelkopf?'

'Oh, that is nothing! It is a pleasure to me. I do not work for money; I live entirely for my art.'

Lord Arthur laid down 4 pounds, 2s. 6d. on the table, thanked the little German for his kindness, and, having succeeded in declining an invitation to meet some Anarchists at a meat-tea on the following Saturday, left the house and went off to the Park.

For the next two days he was in a state of the greatest excitement, and on Friday at twelve o'clock he drove down to the Buckingham to wait for news. All the afternoon the stolid hall-porter kept posting up telegrams from various parts of the country giving the results of horse-races, the verdicts in divorce suits, the state of the weather, and the like, while the tape ticked out wearisome details about an all-night sitting in the House of Commons, and a small panic on the Stock Exchange. At four o'clock the evening papers came in, and Lord Arthur disappeared into the library with the Pall Mall, the St. James's, the Globe, and the Echo, to the immense indignation of Colonel Goodchild, who wanted to read the reports of a speech he had delivered that morning at the Mansion House, on the subject of South African Missions, and the advisability of having black Bishops in every province, and for some reason or other had a strong prejudice against the Evening News. None of the papers, however, contained even the slightest allusion to Chichester, and Lord Arthur felt that the attempt must have failed. It was a terrible blow to him, and for a time he was quite unnerved. Herr Winckelkopf, whom he went to see the next day was full of elaborate apologies, and offered to supply him with another clock free of charge, or with a case of nitro-glycerine bombs at cost price. But he had lost all faith in explosives, and Herr Winckelkopf himself acknowledged that everything is so adulterated nowadays, that even dynamite can hardly be got in a pure condition. The little German, however, while admitting that something must have gone wrong with the machinery, was not without hope that the clock might still go off, and instanced the case of a barometer that he had once sent to the military Governor at Odessa, which, though timed to explode in ten days, had not done so for something like three months. It was quite true that when it did go off, it merely succeeded in blowing a housemaid to atoms, the Governor having gone out of town six weeks before, but at least it showed that dynamite, as a destructive force, was, when under the control of machinery, a powerful, though a somewhat unpunctual agent. Lord Arthur was a little consoled by this reflection, but even here he was destined to disappointment, for two days afterwards, as he was going upstairs, the Duchess called him into her boudoir, and showed him a letter she had just received from the Deanery.

'Jane writes charming letters,' said the Duchess; 'you must really read her last. It is quite as good as the novels Mudie sends us.'

Lord Arthur seized the letter from her hand. It ran as follows:—

THE DEANERY, CHICHESTER,

27th May.

My Dearest Aunt,

Thank you so much for the flannel for the Dorcas Society, and also for the gingham. I quite agree with you that it is nonsense their wanting to wear pretty things, but everybody is so Radical and irreligious nowadays, that it is difficult to make them see that they should not try and dress like the upper classes. I am sure I don't know what we are coming to. As papa has often said in his sermons, we live in an age of unbelief.

We have had great fun over a clock that an unknown admirer sent papa last Thursday. It arrived in a wooden box from London, carriage paid, and papa feels it must have been sent by some one who had read his remarkable sermon, 'Is Licence Liberty?' for on the top of the clock was a figure of a woman, with what papa said was the cap of Liberty on her head. I didn't think it very becoming myself, but papa said it was historical, so I suppose it is all right. Parker unpacked it, and papa put it on the mantelpiece in the library, and we were all sitting there on Friday morning, when just as the clock struck twelve, we heard a whirring noise, a little puff of smoke came from the pedestal of the figure, and the goddess of Liberty fell off, and broke her nose on the fender! Maria was quite alarmed, but it looked so ridiculous, that James and I went off into fits of laughter, and even papa was amused. When we examined it, we found it was a sort of alarum clock, and that, if you set it to a particular hour, and put some gunpowder and a cap under a little hammer, it went off whenever you wanted. Papa said it must not remain in the library, as it made a noise, so Reggie carried it away to the schoolroom, and does nothing but have small explosions all day long. Do you think Arthur would like one for a wedding present? I suppose they are quite fashionable in London. Papa says they should do a great deal of good, as they show that Liberty can't last, but must fall down. Papa says Liberty was invented at the time of the French Revolution. How awful it seems!

I have now to go to the Dorcas, where I will read them your most instructive letter. How true, dear aunt, your idea is, that in their rank of life they should wear what is unbecoming. I must say it is absurd, their anxiety about dress, when there are so many more important things in this world, and in the next. I am so glad your flowered poplin turned out so well, and that your lace was not torn. I am wearing my yellow satin, that you so kindly gave me, at the Bishop's on Wednesday, and think it will look all right. Would you have bows or not? Jennings says that every one wears bows now, and that the underskirt should be frilled. Reggie has just had another explosion, and papa has ordered the clock to be sent to the stables. I don't think papa likes it so much as he did at first, though he is very flattered at being sent such a pretty and ingenious toy. It shows that people read his sermons, and profit by them.

Papa sends his love, in which James, and Reggie, and Maria all unite, and, hoping that Uncle Cecil's gout is better, believe me, dear aunt, ever your affectionate niece,

JANE PERCY.

PS. — Do tell me about the bows. Jennings insists they are the fashion.

Lord Arthur looked so serious and unhappy over the letter, that the Duchess went into fits of laughter.

'My dear Arthur,' she cried, 'I shall never show you a young lady's letter again! But what shall I say about the clock? I think it is a capital invention, and I should like to have one myself.'

'I don't think much of them,' said Lord Arthur, with a sad smile, and, after kissing his mother, he left the room.

When he got upstairs, he flung himself on a sofa, and his eyes filled with tears. He had done his best to commit this murder, but on both occasions he had failed, and through no fault of his own. He had tried to do his duty, but it seemed as if Destiny herself had turned traitor. He was oppressed with the sense of the barrenness of good intentions, of the futility of trying to be fine. Perhaps, it would be better to break off the marriage altogether. Sybil would suffer, it is true, but suffering could not really mar a nature so noble as hers. As for himself, what did it matter? There is always some war in which a man can die, some cause to which a man can give his life, and as life had no pleasure for him, so death had no terror. Let Destiny work out his doom. He would not stir to help her.

At half-past seven he dressed, and went down to the club.

Surbiton was there with a party of young men, and he was obliged to dine with them. Their trivial conversation and idle jests did not interest him, and as soon as coffee was brought he left them, inventing some engagement in order to get away. As he was going out of the club, the hall-porter handed him a letter. It was from Herr Winckelkopf, asking him to call down the next evening, and look at an explosive umbrella, that went off as soon as it was opened. It was the very latest invention, and had just arrived from Geneva. He tore the letter up into fragments. He had made up his mind not to try any more experiments. Then he wandered down to the Thames Embankment, and sat for hours by the river. The moon peered through a mane of tawny clouds, as if it were a lion's eye, and innumerable stars spangled the hollow vault, like gold dust powdered on a purple dome. Now and then a barge swung out into the turbid stream, and floated away with the tide, and the railway signals changed from green to scarlet as the trains ran shrieking across the bridge. After some time, twelve o'clock boomed from the tall tower at Westminster, and at each stroke of the sonorous bell the night seemed to tremble. Then the railway lights went out, one solitary lamp left gleaming like a large ruby on a giant mast, and the roar of the city became fainter.

At two o'clock he got up, and strolled towards Blackfriars. How unreal everything looked! How like a strange dream! The houses on the other side of the river seemed built out of darkness. One would have said that silver and shadow had fashioned the world anew. The huge dome of St. Paul's loomed like a bubble through the dusky air.

As he approached Cleopatra's Needle he saw a man leaning over the parapet, and as he came nearer the man looked up, the gas-light falling full upon his face.

It was Mr. Podgers, the cheiromantist! No one could mistake the fat, flabby face, the gold-rimmed spectacles, the sickly feeble smile, the sensual mouth.

Lord Arthur stopped. A brilliant idea flashed across him,

and he stole softly up behind. In a moment he had seized Mr. Podgers by the legs, and flung him into the Thames. There was a coarse oath, a heavy splash, and all was still. Lord Arthur looked anxiously over, but could see nothing of the cheiromantist but a tall hat, pirouetting in an eddy of moonlit water. After a time it also sank, and no trace of Mr. Podgers was visible. Once he thought that he caught sight of the bulky misshapen figure striking out for the staircase by the bridge, and a horrible feeling of failure came over him, but it turned out to be merely a reflection, and when the moon shone out from behind a cloud it passed away. At last he seemed to have realised the decree of destiny. He heaved a deep sigh of relief, and Sybil's name came to his lips.

'Have you dropped anything, sir?' said a voice behind him suddenly.

He turned round, and saw a policeman with a bull's-eye lantern.

'Nothing of importance, sergeant,' he answered, smiling, and hailing a passing hansom, he jumped in, and told the man to drive to Belgrave Square.

For the next few days he alternated between hope and fear. There were moments when he almost expected Mr. Podgers to walk into the room, and yet at other times he felt that Fate could not be so unjust to him. Twice he went to the cheiromantist's address in West Moon Street, but he could not bring himself to ring the bell. He longed for certainty, and was afraid of it.

Finally it came. He was sitting in the smoking-room of the club having tea, and listening rather wearily to Surbiton's account of the last comic song at the Gaiety, when the waiter came in with the evening papers. He took up the St. James's, and was listlessly turning over its pages, when this strange heading caught his eye:

Suicide of a Cheiromantist.

He turned pale with excitement, and began to read. The paragraph ran as follows:

Yesterday morning, at seven o'clock, the body of Mr. Septimus R. Podgers, the eminent cheiromantist, was washed on shore at Greenwich, just in front of the Ship Hotel. The unfortunate gentleman had been missing for some days, and considerable anxiety for his safety had been felt in cheiromantic circles. It is supposed that he committed suicide under the influence of a temporary mental derangement, caused by overwork, and a verdict to that effect was returned this afternoon by the coroner's jury. Mr. Podgers had just completed an elaborate treatise on the subject of the Human Hand, that will shortly be published, when it will no doubt attract much attention. The deceased was sixty-five years of age, and does not seem to have left any relations.

Lord Arthur rushed out of the club with the paper still in his hand, to the immense amazement of the hall-porter, who tried in vain to stop him, and drove at once to Park Lane. Sybil saw him from the window, and something told her that he was the bearer of good news. She ran down to meet him, and, when she saw his face, she knew that all was well.

'My dear Sybil,' cried Lord Arthur,   'let us be married tomorrow!'

'You foolish boy! Why, the cake is not even ordered!' said Sybil, laughing through her tears.

# 6

When the wedding took place, some three weeks later, St. Peter's was crowded with a perfect mob of smart people. The service was read in the most impressive manner by the Dean of Chichester, and everybody agreed that they had never seen a handsomer couple than the bride and bridegroom. They were more than handsome, however — they were happy. Never for a single moment did Lord Arthur regret all that he had suffered for Sybil's sake, while she, on her side, gave him the best things a woman can give to any man — worship, tenderness, and love. For them romance was not killed by reality. They always felt young.

Some years afterwards, when two beautiful children had been born to them, Lady Windermere came down on a visit to Alton Priory, a lovely old place, that had been the Duke's wedding present to his son; and one afternoon as she was sitting with Lady Arthur under a lime-tree in the garden, watching the little boy and girl as they played up and down the rose-walk, like fitful sunbeams, she suddenly took her hostess's hand in hers, and said, 'Are you happy, Sybil?'

'Dear Lady Windermere, of course I am happy. Aren't you?'

'I have no time to be happy, Sybil. I always like the last person who is introduced to me; but, as a rule, as soon as I know people I get tired of them.'

'Don't your lions satisfy you, Lady Windermere?'

'Oh dear, no! lions are only good for one season. As soon as their manes are cut, they are the dullest creatures going. Besides, they behave very badly, if you are really nice to them. Do you remember that horrid Mr. Podgers? He was a dreadful impostor. Of course, I didn't mind that at all, and even when he wanted to borrow money I forgave him, but I could not stand his making love to me. He has really made me hate cheiromancy. I go in for telepathy now. It is much more amusing.'

'You mustn't say anything against cheiromancy here, Lady Windermere; it is the only subject that Arthur does not like people to chaff about. I assure you he is quite serious over it.'

'You don't mean to say that he believes in it, Sybil?'

'Ask him, Lady Windermere, here he is'; and Lord Arthur came up the garden with a large bunch of yellow roses in his hand, and his two children dancing round him.

'Lord Arthur?'

'Yes, Lady Windermere.'

'You don't mean to say that you believe in cheiromancy?'

'Of course I do,' said the young man, smiling.

'But why?'

'Because I owe to it all the happiness of my life,' he murmured, throwing himself into a wicker chair.

'My dear Lord Arthur, what do you owe to it?'

'Sybil,' he answered, handing his wife the roses, and looking into her violet eyes.

'What nonsense!' cried Lady Windermere.   'I never heard such nonsense in all my life.'

# W. H.先生的畫像

十四行詩是帶有悲劇含義的嚴肅詩作，
摔出了莎士比亞內心的苦痛，
卻用甜言蜜語使之變得愉悅芬芳，
這些詩作討論了理想自我、理想人性、美的精神……

## 1

厄斯金邀我到他家共進晚餐，他的漂亮小房子坐落於鳥籠小徑。飯後，我們坐在書房裡喝咖啡、抽菸，話題不知怎地突然轉到文學偽造的問題上。如今我已記不得當時怎麼突然談到這個有點不太尋常的奇特主題，不過我知道我們討論了麥佛森、艾爾藍和查特頓①許久。

對於查特頓，我堅持他的偽作其實只是一種追求完美表現的藝術渴望，我們無權與藝術家爭論他想在什麼樣的條件底下呈現自己的作品。況且，所有的藝術在一定程度上都是一種表演方式，企圖掙脫真實人生的橫禍與限制束縛，在某個想像的水平上展現自己的個人魅力。因此，為了偽造而譴責藝術家，等於是將倫理問題與美學問題混為一談。

厄斯金比我年長許多，這位四十歲的男人抱著興味盎然的尊重，原本靜靜聆聽著我大發議論。突然間，他拍拍我的肩膀，問道：「如果有個年輕人對某件藝術作品抱持某種奇特的論點，並且深信不疑，甚至為了加以證明，不惜假造出一件贗品，你會怎麼看待？」

　　「啊，那可是完全不同的兩碼事！」

　　聽了我的回答後，厄斯金靜默了好一會兒，兩眼盯著他手上香菸冉冉浮起的細細灰線。「沒錯，」他終於開口說話，卻又頓了一下，「完全不同。」

　　他的聲音帶有某種情緒，該說是一抹苦澀嗎，那勾起了我的好奇心。「你認識誰做過那樣的事嗎？」我急忙問道。

　　「有的，」厄斯金將手上的香菸扔進火堆中，接著說：「西里爾・葛拉罕，他是我很重要的朋友。他非常迷人，非常傻氣，非常薄情，可是卻將遺產留給了我，那也是我此生目前唯一收到的遺產。」

　　「是什麼？」我急急追問。

　　厄斯金從座位站起身，走到兩扇窗之間的一座雕花高櫃旁，開鎖，旋即回到我坐的地方。他手中拿著一小幅畫，裝裱在一只老舊且帶點汙損的伊莉莎白式畫框中。

　　那是一幅年輕男子的全身肖像，畫中人身穿十六世紀晚期服裝，站在一張桌子旁，右手擱在一本打開的書上。他看起來年約十七，長相十分俊俏，而且顯然帶點脂粉氣。真的，撇開那身打扮和一頭極短短髮，就憑那對飽含欲望的迷離眼眸、兩瓣嬌嫩的紅豔雙唇，任誰都會說那是張女孩的臉龐。從畫風，尤其是手部的處理方式，在在都提示這是弗朗索瓦・克盧埃晚期的作品。

　　黑色絲絨緊身上衣綴有金光閃閃、極為出色的小點，孔雀藍的背景使畫中人物顯得討喜，也提高了畫作的明度，這些都

很符合克盧埃的風格。至於從大理石雕像底座懸垂而下的悲劇和喜劇兩張面具，則帶有冷硬嚴肅筆觸，這一點和著重流暢優雅的義大利畫家非常不同。看來，就算身處法國宮廷，克盧埃這位了不起的法蘭德斯大師也從未忘本，這一直是北方人脾氣的特徵②。

「真是一幅迷人的傑作！」我高聲讚嘆，「不過，這個美少年是誰呀？多虧藝術將他的美如實保留下來，供後世欣賞。」

「這是W. H.先生的畫像，」厄斯金說，唇邊還掛著悲傷的笑容。儘管可能只是光線的關係，但我似乎看見他的雙眼因淚水而發亮。

「W. H.先生！」我驚呼，「誰是W. H.先生呀？」

「你不記得了嗎？」厄斯金答道，「看看他的手歇息在哪本書上？」

「我只看得見那裡有字，卻無法分辨它寫些什麼。」

「唔，用這把放大鏡再試一次，」厄斯金說，唇邊那個悲傷的笑容依舊。

我接過放大鏡，將油燈挪近些，開始拼湊潦草的十六世紀手寫字跡。「『謹將以下十四行詩獻給它們的父親……』」我忍不住大喊，「老天，是莎士比亞的W. H.先生嗎？」

「西里爾・葛拉罕以前常這麼說。」厄斯金低聲嘟噥。

「可是這一點也不像潘卜洛克勛爵啊③，」我接著說，「我對潘思赫斯特大宅④的肖像畫可是瞭如指掌。幾週前，我才在那附近待過。」

「這麼說，你真的認為那些十四行詩是獻給潘卜洛克勛爵嘍？」厄斯金追問。

「我敢肯定，」我說，「潘卜洛克、莎士比亞和瑪莉・費通夫人⑤，是這些十四行詩的三大要角，這一點無庸置疑。」

「嗯，我同意你的看法，」厄斯金說，「不過我並不是一

直都這麼認為。我過去相信——嗯，我想我過去相信西里爾‧葛拉罕和他的論點。」

「什麼樣的論點？」我隨口問著，目光卻忍不住瞧向那幅出色的肖像畫，它已經開始對我產生某種奇怪的魔力了。

「這個故事很長，」厄斯金一邊說，一邊把畫從我眼前拿走（當時，我覺得他的舉止相當無禮），「說來話長，不過你要是想聽，我就說給你聽吧。」

「我熱愛有關十四行詩的各種論點，」我熱切地說，「可惜的是，大概沒有任何新的見解能說服我改變想法。這件事對任何人來說早就不是什麼懸案了，說真的，我倒對它曾是一樁懸案感到百思不解。」

「反正我也不信那套論點，所以大概沒辦法讓你改變想法，」厄斯金笑著說，「不過你或許會有興趣聽聽它的主張。」

「當然好，請務必說給我聽，」我答道，「假如它有那幅畫的一半精彩，我就很滿足了。」

厄斯金點了根菸，開口說道：「好，我得從西里爾‧葛拉罕這個人開始講起。他和我在伊頓公學時期住在同一間宿舍。我比他年長一、兩歲，但我們很要好，不僅一起唸書、做許多事，也一塊兒玩耍。認真算算，當時玩耍的時間遠多過做正經事，不過回想起來並不覺得懊悔。沒有接受徹底商業化的教育始終是個優點，更何況，我在伊頓運動場上學到的種種跟劍橋教我的一切同樣管用。

「我得告訴你，當時，西里爾的父母都已經過世了，他們在懷特島外海一場嚴重的遊艇事故中雙雙溺斃。父親是一位外交官，娶了老克雷迪頓勳爵的女兒。由於母親是勳爵的獨生女，所以勳爵在自己的女兒、女婿亡故後，便成了孫子西里爾的監護人。但我不認為克雷迪頓勳爵很關心西里爾，因為他始終無法原諒女兒下嫁給一個沒有頭銜的平民。

「勛爵是個非常老派的貴族，罵人時像街頭叫賣的小販，待人接物的規矩跟農夫沒有兩樣。我記得有一回在畢業典禮上遇見他，他衝著我咆哮，賞我一枚一英鎊金幣，叮囑我長大後千萬別像我父親那樣成為『一個該死的激進分子』。

「西里爾對他沒什麼感情，寧願將自己絕大部分的假期花在蘇格蘭，和我們共度。他們祖孫倆的相處從來就談不上和睦融洽，西里爾當他是頭熊，他則認為西里爾沒有男子氣概——儘管西里爾騎術精湛、劍術一流（事實上，早在離開伊頓前，他的劍術已無人能敵），但我認為他在某些方面確實有點優柔寡斷，可惜他的舉止漫不經心，又自負於長相俊美，更別提他非常討厭足球。

「真正能為他帶來快樂的兩件事情，是詩歌和表演。在伊頓時，他總是盛裝打扮，吟誦莎士比亞的作品，等我們進入三一學院後，他在第一個學期就成為Ａ．Ｄ．Ｃ．⑥的一員。我記得自己一直都很嫉妒他的表演天分。我對他一直無比忠誠，我想是因為我們在某些事情上是如此不同吧。那時的我是個相當笨拙、軟弱的小伙子，一雙大腳，臉上還長滿雀斑。雀斑在蘇格蘭家庭之常見，正如痛風之於英格蘭家庭的普遍；西里爾曾經說過，若非得兩者擇一，他寧可選擇痛風。

「他總是過度推崇一個人美貌的價值，有一次，他還當著辯論社社員的面大聲朗誦一篇文章，用以證明長得好看勝過循規蹈矩。毫無疑問，他長得非常帥氣俊俏。那些不喜歡他的人，包括大老粗和學院裡的指導教師，還有攻讀神學的年輕人，總是說他空有一副好看的皮相；但我認為他的臉不只是俊秀，還蘊含了好多其他的事物。

「我認為他是我見過最出色的傢伙，沒有人能勝過他優雅的姿態、翩翩的魅力風度。他總能迷倒每個值得吸引的人，以及很多不值得的人。他時常很任性，性格又莽撞，我以前總

認為他很不誠懇，我想這主要是因為他太想取悅別人了，可憐的西里爾。有一次我告訴他，他太容易滿足於那種很廉價的成功，他卻只是笑個不停。他完全被寵壞了，我猜那些深富魅力的人全都被寵壞了，但那正是他們渾身散發吸引力的祕密。

「不過，我必須跟你說說西里爾的演技。你知道，A．D．C．並不允許女演員上臺表演，我不清楚現在如何，但至少在我那年代是如此。可想而知，西里爾總是扮演女孩的角色，演出《皆大歡喜》時，他飾演蘿莎琳，那是非常精彩的表演。其實，西里爾‧葛拉罕是我看過唯一能完美詮釋蘿莎琳這個角色的人，要想向你描述他表演的美感、無懈可擊的細膩、姿態之文雅是絕對不可能的。它造成了大轟動，讓那間討人厭的小劇場那陣子每晚都爆滿。就連現在我閱讀那部劇本時，都不禁會想起西里爾。這個角色很可能是為他而寫。

「下一個學期，他拿到學位，接著來到倫敦攻讀外交。不過，他從未完成任何作品。白天他閱讀莎士比亞的十四行詩，晚上則在劇場流連。他當然很想成為職業演員，而我和克雷迪頓勛爵所能做的，就是全力阻止他。但如果那時他能當演員，或許現在他還活著。給人建議永遠是件蠢事，但給人好建議是絕對致命的事。我希望你永遠不會犯下那樣的錯誤，否則你肯定會後悔一輩子。

「好，言歸正傳，有一天我收到西里爾的信，要我當天傍晚到他家。他在皮卡底里有間迷人的公寓，可以俯瞰格林公園。其實那時我每天都會去看他，所以他特地寫信邀請我讓我很驚訝。我當然依約前往，抵達時，我發現他整個人處於很興奮的狀態。

「他告訴我，他終於發現了莎士比亞十四行詩的真正祕密，所有的學者和評論家全都弄錯了。而他是第一個純粹憑詩作本身存在的證據，發現誰才是真正W．H．先生的人。他樂瘋

了，一直不肯說明他的論點，最後才拿出一大疊筆記，從壁爐臺上取來他那本《莎士比亞十四行詩集》，坐下來，就這個主題為我講解了許久。

「首先他指出，莎士比亞之所以會在這些不尋常的熱情詩作中特別提到某人，代表那人必定是他戲劇藝術發展的真正關鍵，因此不可能是指潘卜洛克勛爵或南安普頓勛爵⑦。其實無論他是誰，都不可能是出身高貴的人，因為在第廿五首詩中，莎士比亞拿自己和那些『王公貴族』的寵兒相比，他講得很明白——『且讓那些吉星高照之人／誇耀其顯赫名聲與輝煌頭銜／而我，本就與這些榮寵無緣／卻從我最敬重的人得到意外喜悅』。這首十四行詩，最終以暗自慶幸能和心儀之人愛得對等作結——『我多麼幸福，愛人且被愛／既不會移情，也不會失寵』。

「西里爾宣稱，如果我們猜想這些詩作是獻給潘卜洛克勛爵或南安普頓勛爵，那麼這首詩就很難說得通，因為這兩人已經是英格蘭地位最高的人，完全有資格被稱作『王公貴族』。而為了證實自己的觀點，他又為我朗讀了第一二四首、第一二五首詩。在這兩首詩作中，莎士比亞告訴我們，他的愛不是『國家的孩子』，它『不在微笑的榮寵中擔憂受苦』，也『絕非建立在偶然之上』。我興趣濃厚地聆聽他的發言，因為這個觀點過去不曾有人提出，但隨之而來的，仍舊是更多的疑點。

「當時，西里爾的觀點讓我完全捨棄了那人是潘卜洛克的主張。我們從米爾斯⑧的作品得知，十四行詩是在一五九八年之前寫成，而第一〇四首詩作則告訴我們，莎士比亞和W.H.先生的友誼已持續了三年之久。既然一五八〇年出生的潘卜洛克勛爵直到十八歲才來到倫敦，也就是說他到倫敦的那年是一五九八年，而莎士比亞與W.H.先生必定相識於一五九四年，

或最遲在一五九五年。因此，莎士比亞認識潘卜洛克勛爵的時候，十四行詩早已寫成。西里爾也指出，潘卜洛克勛爵的父親死於一六〇一年，但從以下這句詩——『你有父親；讓你的孩子也能這樣驕傲地誇口』可以看出，W. H.先生的父親很顯然一五九八年已不在人世。

「此外，書中這篇題獻乃出自出版商之手，但光是想像當時竟有任何出版商膽敢稱呼威廉‧賀伯（也就是潘卜洛克伯爵）為W. H.先生，就知道這說法有多荒謬。若想以『巴克赫斯特勛爵，被稱為薩克維爾先生』當作例子，則完全不可相提並論，因為巴克赫斯特勛爵在當時還不是貴族，只是貴族的幼子，所以巴克赫斯特勛爵只是個禮貌性尊稱。況且，他在《英國文壇》一書中被提到的那段文字，並非正式且莊重的獻辭，只不過是隨意間接地被提及⑨。到目前為止，西里爾輕輕鬆鬆推翻『潘卜洛克勛爵理應是W. H.先生』的說法，讓我聽得嘖嘖稱奇。

「至於南安普頓勛爵，西里爾處理起來更是沒有什麼困難。南安普頓很年輕時便和伊莉莎白‧佛農⑩相戀，因此他根本不需要懇求對方與他成親。他長得並不英俊，樣貌也不像母親，但W. H.先生卻和母親的容貌相彷——『你是你母親的鏡子，從你身上／喚回她風華正盛的青春四月』。最重要的是，南安普頓的教名是亨利，而那帶有一語雙關意思的第一三五、第一四三首詩則顯示，莎翁『那位朋友』的教名和他自己一樣，都是『威爾』。

「至於那些可嘆評注者的其他論點，像是W. H.先生是W. S.先生（意指威廉‧莎士比亞先生）的誤植；或W. H. all先生應該讀為W. Hall先生；或W. H.先生是威廉‧海瑟威先生，或是『祝』（wisheth）字後頭應該加上句號，讓W. H.先生變成作者，並非題獻的對象⑪……西里爾也在極短時間內將這

些觀點全都推翻。他所根據的理由不值得在此複述,儘管我還記得他為我唸了一段德國評注者邦思朵夫的文章(幸好不是德文),害我笑得前仰後合,因為這名德國人堅持W. H.先生的身分絕不會低於『威廉‧莎士比亞先生本人』。

「西里爾也絕不認同莎翁的十四行詩,只是用來諷刺杜雷頓、赫里福德的約翰‧戴維斯⑫之作罷了。對他來說(其實於我也是),十四行詩是帶有悲劇含義的嚴肅詩作,擰出了莎士比亞內心的苦痛,卻用甜言蜜語使之變得愉悅芬芳。西里爾也不認同這些十四行詩僅僅是一種哲學寓言,莎士比亞實則藉著它們討論自己的理想自我、理想人性、美的精神、理性、神聖之道或天主教會。西里爾認為(事實上,我覺得我們全都必須體認),這些十四行詩是向某個人訴說,而那人是某個年輕男子,但出於某種原因,此男的性格為莎士比亞的靈魂帶來了無比的喜悅,卻也帶來無比的絕望。

「西里爾以他的方式掃除了立論障礙,要我拋棄對這個主題的既定想法,而後公正且無偏見地聆聽他的自創觀點。他指出,關鍵的問題是——在莎士比亞的年代,誰會是那個出身寒微、甚至本性也不特別高貴的年輕男子?值得詩人用如此熱烈崇拜的話語向他傾訴,讓後人只能好奇這奇特的愛慕是怎麼回事,另一方面卻又害怕轉動鑰匙,解開有關詩人內心的謎團。誰會是那個外貌俊美、是莎士比亞創作基礎、靈感泉源、理想化身的人?

「倘若只把此人視為書中某些愛情詩的寫作對象,無疑會誤解這些詩作的整體意義。因為,莎士比亞在十四行詩中探討的藝術並非只是十四行詩本身,對他而言那些只是不重要的私事,他真正在意的是劇本創作藝術。莎士比亞對此人說——『但你是我的才思/讓我從粗魯無知變得文雅淵博』;莎士比亞也向他允諾不朽——『你將生氣蓬勃,活在眾人之口』

「莎士比亞創造了薇奧拉與伊摩琴、茱麗葉與蘿莎琳、波西亞與苔絲狄蒙娜，以及克麗奧佩托拉她本人⑬，為的當然正是這名年輕男演員。這就是西里爾‧葛拉罕的論點。

「如你所見，它純粹是從十四行詩本身逐步推展而成，能否為人接受，所仰賴的大半不是顯而易見的證明或正式的證據，而是一種精神與藝術層面的感受能力。西里爾宣稱，只要憑藉靠那種感受力，就能察覺這些詩作的真正含義。我還記得，他為我朗讀了一首優美的十四行詩，並指出它如何完全證實了他的論點──

> 我的繆思怎麼會缺少主題，
> 只要你活著，就能為我的詩篇注入
> 美妙意趣，你色藝絕倫
> 豈是任何庸俗文章能形容
> 噢，謝你自己吧，若我詩中
> 有幾句你能看得上眼：
> 因為你帶給別人創作的靈感，
> 誰會那麼笨，不寫詩獻給你？
> 因為你帶給別人創作的靈感，
> 誰會那麼笨，不寫詩獻給你？
> 做第十個繆思，你十倍高明
> 遠勝過眾詩人祈求的那九個老繆思；
> 有誰召喚你，就讓他獻出
> 能流傳久遠的不朽詩歌。

「事實上，西里爾仔細推敲研究了每一首十四行詩，證明（或自負地認為證明了）根據他對這些詩作意義的全新解釋，那些原本晦澀難懂、邪惡或誇張的事物，如今變得清楚明白、

合理，並具有高度藝術內涵，說明了莎士比亞對『表演藝術與劇本創作藝術之間的真實關係』所抱持的觀念。

「顯而易見的是，莎士比亞的劇團中必定有個長相十分俊美、演技又出眾的年輕男演員，讓莎士比亞詮釋筆下貴族女主角的責任託付給他。因為，莎士比亞不單是個富有想像力的詩人，也是個務實的劇場經理。

「事實上，西里爾·葛拉罕已經發現那名年輕男演員的名字，他叫做『威爾』，不過莎士比亞比較喜歡喊他『威利·休斯』。西里爾找到威爾這個教名的地方，當然是在那一語雙關的第一三五和第一四三首詩。而根據西里爾的說法，此人的姓氏藏在第廿首詩的第七句，它描述了W. H.先生的外型——『你風姿瀟灑，凌駕眾美男子之上』（A man in hew, all HEWS in his controwling.）

「在原始版本的十四行詩中，『Hews』是用斜體的大寫字母標示。西里爾宣稱，這清楚表明它是個文字遊戲，此觀點可從那些十四行詩中得到大量佐證，像是『use』和『usury』這兩個字常被拿來做成令人玩味的雙關語。於是，我立刻改變了想法——威利·休斯於我，就像莎士比亞，是個再真實不過的活人。

「我對這個論點只有一個異議，那就是——威利·休斯這個名字並未出現在《第一對開本》⑭的莎士比亞劇團演員表上。然而西里爾指出，威利·休斯的名字不在演員表上正坐實了這個論點，因為顯然可以從第八十六首詩得知，威利·休斯離開了莎士比亞的劇團，轉而在競爭對手的劇場表演，說不定表演的還是查普曼⑮的劇作。

「關於這一點，在談及查普曼了不起的十四行詩時，莎士比亞則對威利·休斯說——『可是，當他的詩句盡得你的贊同／我就靈感全無，我的詩也暗淡無光』。『當他的詩句盡得你的贊同』這說法很明顯是指，這個年輕演員的美為查普曼的詩

篇注入生命，使它活靈活現，增添迷人風采。

　　「同樣的想法，也出現在第七十九首詩——『當初只有我一人向你求助／我的詩曾獨享你的美好風韻／可如今，我已江郎才盡／只得將霸主寶位讓予他人』。

　　「而且在第七十八首詩中，莎士比亞還說——『那些外來的詩人奪走了我的立場（USE）／在你的應允下，將他們的詩廣為散播』。這些詩句很明顯是在玩弄文字遊戲（use的發音近似Hughes），而這句『在你的應允下，將他們的詩廣為散播』意思是『透過你身為演員的協助，將他們的作品呈現在眾人眼前』。

　　「那是個美妙的夜晚，西里爾和我徹夜未眠，不斷反覆朗讀這些十四行詩，直到幾乎天明。然而，過了一段時間以後我開始明白，若要將這個論點以真正完美的形式呈現在世人眼前，就必須先證明威利‧休斯這個年輕演員真的存在，確有其人；一旦成立，此人是W. H.先生的事就沒什麼可懷疑的，否則這個論點將會一敗塗地。

　　「我強烈地向西里爾主張這一點，但他實在不敢領教我這種俗不可耐的想法，並對此感到憤憤不平。儘管如此，為了他好，我還是要他答應，除非得到確鑿的證據、讓整件事毫無疑點，否則他絕不會發表自己的發現。

　　「後來，我們接連好幾個星期搜尋倫敦市內各教堂的登記名冊、達利奇學院的艾黎恩手稿、公眾檔案處，以及宮務大臣發布的文件⑯；事實上，我們找遍了所有可能會提到威利‧休斯的資料，結果什麼也沒找著。在我看來，威利‧休斯的存在愈來愈可疑。

　　「西里爾處於一種糟透了的狀況，日復一日地想著整個問題，並懇求我相信。但我無法忽略此論點中的這個瑕疵，因而拒絕被說服，除非伊莉莎白時代確實存在著威利‧休斯這個年

輕演員。

「有一天，西里爾出城去探望外祖父，我想應該就是那個時候發生的事（不過，後來我聽克雷迪頓勛爵說，事情並非如此）。大約兩星期後，我接到一封西里爾從華瑞克打來的電報，要我當天晚上八點到他家吃飯。一抵達，他便對我說：『使徒中唯一沒資格要求證據的是聖多馬，偏偏聖多馬是唯一取得佐證的人。』

「我問他，這話是什麼意思。他回答，他不僅發現一個名叫威利‧休斯的十六世紀年輕演員的存在，還能用最具說服力的證據證實他就是十四行詩中的W. H.先生。在那當下，他不願透露更多，直到吃完晚飯後，才鄭重出示我讓你看的那幅畫作，說在華瑞克郡一處被他買下的農家裡，偶然發現它被釘在一只老舊箱子的側板中。

「這口箱子本身就是伊莉莎白時代細緻之作的典範；當然，他把它帶回了倫敦。這口箱子正面面板中央，無疑刻有W. H.的首字母，正是這花押字引起了他的注意。他告訴我，在取得這口箱子好幾天以後，才想到應該仔細檢查箱子內側。不過，有天早上他發現，箱子某一側遠比另一側厚上許多，於是湊近細看，不得了，竟有一幅已裝框裱褙的畫被固定在上頭。

「將畫取出後，他發現它非常骯髒，表面全是黴，但仍設法清理乾淨；結果很開心地看見，自己竟偶然發現了一直在尋找的那件東西。這就是貨真價實的W. H.先生肖像畫，畫中人的手擱在十四行詩的題獻頁上；而且在褪色的金色畫框上，還能隱約看見有人用黑色的安色爾字體書寫這個年輕人的名字——『威爾‧休斯少爺。』

「嗯，我該怎麼說呢？我從沒想過西里爾‧葛拉罕會捉弄我，或是居然會用一幅贗品來證明自己的論點。」

「難道那幅畫是假造的？」

厄斯金回答：「它當然是假的，那幅偽畫非常傑出，可惜依舊是假貨。我想，那時西里爾對這整件事的態度相當沉著。不過我還記得，他不只一次告訴我，自己並不需要這類證據，就算沒有那幅畫，他也認為自己的論點是完整的。我嘲笑他，說這個論點少了它就無法成立，因此我熱烈恭喜他這奇妙的發現。接著，我們討論那幅畫應該要蝕刻或描摹，當作西里爾版本十四行詩的卷首插圖。然後我們花了三個月的時間啥事也不做，成天只是逐行重溫每一首詩，直到我們解決了文句或意義的每一道難題。

「有一天運氣不太好，我在侯爾蹦的一家版畫店看見櫃檯有幾張非常漂亮的銀筆畫作，我實在太喜歡了，便出手買下它們。那家店的店東名叫羅令思，他告訴我，這些是年輕畫家愛德華・莫頓的作品。此人非常聰明，卻窮得跟教堂老鼠一樣。我向那位版畫商要了莫頓的地址，過了幾天登門拜訪，發現他是個面色蒼白的有趣年輕人，討了個長相很平凡的老婆——後來我才知道，他的模特兒就是他老婆。我告訴他，我很欣賞他的畫，他聽了十分開心，接著我又問能否讓我看看其他作品。

「我們翻閱著一本作品集，裡頭充滿非常迷人的事物，因為莫頓的筆觸至為纖細清秀、賞心悅目。突然間，我瞥見了W. H.先生的畫像——毫無疑問，絕對是它。它幾乎算是一張描摹之作，唯一的不同是，悲劇和喜劇那兩張面具並不是從大理石底座懸垂而下（如西里爾手中那張肖像畫那樣），而是擺在畫中那名年輕男子的腳邊。

「我問：『你究竟從哪兒得到這張畫？』他先是有點迷惑不解，接著便說：『噢，那沒什麼。我不知道它也在作品集裡，它是非賣品。』他妻子則喊道：『那是你幫西里爾・葛拉罕先生畫的作品，假如這位先生想買下它，就賣給他吧。』

「我不可置信地問：『為西里爾・葛拉罕先生畫的？W.

H.先生的畫像是你畫的嗎？』並自問了好幾遍。他回答：『我不懂您的意思。』臉色脹得通紅。

「唉，這整件事糟透了。畫家的妻子將事情始末全盤托出。我離開的時候，給了她五英鎊。如今我實在不忍想起這件事，但當時我自然怒不可遏。我立刻上西里爾家，在那兒等他等了三個鐘頭，而那彌天大謊就清清楚楚地擺在我眼前。我告訴西里爾，他的偽造罪行已經被我揭穿了。

「他臉色發白，吞吞吐吐地說：『我這麼做純粹是為你著想，因為其他方式都說服不了你。但這幅畫並不影響那個論點的真實性。』

「我驚呼：『那個論點的真實性！我們最好別談那件事。你自己甚至從來沒有相信過它。如果你信，就不會用一件假貨來證明它是真的。』我們指責彼此，脫口說出氣話，大吵一架。我敢說，我當時說的話對他並不公平。第二天上午他就死了。」

「死了！」我大喊。

「嗯，他用左輪手槍結束了自己的生命，有幾滴血還濺到那幅畫的畫框上，就在寫有名字的那個地方。槍響後，他的僕役立刻請我過去，但在我趕到之前，警方已經來了。他留了一封信給我，顯然是在心情極度焦躁不安、既痛苦又煩惱的狀態下寫的。」

「信裡寫了些什麼？」我急忙追問。

「噢，無非是他絕對相信威利‧休斯真有其人，假造那幅畫為的只是向我讓步，但它一點也無損那個論點的真實性。為了向我證明他對這整件事的信念有多麼堅定且無懈可擊，他願意為十四行詩的這個祕密獻上自己的性命。這根本是一封愚蠢又瘋狂的信。我記得最後他說，他把威利‧休斯論點託付給我，請我向全世界公布，破解莎士比亞內心的祕密。」

「這真是個悲慘的故事，」我驚呼，「可是，你為什麼不肯執行他的遺願？」

厄斯金聳了聳肩，回答：「因為它從頭到尾都是個完全不合邏輯的論點呀。」

「我親愛的厄斯金，」我從座位站起來，說：「就這整件事來說，你完全錯了。它是探討莎士比亞十四行詩不可或缺的唯一關鍵，它讓所有的細節變得完整。我相信，威利‧休斯是真有其人。」

「千萬別那麼說，」厄斯金神情嚴肅地表示，「我認為這個想法帶有某種毀滅的特質，就理智上而言，它真的沒什麼好說的。我曾深入探究此事，因此可以向你保證，這個論點完全是騙人的。在某種程度上，會覺得它聽起來有道理，接著它就打住了。我親愛的孩子，看在老天爺的分上，千萬別繼續追蹤威利‧休斯這檔事，你會為它心碎的。」

「厄斯金，」我回答，「將這個論點公諸於世是你的責任。如果你不願意做，我來。隱瞞它，等於讓西里爾‧葛拉罕這名最年輕、最了不起的文學烈士所懷抱的文學回憶受到冤屈。我求你還他一個公道，他已為此喪命，別讓他白白犧牲。」

厄斯金愣住了，看著我：「你被這整件事的情緒牽著鼻子走。你忘了事情未必會因為有人為它捨命就成真。西里爾‧葛拉罕是我的摯友，他的死對我是個沉重的打擊。多年來，我一直走不出這傷痛，也不認為自己能恢復過來。可是威利‧休斯？有關威利‧休斯的想法，裡頭什麼東西也沒有，這個人根本不存在。至於把這整件事公諸於世——世人都以為西里爾‧葛拉罕是意外誤殺了自己，唯一能證明他自殺的證據，就在他寫給我的信裡，偏偏大家從未聽說過這封信的存在。直到今天，他外祖父克雷迪頓勛爵仍然認為這件事純屬意外。」

「西里爾・葛拉罕為了一個偉大的想法獻上自己的性命，」我回答，「如果你不願說出他以身殉道的事，至少也該廣為宣揚他的信念。」

「他的信念，」厄斯金說，「牢牢建築在一件虛假、不合邏輯的事情上，沒有半個莎士比亞學者會接受這件事。這個論點會被狠狠地嘲笑。別做傻事讓自己出醜，也別沿著通不到任何地方的路走。你一開始便假定這個人存在，但他是否存在有待證明。更何況，十四行詩是獻給潘卜洛克勛爵的，此事人盡皆知。這事就這麼決定，別再提了。」

「事情還沒定案！」我大喊，「我要從西里爾・葛拉罕放手的地方繼續發揚光大這論點，我會向世人證明他是對的。」

「傻孩子，」厄斯金說，「回家休息吧。現在已經過了半夜兩點，別再想著威利・休斯了。我實在不該告訴你這件事，更後悔害你改信一件我自己根本不信的事。」

「你給了我開啟現代文學最大祕密的鑰匙，」我回答，「除非你和世人能認同，西里爾・葛拉罕是我們這個時代最敏銳的莎士比亞評論家，否則我絕不罷手。」

當我穿過聖詹姆士公園準備走路回家時，倫敦正要迎接破曉。白天鵝在閃閃發亮的湖面沉沉入睡，那單調乏味的宮殿建築在淡綠色天空的襯托下顯現出皇室風範。我想著西里爾・葛拉罕，眼中滿是淚水。

## 2

等我醒來時，已經過了正午，沙金色的斜陽光束穿透窗簾，照進了我房間。我吩咐僕人別讓任何人知道我在家。喝完一杯巧克力，吃下一個小圓麵包後，從書架取下我那本《莎士比亞十四行詩集》，開始仔細閱讀它們。在我看來，每首詩似乎都證實了西里爾・葛拉罕的論點。我感覺自己彷彿將手放

在莎士比亞的心上，能數算每一次的跳動，感受那股熱情的悸動。我想著那個表現亮眼的年輕演員，在每一行詩句中看見了他的臉龐。

我記得有兩首詩特別打動我，分別是第五十三首、第六十七首。在這兩首詩的開頭，莎士比亞讚揚威利・休斯的演技千變萬化——「你的本質是什麼，你是什麼樣的人／竟有萬千怪奇縮影任你差遣／因為凡人只有一種面貌／而你，卻能化為千面人」，稱許他能詮釋的角色範圍很廣泛（從蘿莎琳到茱麗葉，從碧翠絲到歐菲莉亞⑰）假使這些句子並非向某位演員傾訴，無疑會讓人覺得莫名其妙，因為在莎士比亞的時代，「shadow」這個字有其中一種字面意義和戲劇表演相關——像是在《仲夏夜之夢》中，忒休斯便說「最好的戲劇也不過是人生的縮影」，當時的文學有許多類似的引喻。

這些十四行詩顯然是莎士比亞探討表演藝術本質的一系列作品，其中也探究完美的舞臺表演者不可或缺的奇特珍稀氣質。莎士比亞忍不住問威利・休斯：「怎麼回事，你怎麼會有那麼多種性格？」

接著他又繼續指出威利・休斯的美，似乎能實現各種形式與方向的想像，具體展現創造性想像的每一個夢想，而這想法在接下來的第五十四首詩當中有進一步的闡述，而且一起頭即是——「噢，美麗若有真誠助陣／不知看起來能美上多少倍」。莎士比亞邀請我們留意，表演的真實性和舞臺演出的真實性，是如何為詩歌增添光采，讓它的美好鮮活有勁，並具體落實了它的理想形式。

但莎士比亞又在第六十七首詩當中，要求威利・休斯放棄舞臺的矯揉造作，放棄用彩繪臉龐與虛假戲服拙劣地模仿人生，放棄它不道德的影響與暗示，放棄它與真實世界的高貴行動、真誠話語如此脫節——「啊，為什麼他要與臭腐同居／用

他翩翩風采粉飾邪惡／讓罪孽因他得逞／靠著與他交際來往而自抬身價／為什麼要塗脂抹粉，模仿他的臉龐／從他飛揚的神采盜取無神的外貌／既然他才是真正的玫瑰／可憐的美人何苦東施效顰」。

這似乎有點奇怪，像莎士比亞這樣了不起的劇作家，在舞臺創作與舞臺表演的理想層次上，實現了作為藝術家的完美追求，以及生而為人的人性探尋，怎麼會用這些話來書寫「劇場」這個主題呢？

但我們必須牢記，莎士比亞在第一一〇、第一一一首詩作中向我們坦承，他也厭倦了傀儡世界，同時對於讓自己「在眾人面前出醜」充滿羞愧。第一一一首詩尤其苦澀——「噢，你該為我譴責命運不公／我不端的行為就是她的過錯／她沒有給我體面的生活／而是要我拋頭露臉，賺錢謀生／結果使我名字烙上恥辱標記／我的本性也幾乎屈服於／我從事的行業，就像染工的手／你該可憐我，祝我重獲新生」。

其他十四行詩當中，也用了許多暗號表達相同的感受，它們是莎士比亞所有真正的傳人都熟知的暗號。

閱讀十四行詩的時候，有一點讓我覺得非常困惑，並且直到幾天前才突然想出真正的解釋，這一點，西里爾·葛拉罕似乎沒有注意到——我不明白莎士比亞為什麼會為他年輕朋友的婚事，設下那麼高的標準。他自己年紀輕輕就結婚，但婚後一直不幸福，因此不大可能要求威利·休斯犯下同樣的錯誤。這位飾演蘿莎琳的年輕男演員，並無法從婚姻、從現實生活的激情當中得到什麼好處。

前面列出的那些十四行詩經常突兀地懇求生育小孩，在我看來是個極不協調的音符，而這個謎團的答案也來得極為突然，我是從那令人玩味的題獻中找到它的。此書的題獻原文是這麼寫的——

獻給下列十四行詩

的唯一促成者

W．H.先生　願所有幸福

與永恆的名聲為您所有

由

我們永垂不朽的詩人

承諾

祝

冒險者

出版

此書

大獲成功

Ｔ．Ｔ．

　　有些學者假定，這篇題獻中的「促成者」，單純是指取得這些十四行詩的人，也就是出版商湯瑪斯·索普（Thomas Thorpe）。不過，這個觀點如今已被普遍揚棄；權威人士多半同意，這處隱喻應該是藉由比擬現實生活而得，指的應該是鼓舞詩人、激發其靈感的人。如今，我看見莎士比亞在不同的詩篇中運用了相同的隱喻，而這讓我踏上正確的道路。

　　最後，我有了重大的發現——莎士比亞向威利·休斯遊說的婚事，是指和莎士比亞的繆思成婚，這個說法在第八十二首詩當中曾明確地被提出。在此詩中，莎士比亞想起自己曾為這名年輕演員寫出令人難忘的角色，以及他的美確實賦予這些角色生命，因此他的背叛令人滿懷苦澀悲痛，於是開門見山抱怨道——「我承認你並沒有與我的繆思成親」。而莎士比亞乞求對方生育的子嗣，指的也不是血肉之軀的孩童，而是不朽的永

世聲名。

　　前面的整個組詩，純粹是莎士比亞邀請威利・休斯走上舞臺，成為演員。他說，你的美貌倘若沒有妥善運用，將會多麼無趣又無意義——「四十載寒冬包圍你的額頭／在你美貌上刻鏤深刻溝渠／自豪的青春華服，此刻眾人豔羨／他日將成一文不值破爛衫／若人問起當年美色如今安在／少壯年華的寶藏流落何方／你說，藏在那深陷的空洞眼底／只剩無邊的羞愧與無用的虛榮」。

　　你必須在表演藝術上創造些什麼，我的詩篇「受你影響，因你而生」；只要你聽我的，我會「獻出流傳久遠的不朽詩歌」，而你則該在舞臺的虛構世界以你原本的樣貌生活。莎士比亞繼續遊說道，你孕育的這些孩子不會像肉身子女那樣凋亡，但是你得活在它們之間，活在我的戲劇裡；就算不為這些理由，也希望你能——「為了愛我，造另一個你／讓美在你孩子或你身上永留存」。

　　我蒐集了所有在我看來能證實這個觀點的詩句，它們帶給我強烈印象，並讓我看清西里爾・葛拉罕的論點有多完整。我也發現，其實很容易就能分辨出哪些詩句談論的是十四行詩本身，哪些說的是莎士比亞傑出的劇作；但直到西里爾・葛拉罕指出這個論點之前，所有的評論家全都忽略了它，然而它卻是整個組詩當中最重要的一點。

　　莎士比亞對十四行詩本身多少有一點冷淡，他並不期待靠它們博得美名。對他來說，它們不過是「微不足道的繆思」。如同米爾斯告訴我們的，這些十四行詩只在極少數朋友之間私下流傳。另一方面，莎士比亞非常清楚自己的戲劇作品藝術價值極高，展現他自恃的崇高戲劇才華，因此他對威利・休斯說——「但你的夏天永不消逝／你的美也永不折損／死神無法誇口你行過死蔭／因你在不朽臺詞間與時同在／只要有人還能

呼吸，還能閱讀／這齣戲就活著，就能予你生命」。

「不朽臺詞」這個說法，清楚暗示莎士比亞當時送了一部自己的劇作給對方；正如結尾的對句所指出，莎士比亞深信自己的劇作永遠都會被演出。此外，從他對戲劇繆思說的話（第一○○首、第一○一首），我們也能找到相同的感受——「你在哪裡？繆思，竟長久忘了／讚美賦予你所有力量的對象／為何在無用俗歌揮霍靈感／消耗才華，只為照亮卑微瑣事」。

莎士比亞大聲疾呼，接著繼續斥責悲劇繆思和喜劇繆思，因為她們「怠慢浸染著美的真」，他說——「因為他不需要讚美，你就不開口／別為沉默找藉口，問題全在於你／讓他比鍍金墓碑更恆久／為世世代代稱頌謳歌／繆思，我教你怎麼盡職／讓他在未來一如今日，永遠風光」。

然而，最能完整表達莎士比亞這個念頭的，也許是第五十五首詩作——

> 王公貴族的大理石或鍍金墓碑
> 都敵不過這強勁有力韻文的恆久：
> 你在文字裡能永遠熠熠生輝
> 你在石碑上只會蒙塵、為世人遺忘。
> 毀天滅地的戰爭會把銅像推倒，
> 也會將巍峨石造宮殿連根燒光，
> 但戰神利劍或無情兵燹毀不掉
> 你留在眾人腦中的鮮明印象。
> 無視死亡與毀壞一切的不和
> 你將邁步前行；在後代子孫眼中
> 你不朽的美永遠有一席之地
> 直到他們耗損世界，迎來末日。
> 因此，在你起身迎接審判日來臨前

你將活在臺詞間，活在情人眼底。

　　但若以為詩中第二行的「強勁有力韻文」，指的是這首十四行詩本身，那可就完全誤解莎士比亞的意思。從十四行詩的共同特性來看，它極有可能是指某齣戲，而這齣戲除了《羅密歐與茱麗葉》，不作他想。尤其值得注意的是，莎士比亞在這首詩以及其他詩篇中，向威利・休斯允諾不朽，是極盡挑逗之能事的。莎士比亞所訴求的不朽，乃出自男性的眼光——意即，以引人注目的形體，在戲劇表演中贏得眾人的觀看凝視。

　　整整兩個星期，我努力研讀十四行詩，幾乎足不出戶，也回絕了所有的邀約。每一天，我似乎都能發現新事物。威利・休斯於我，成了一種精神支柱，一個總是很顯眼的人。我幾乎可以想像自己看見了他，他就站在我房間的陰暗處。莎士比亞將他描述得很完整——金髮，溫柔如花的翩翩風度，迷離深邃的眼眸，纖細靈活的四肢，還有那雙白百合般的纖纖玉手。

　　他的名字使我著迷——威利・休斯！威利・休斯！多麼富有音樂性！沒錯，除了他，誰能是莎士比亞傾注所有熱情的情郎兼情婦；誰能是莎士比亞甘願臣服、永遠效忠的愛情領主，是歡愉的嬌嫩寵兒，是全世界的玫瑰，是春天的使者，是那個用自豪的青春華服裝扮自己、像甜美音樂般可愛的男子。他的美貌是莎士比亞內心得體的衣裳，他的整個人是莎士比亞戲劇創作的力量礎石。

　　如今看來，他對莎士比亞的背叛與恥辱，導致這整齣悲劇是多麼苦澀！——儘管他的性格魅力讓恥辱變得嬌媚可愛，但那仍舊是恥辱。不過，既然莎士比亞都不計前嫌，我們又何妨原諒他？我無意刺探他的罪孽謎團。

　　但他背棄莎士比亞的劇團則是另外一回事。我花了很多時間調查此事，最後得到的結論是——西里爾・葛拉罕認定第

八十首詩所指競爭對手是查普曼，這一點是錯的；此人應當是馬羅⑱，莎士比亞曾間接提到他。儘管類似「他雄渾的詩句滿帆風使」的說法，或許適合套用在查普曼後來於詹姆士一世時代所創作的戲劇作品，但在十四行詩寫成的時候，它絕不可能用來形容查普曼的作品，絕不可能。

馬羅顯然才是莎士比亞以讚美字眼指稱的那個競爭敵手；此外，「和藹可親的邪惡靈魂／夜夜用智慧欺騙他」，指的就是馬羅那部《浮士德博士》中的梅菲斯托費勒斯 —— 毫無疑問，馬羅為這名年輕演員的美貌與風采傾倒，便許諾他可以在《愛德華二世》這齣戲中扮演蓋維斯頓一角，引誘他遠離莎士比亞劇團所在的「黑衣修士劇院」。

從第八十七首十四行詩可明白得知，莎士比亞其實有合法權利可將威利・休斯留在自己的劇團，他是這麼說的——

> 再會！你太珍貴，我高攀不起，
> 你大概也清楚自己的身價：
> 你的身價足已贖回你的自由：
> 我和你的契約就此一筆勾消。
> 除非你同意，我怎能留住你？
> 可我哪配得上那樣的福氣？
> 贈予我這份厚禮的理由已消失，
> 我獨享的權益也該歸還於你。
> 當初你不識自己價值，以身相許，
> 或是錯看了我，予我深情；
> 所以這份基於錯愛的大禮，
> 在明智決斷下，合該物歸原主。
> 我曾擁有你，如同黃粱一夢，
> 在夢中為王，醒來卻一場空。

既然無法用愛留住對方，莎士比亞也不願用其他強制力量約束對方。威利‧休斯成為潘卜洛克勛爵劇團的一員，而且也許曾在紅牛客棧的空地上，擔綱演出愛德華二世的俊美寵臣。馬羅過世後，他似乎又回來投靠莎士比亞。莎士比亞才不管自己的合作夥伴會怎麼看待這件事，很快就原諒了這名年輕演員的任性與變節。

　　莎士比亞是多麼擅長勾勒舞臺演員的性情啊！威利‧休斯正是那種「有驚世美貌，卻不趁機風流／能讓人心緒震盪，自己卻不動如石」的演員。他能演出愛戀的感覺，卻感受不到那種怦然心動，他能在不理解愛情的狀況下模仿激情。

　　「許多人虛情假意，一眼就被看穿／心緒全在反常表情顯露無遺」──但威利‧休斯可不是如此彆腳的演員。莎士比亞在一首瘋狂崇拜的十四行詩中說──「上蒼創造你時便已注定／柔情蜜意將在你臉龐永遠逗留／管你腦子有什麼念頭／你的表情只是一貫甜美溫柔」。

　　從威利‧休斯的「反覆無常」和「虛情假意」，很容易辨識出不真誠與背叛；不知怎地，這兩者似乎無法與藝術的本質分割，正如同威利‧休斯喜愛受人稱讚，渴望得到立即的肯定那樣，也全是演員常見的特質。

　　然而威利‧休斯比其他演員幸運的是，他知道什麼是不朽，他與莎士比亞的戲劇密不可分，他活在戲劇之間──「你的名字從此將永垂不朽／而我，一旦死了，就會被世人遺忘／大地只會為我騰出一口棺材之地／而你卻長眠在眾人眼裡／我溫柔詩篇將化作你的墓銘／未來的眼睛會對它百讀不厭／未來的舌頭會散播你的美名／哪怕現在活著的人都離開人間」。

　　十四行詩中也有無窮的暗示，間接提到威利‧休斯對觀眾施展的魅力，莎士比亞稱觀眾為「凝視者」。不過，最完美

描述威利・休斯對戲劇表演的巧妙掌控，或許得往〈愛人的怨訴〉這首詩裡找；莎士比亞在詩中說他——

> 他有滿腹騙人的把戲，
> 幻化成各種模樣，施行各式詭計，
> 忽而滿面羞慚，忽而哭哭啼啼，
> 忽而暈厥癱倒：各種手法交替使喚，
> 端看哪種較適合，能發揮最大魅力，
> 開黃腔就臉紅，聞苦惱就啜泣，
> 遭逢不幸就面無血色、暈倒癱軟。
> （中略）
> 於是他巧言令色的舌尖，
> 滔滔雄辯各種論據，侃侃談論深奧問題，
> 全都應答如流，理由堅強，
> 隨何者有利於己或高談闊論或緘默不語，
> 讓人破涕為笑，教人斂笑為泣。
> 他能操多種語言，精通不同技巧，
> 隨心所欲，讓所有人為他傾心。

我曾一度以為，自己真的在伊莉莎白時代的文學中，找到了威利・休斯的蹤跡。艾塞克斯伯爵的牧師湯瑪斯・內爾，曾在一篇出色文章中栩栩如生描繪了臨終前的伯爵。內爾告訴我們，伯爵過世前一夜——「他召喚樂師威廉・休斯演奏古鍵琴並唱歌。他親暱地喊著：『威爾・休斯，演奏我的歌，我自個兒來唱。』於是他非常開心地歌唱，不是像嚎叫的天鵝那樣眼光低垂，一路哭喊到底，而像隻甜美的雲雀，在清澈夜空的襯托下，高舉雙手，抬起雙眼，凝望著上帝的方向，將他精神抖擻的歌聲傳送到最高的天堂頂端。」

這個為席德尼筆下星星⑲垂死的父親彈奏古鍵琴的青年，肯定是莎士比亞十四行詩題獻的那位，因為莎士比亞告訴我們，此人甜美得「如悅耳的音樂」。只是，艾塞克斯伯爵死於一五七六年，當時莎士比亞自己才十二歲；意即，伯爵的樂師不太可能是十四行詩所題獻的 W. H. 先生。或許莎士比亞的年輕朋友，是這名樂師的兒子？但至少可以確定，威爾・休斯是個伊莉莎白時代的名字。其實，「休斯」這個姓似乎與音樂、與舞臺有密切連結。第一位英格蘭女演員是美麗的瑪格莉特・休斯，魯柏特王子瘋狂地愛慕她。還有什麼人選，會比她和艾塞克斯伯爵樂師生下的孩子，更善於表演莎士比亞的戲劇呢？但證據、連結在哪兒，唉，我找不到。我怎麼老是敗在徹底證實這一關，要是真能辦到就好了。

我的思緒很快從威利・休斯的生跳到他的死。之前我總是納悶，他的人生終章是什麼模樣。

也許他是那群在一六○四年跨海前去德國的英格蘭演員之一。這群人在布倫瑞克的亨利・尤利烏斯公爵面前表演。公爵自己也是個傑出的劇作家，也在古怪的布蘭登堡選侯的宮殿表演。據說選侯非常迷戀美人，他曾看上某個希臘行商的年輕兒子，後來用相當於那年輕人體重的琥珀買下他。也曾為了紀念他的一名奴隸，而在一六○六、一六○七這個大荒年裡連續舉辦多次慶典；當時，城裡到處可見餓死骨，而且已經七個月沒下雨了。

無論如何，《羅密歐與茱麗葉》於一六一三年在德勒斯登推出，同時上演的還有《哈姆雷特》和《李爾王》。一六一五年，莎士比亞的死亡面具，透過英國大使隨從之手被帶到德國交給某人，這個某人肯定是威利・休斯，不是別人；這蒼白面具，是曾如此深愛他的已逝偉大詩人留給他的紀念品。

確實，理應有證據特別符合這個想法，意即——這名年輕

演員的美貌，是莎士比亞藝術中寫實主義與浪漫傳奇非常重要的元素，因此，他應當是第一批將新文化種子帶到德國的人，並踏上成為十八世紀啟蒙運動先驅的道路。這場壯闊的運動雖始於萊辛與赫爾德，並在歌德的推波助瀾下成為完整且完美的議題，但也得到了弗里德里希‧施羅德[20]這名演員不小的幫助。施羅德喚醒公眾的意識，並透過舞臺表演的假裝激情與模仿擬態，展現現實人生與文學之間至為重要的親密連結。

若真是如此（你肯定找不到證據否決），威利‧休斯便可能是那些英格蘭喜劇演員（古老的編年史稱他們為「從不列顛來的演員」）之一，他在紐倫堡一場突發暴動中遭殺害，並被人偷偷埋在城外的一小片葡萄園中，埋屍者是個年輕人——「從他們的表演中得到樂趣，因而希望有幸學習這門全新藝術的奧祕」。

肯定沒有其他地方，比城牆外的這座小葡萄園更適合威利‧休斯，更適合莎士比亞說「你是我的才思」的這個人。因為，酒神戴奧尼修斯的哀痛不正是悲劇出現的緣由？喜劇輕快的笑聲，無憂無慮的歡鬧和快問快答，最初不就是從西西里葡萄園丁口中傳出來的嗎？還有，是沾在人們臉龐與四肢的那紫紅色葡萄泡沫汁液，率先指出了偽裝的迷人魅力，於是讓隱藏自我的渴望和客觀價值的意識，成了藝術粗陋的開端。

不管怎樣，無論他葬在何處，管它是中世紀小鎮城門外的小葡萄園，或是倫敦某個不起眼的教堂墓地，都不會有豪華的紀念碑標示威利‧休斯的長眠之處。

一如莎士比亞早已預見，威利‧休斯真正的墳塋坐落在詩人的詩篇中，威利‧休斯真正的紀念碑是戲劇的不朽。威利‧休斯的美，賦予了每個時代嶄新的創作衝動——比提尼亞奴隸那象牙色的身體，在尼羅河的綠色淤泥中腐朽，雅典青年的骨灰被灑在塞瑞米克斯的黃色山丘上；但，安提諾烏斯活在雕塑

中，而查密迪斯則活在哲學裡㉑。

# 3

　　三個星期過去了，我決定向厄斯金提出強烈呼籲，一是公正地對待西里爾‧葛拉罕的回憶，二是將西里爾‧葛拉罕對十四行詩的精彩詮釋公諸於世，因為那是唯一能徹底回答問題的解釋。遺憾的是，我並沒有保留這封信的副本，也無法取得正本，但我記得我回顧了整個主題，花了很多篇幅熱烈重申我研究所得的論點和證據。在我看來，這不只是重建西里爾‧葛拉罕在文學史的正確地位，也可從這無比迂迴冗長的古舊文本架構中挽救莎士比亞本人的名聲。我將所有的熱情與信念全都貫注到那封信中。

　　其實呢，信才剛寄出，我便忽然感覺內心湧出一股奇特的反應，彷彿我已將自己相信威利‧休斯論點的所有能力隨信送了出去，彷彿那種情感已不復存在，而我對這個主題已完全無感。究竟發生了什麼事，我也說不清——也許是，憑著熱情四處尋找完美表現的過程中，我耗盡了那股熱情；畢竟，情感力量就像現實生活中的各種力量，是有明確限度的。也許是，想讓任何人改信某種論點的純粹努力，會磨損你相信事物的能力。也許，我只是厭倦了這整件事，熱情已熄滅，理智只剩心平氣和的判斷力。無論它是怎麼發生的，我都不想假裝我能解釋它。毫無疑問地，對我來說，威利‧休斯突然變成只是個單純的神話，一場白日夢，一個年輕人的孩子氣幻想，而那個年輕人就像大多數熱心腸的人，比起說服自己，更急於讓人信服。

　　由於我在信中對厄斯金說了些很不公道又刻薄的話，便決定馬上登門拜訪，當面向他致歉。因此，第二天早上我駕車前往鳥籠小徑。一到，發現厄斯金正坐在書房裡，而那幅威利‧休斯的仿造畫像就擺在他面前。

「我親愛的厄斯金！」我高聲喊道，「我是來向你道歉的。」

「向我道歉？」他說，「為什麼？」

「為了我寫的信。」我回答。

「你的信沒有什麼需要後悔的地方，」他說，「相反地，你已盡了最大能力幫助我知道，西里爾·葛拉罕的論點是完全合理的。」

「你該不會是相信，威利·休斯真的存在吧？」我驚呼。

「是啊，」他回答，「你向我證明了這件事。你以為我無法衡量證據的價值嗎？」

「但是根本沒有證據可言。」我重重地跌進一張椅子，悲歎地說，「我寫信給你的時候，正受到全然愚蠢的熱情影響。我被西里爾·葛拉罕殉身的故事感動，著迷於他浪漫的論點，被整個想法的新鮮奇妙深深吸引。如今，我已看清這個論點奠基於妄想，威利·休斯存在的唯一證據就是你眼前的那幅畫，而它卻是個贗品。別只因為你對這件事懷有感情，就被沖昏了頭。無論這浪漫傳奇如何訴說威利·休斯真有其人，理智都會堅決反對它。」

「我真搞不懂你，」厄斯金驚訝地看著我，「為什麼呢？你不是明明寫信說服我，說威利·休斯真有其人。為什麼你自己卻改變了心意？還是，你對我說的一切全都只是個笑話呢？」

「我沒辦法向你解釋，」我答道，「不過，現在我知道實在無法多說些什麼來支持西里爾·葛拉罕的詮釋。十四行詩是獻給潘卜洛克勛爵的。看在老天爺的分上，別浪費時間尋找一個從不曾存在於伊莉莎白時代的年輕演員，並將一個幽靈傀儡放在莎士比亞十四行詩了不起的組詩中央。」

「依我看，你不懂這個論點。」他回應道。

「我親愛的厄斯金，」我大聲抗議，「我不懂它！什麼，我感覺它像是我一手創造的呢！我的信肯定說明了我不只深入

探究這整件事，還提出了各式各樣的證明。這個論點的一大缺陷是——它以此人的存在為前提，但他是否真的存在是有爭議的。如果我們同意莎士比亞的劇團裡有個年輕演員名叫威利‧休斯，那麼讓他成為十四行詩的寫作對象並非難事。可是就我們所知，在環球劇場表演的劇團成員中，沒有人叫這個名字，實在找不到理由再進一步往下追查。」

「但那正是我們不明白的地方。」厄斯金說，「他的名字確實沒有出現在《第一對開本》的名單上，可是正如西里爾指出的，如果我們還記得他背叛離棄了莎士比亞，轉而為競爭敵手效力，那麼這一點應該算是支持威利‧休斯確實存在，而非否定他存在的證明。」

我們為此事爭辯了好幾個小時，可是我所說的一切都無法讓厄斯金放棄他對西里爾‧葛拉罕詮釋版本的信念。他告訴我，他打算獻出自己的一生來證明這個論點，並決心要還西里爾‧葛拉罕一個公道。任憑我怎麼哀求、譏諷、懇求，他都不改其志。最後分別時，應該算不上是不歡而散，但我們之間肯定已留下一層陰影——他認為我膚淺，我覺得他愚蠢。當再次登門拜訪，他的僕人告訴我，他早就去了德國。

兩年後的某一天，我走進俱樂部，門房交給我一封信，上頭蓋著外國郵戳。信是厄斯金寄來的，發信地點是坎城的丹格利特旅館。讀完信後，我整個人嚇呆了，儘管我不大相信他會如此瘋狂地決心付諸實現。這封信的大意是，他已試過各種方法證實威利‧休斯論點，結果還是失敗了。由於西里爾‧葛拉罕為這個論點捨棄了生命，他決定也要為了相同的理由獻出自己的性命。這封信的結尾是這麼寫的——「我仍舊相信威利‧休斯真有其人。當你收到這封信的時候，我應該已經為了威利‧休斯而親手了結自己的性命。為了他，也為了西里爾‧葛拉罕，由於我膚淺的懷疑態度與一派無知的缺乏信心，把西里

爾逼上了絕路。真相曾向你揭露，卻被你揚棄，現在，它帶著兩條性命的血腥回來找你，不要拒它於門外。」

那是個恐怖的片刻。我覺得很痛苦，又覺得難以置信。為了神學信念送命是一個人運用其生命最差勁的方法，更何況是為了某個文學意見送死！這實在是匪夷所思。

我查看郵戳日期，發現信已送達一個星期。某種不幸的巧合讓我這幾天都沒到俱樂部來，否則就能及時收到信，趕去救他。或許，現在也還不遲。我速速驅車回家，打包行李，從查令十字火車站搭夜間郵務列車前往。這趟旅程十分難捱，我感覺自己永遠到不了。一抵達坎城，我立刻搭車前往丹格利特旅館。他們告訴我，兩天前，厄斯金已經安葬在英國人墓園了。這整件悲劇潛伏著某種駭人的荒誕。我滿口胡言亂語，惹得大廳裡每個人全都好奇地看著我。

突然間，哀慟憔悴的厄斯金夫人正好走過旅館門廳。她看見我，便走了過來，低聲說些她可憐兒子之類的話，接著忍不住淚流滿面。我陪她走進她套房的客廳，裡頭有位年長的紳士正在等她。他是個英國醫生。

我們聊了很多厄斯金的事，不過我沒提他自殺的動機。顯然他沒有告訴母親，驅使他做出如此致命、如此瘋狂舉動的理由是什麼。最後，厄斯金夫人站起身，說：「喬治留了件東西給你做紀念，那是他非常珍惜的東西。我去拿來給你。」

等她一離開房間，我便轉向醫生，說：「這件事對厄斯金夫人來說肯定是很難受的打擊吧！我真懷疑她能否承受得住。」

「噢，她早在好幾個月前就先有了心理準備。」他答道。

「好幾個月前就先知道！」我不禁放聲大喊，「那她為什麼不阻止他？她怎麼沒找人看住他？他肯定是瘋了。」

醫生滿腹狐疑地看著我說：「我不懂你的意思。」

「這麼說吧，」我嘆道，「假如一個做母親的知道自己兒

子打算自殺……」

「自殺！」他回應，「可憐的厄斯金沒有自殺，而是死於肺癆。他特地來這裡等死。我看見他的那一刻，就知道他來日無多了。有一半的肺早就失去功能，另一半的肺也嚴重受損。就在他過世的前三天，他問我他還有希望嗎？我坦白告訴他已經沒救了，他只剩幾天可活。聽完我這番話，他提筆寫了幾封信。他很認命，直到最後，他的神智都很清醒。」

就在那一刻，厄斯金夫人走進房間，手上拿著威利・休斯那幅致命的畫作：「喬治死前拜託我將這個交給你。」從她手上接過這幅畫時，她的眼淚正好滴在我手上。

如今，這幅畫掛在我的書房中，我熱愛藝術的許多朋友對它總是讚譽不絕。他們認定它不是克盧埃的畫，而是烏德利㉒的作品。我從沒想過要把它真正的來歷告訴他們。但有時候，我看著它不禁會想，莎士比亞十四行詩的威利・休斯論點，還真的有很多內容可說。

## 譯註

① 這三人都曾偽造文藝作品——詹姆士・麥佛森（James Macpherson，1736～1796）曾出版他宣稱由蓋爾語翻譯而成的詩集《莪相集》（Ossian），但其實是一部憑空虛構的偽作。

威廉・亨利・艾爾藍（William Henry Ireland，1777～1835）曾偽造莎士比亞的手稿。

湯瑪斯・查特頓（Thomas Chatterton，1752～1770）則假借中世紀僧侶湯瑪斯・羅立（Thomas Rowley）之名，創作了許多中世紀詩歌。

② 弗朗索瓦・克盧埃（Francois Clouet，1520～1572），法國文藝復興時期傑出的宮廷肖像畫家。事實上，真正誕生於

比利時法蘭德斯地區的，是弗朗索瓦那同為肖像畫家的父親讓‧克盧埃（Jean Clouet）才對。

③ 指威廉‧賀伯這個人，他是第三代潘卜洛克伯爵（William Herbert，third Earl of Pembroke，1580～1630），是許多詩人的贊助者。他是莎翁劇作集《第一對開本》（First Folio）的題獻對象，許多人認為他就是莎翁十四行詩裡的 W. H.先生。

④ 位於肯特郡的潘思赫斯特大宅（Penshurst Place），是英國詩人菲利普‧席德尼爵士（Sir Philip Sidney，1554～1586）的出生地。
潘卜洛克伯爵的肖像畫，實則陳列在索爾茲伯里附近的威爾頓大宅（Wilton House）。

⑤ 瑪莉‧費通（Mary Fitton，1578～1647）是伊莉莎白一世的未婚侍女，也是威廉‧賀伯（第三代潘卜洛克伯爵）的情婦。後人認為，她是莎翁十四行詩中「黝黑的女郎」（Dark Lady）原型。

⑥ 指劍橋大學業餘戲劇同好會（Amateur Dramatic Club）。

⑦ 指亨利‧瑞歐茲里這個人；他是第三代南安普頓伯爵（Henry Wriothesley，third Earl of Southampton，1573～1624）。他和潘卜洛克伯爵一樣，是許多詩人的贊助者（包括莎翁），也有許多人認為W. H.先生指的是他。

⑧ 英國牧師弗朗西斯‧米爾斯（Francis Meres，1565～1647）於一五九八年出版了《智慧寶庫》（Palladis Tamia: Wits Treasury）一書，探討從喬叟時代到他那個年代的英國文學史，是後人建立莎翁劇作年表的重要依據。

⑨ 湯瑪斯‧薩克維爾（Thomas Sackville，1536～1608）是英國政治家、詩人暨劇作家。於一五六七年受封為巴克赫斯特男爵（Baron Buckhurst），一六〇四年被封為多塞特伯爵

（Earl of Dorset）。

由羅柏・艾洛特（Robert Allott）所編纂、出版於一六〇〇年的《英國文壇》選集（England's Parnassus），收錄了薩克維爾的作品，書裡的署名為M. 薩克維爾。

⑩ 伊莉莎白・佛農（Elizabeth Vernon，1572～1655）是第二代艾塞克斯伯爵的姪女。她原是第三代南安普頓伯爵的情婦，後來扶正成為其妻。

⑪ 其實這些全是一八五〇、六〇年代的莎士比亞學者所提說法。威廉・海瑟威先生，是莎士比亞的連襟。

⑫ 指詩人麥可・杜雷頓（Michael Drayton，1563～1631）。
指詩人約翰・戴維斯（John Davies of Hereford，1565～1618）。為了與同名者區別，通常會加上他的出生地，因而稱赫里福德的約翰・戴維斯。

⑬ 依序指《第十二夜》、《辛白林》、《羅密歐與茱麗葉》、《皆大歡喜》、《威尼斯商人》、《奧賽羅》、《安東尼奧與克麗奧佩托拉》等戲劇女主角。

⑭ 指一六二三年出版的《莎士比亞的喜劇、歷史劇和悲劇》（Mr. William Shakespeare's Comedies, Histories, & Tragedies）一書，現代學者多稱它為《第一對開本》。這部莎士比亞劇本合集以對開形式印行，收錄莎翁三十六部劇作，由莎翁故舊約翰・賀明斯（John Heminges）和亨利・康得爾（Henry Condell）籌畫出版。

⑮ 喬治・查普曼（George Chapman，1559～1634），英國劇作家、詩人暨翻譯家。他是莎士比亞的好友，也是他的死對頭。他一生創作了十多部劇作，但更重要的貢獻則是翻譯了荷馬史詩《伊利亞德》與《奧德賽》。

⑯ 愛德華・艾黎恩（Edward Alleyn，1566～1626）是伊莉莎白時代著名演員，他成立了達利奇學院（Dulwich

College），該校藏有艾黎恩本人與其岳父所遺贈的大量文件，內容多與專業劇場及戲劇表演有關。

根據「1737年牌照法令」（Licensing Act 1737），宮務大臣（Lord Chamberlain）握有劇院審查權，可否決任何戲劇的演出，直到「1968年劇院法令」（Theatres Act 1968）制定後，才被廢止。

⑰ 依序分別為《無事生非》與《哈姆雷特》的女主角。

⑱ 克里斯多福・馬羅（Christopher Marlowe，1564～1593），英國劇作家、詩人暨翻譯家。擅長無韻詩和悲劇，是非常成功的一流劇作家，可惜英年早逝。莎士比亞深受其影響，在他死後，繼之成為戲劇天王。

⑲ 潘妮洛普・戴福羅（Penelope Devereux）是第一代艾塞克斯伯爵的女兒，後來嫁給里奇勛爵。這裡暗指，她是詩人菲利普・席德尼（Philip Sidney）十四行組詩集《愛星者與星》（Astrophel and Stella）中的女主角。

⑳ 弗里德里希・施羅德（Friedrich Schröder，1744～1816）是將莎士比亞戲劇引入德國表演舞臺的第一人。

㉑ 比提尼亞奴隸指的是「安提諾烏斯」（Antinous），他是羅馬皇帝哈德良的俊美童僕兼情人。

塞瑞米克斯（Cerameicus），是雅典的一個行政區。

查密迪斯（Charmides），是個瀟灑的雅典青年，曾出現在柏拉圖的《對話錄》中。

㉒ 讓—巴蒂斯特・烏德利（Jean-Baptiste Oudry，1686～1755），法國靜物畫家。

# The Portrait
# of
# Mr. W. H.

## 1

I had been dining with Erskine in his pretty little house in Birdcage Walk, and we were sitting in the library over our coffee and cigarettes, when the question of literary forgeries happened to turn up in conversation. I cannot at present remember how it was that we struck upon this somewhat curious topic, as it was at that time, but I know that we had a long discussion about Macpherson, Ireland, and Chatterton, and that with regard to the last I insisted that his so-called forgeries were merely the result of an artistic desire for perfect representation; that we had no right to quarrel with an artist for the conditions under which he chooses to present his work; and that all Art being to a certain degree a mode of acting, an attempt to realise one's own personality on some imaginative plane out of reach of the trammelling accidents and limitations of real life, to censure an artist for a forgery was to confuse an ethical with an aesthetical problem.

Erskine, who was a good deal older than I was, and had been listening to me with the amused deference of a man of forty, suddenly put his hand upon my shoulder and said to me, 'What would you say about a young man who had a strange theory about a certain work of art, believed in his theory, and committed a forgery in order to prove it?'

'Ah! that is quite a different matter,' I answered.

Erskine remained silent for a few moments, looking at the thin grey threads of smoke that were rising from his cigarette. 'Yes,' he said, after a pause, 'quite different.'

There was something in the tone of his voice, a slight touch of bitterness perhaps, that excited my curiosity. 'Did you ever know anybody who did that?' I cried.

'Yes,' he answered, throwing his cigarette into the fire — 'a great friend of mine, Cyril Graham. He was very fascinating, and very foolish, and very heartless. However, he left me the only legacy I ever received in my life.'

'What was that?' I exclaimed. Erskine rose from his seat, and going over to a tall inlaid cabinet that stood between the two windows, unlocked it, and came back to where I was sitting, holding in his hand a small panel picture set in an old and somewhat tarnished Elizabethan frame.

It was a full-length portrait of a young man in late sixteenth-century costume, standing by a table, with his right hand resting on an open book. He seemed about seventeen years of age, and was of quite extraordinary personal beauty, though evidently somewhat effeminate. Indeed, had it not been for the dress and the closely cropped hair, one would have said that the face with its dreamy wistful eyes, and its delicate scarlet lips, was the face of a girl. In manner, and especially in the treatment of the hands, the picture reminded one of Francois Clouet's later work.

The black velvet doublet with its fantastically gilded points, and the peacock-blue background against which it showed up so pleasantly, and from which it gained such luminous value of colour, were quite in Clouet's style; and the two masks of Tragedy and Comedy that hung somewhat formally from the marble pedestal had that hard severity of touch — so different from the facile grace of the Italians — which even at the Court of France the great Flemish master never completely lost, and which in itself has always been a characteristic of the northern temper.

'It is a charming thing,' I cried, 'but who is this wonderful young man, whose beauty Art has so happily preserved for us?'

'This is the portrait of Mr. W. H.,' said Erskine, with a sad smile. It might have been a chance effect of light, but it seemed to me that his eyes were quite bright with tears.

'Mr. W. H.!' I exclaimed; 'who was Mr. W. H.?'

'Don't you remember?' he answered; 'look at the book on which his hand is resting.'

'I see there is some writing there, but I cannot make it out,' I replied.

'Take this magnifying-glass and try,' said Erskine, with the same sad smile still playing about his mouth.

I took the glass, and moving the lamp a little nearer, I began to spell out the crabbed sixteenth-century handwriting. 'To the onlie begetter of these insuing sonnets.' . . . 'Good heavens!' I cried, 'is this Shakespeare's Mr. W. H.?'

'Cyril Graham used to say so,' muttered Erskine.

'But it is not a bit like Lord Pembroke,' I answered. 'I know the Penshurst portraits very well. I was staying near there a few weeks ago.'

'Do you really believe then that the sonnets are addressed to Lord Pembroke?' he asked.

'I am sure of it,' I answered. 'Pembroke, Shakespeare, and Mrs. Mary Fitton are the three personages of the Sonnets; there is no doubt at all about it.'

'Well, I agree with you,' said Erskine, 'but I did not always think so. I used to believe — well, I suppose I used to believe in Cyril Graham and his theory.'

'And what was that?' I asked, looking at the wonderful portrait, which had already begun to have a strange fascination for me.

'It is a long story,' said Erskine, taking the picture away from me — rather abruptly I thought at the time — 'a very long story; but if you care to hear it, I will tell it to you.'

'I love theories about the Sonnets,' I cried; 'but I don't think I am likely to be converted to any new idea. The matter has ceased to be a mystery to any one. Indeed, I wonder that it ever was a mystery.'

'As I don't believe in the theory, I am not likely to convert you to it,' said Erskine, laughing; 'but it may interest you.'

'Tell it to me, of course,' I answered. 'If it is half as delightful as the picture, I shall be more than satisfied.'

'Well,' said Erskine, lighting a cigarette, 'I must begin by telling you about Cyril Graham himself. He and I were at the same house at Eton. I was a year or two older than he was, but we were immense friends, and did all our work and all our play together. There was, of course, a good deal more play than work, but I cannot say that I am sorry for that. It is always an advantage not to have received a sound commercial education, and what I learned in the playing fields at Eton has been quite as useful to me as anything I was taught at Cambridge. I should tell you that Cyril's father and mother were both dead. They had been drowned in a horrible yachting accident off the Isle of Wight. His father had been in the diplomatic service, and had married a daughter, the only daughter, in fact, of old Lord Crediton, who became Cyril's guardian after the death of his parents. I don't think that Lord Crediton cared very much for Cyril. He had never really forgiven his daughter for marrying a man who had not a title. He was an extraordinary old aristocrat, who swore like a costermonger, and had the manners of a farmer. I remember seeing him once on Speechday. He growled at me, gave me a sovereign, and told me not to grow up "a damned Radical" like my father. Cyril had very little affection for him, and was only too glad to spend most of his holidays with us in Scotland. They never really got on together at all. Cyril thought him a bear, and he thought Cyril effeminate. He was effeminate, I suppose, in some things, though he was a very good rider and a capital fencer. In fact he got the foils before he left Eton. But he was very languid in his manner, and not a little vain of his good looks, and had a strong objection to football. The two things that really gave him pleasure were poetry and acting. At Eton he was always dressing up and reciting Shakespeare, and when we went up to Trinity he became a member of the A.D.C. his first term. I remember I was always very jealous of his acting. I was absurdly devoted to him; I suppose because we were so different in some things. I was a rather awkward, weakly lad, with huge feet, and horribly freckled. Freckles run in Scotch families just as gout does in English families. Cyril used to say that of the two he preferred the gout; but he always set an absurdly high value on personal appearance, and once read a paper before our debating society to prove that it was better to be good-looking than to be good. He certainly was wonderfully handsome. People who did not like him, Philistines and college tutors, and young men reading for the Church, used to say that he was merely pretty; but there was a great deal more in his face than mere prettiness. I think he was the most splendid creature I ever saw, and nothing could exceed the grace of his movements, the charm of his manner. He fascinated everybody who was worth fascinating, and a great many people who were not. He was often wilful and petulant, and I used to think him dreadfully insincere. It was due, I think, chiefly to his inordinate desire to please. Poor Cyril! I told him once that he was contented with very cheap triumphs, but he only laughed. He was horribly spoiled. All charming people, I fancy, are spoiled. It is the secret of their attraction.

'However, I must tell you about Cyril's acting. You know that no actresses are allowed to play at the A.D.C. At least they were not in my time. I don't know how it is now. Well, of course, Cyril was always cast for the girls' parts, and when As You Like It was produced he played Rosalind. It was a marvellous performance. In fact, Cyril Graham was the only perfect Rosalind I have ever seen. It would be impossible to describe to you the beauty, the delicacy, the refinement of the whole thing. It made an immense sensation, and the horrid little theatre, as it was then, was crowded every night. Even when I read the play now I can't help thinking of Cyril. It might have been written for him. The next term he took his degree, and came to London to read for the diplomatic. But he never did any work. He spent his days in reading Shakespeare's Sonnets, and his evenings at the theatre. He was, of course, wild to go on the stage. It was all that I and Lord Crediton could do to prevent him. Perhaps if he had gone on the stage he would be alive now. It is always a silly thing to give advice, but to give good advice is absolutely fatal. I hope you will never fall into that error. If you do, you will be sorry for it.

'Well, to come to the real point of the story, one day I got a letter from Cyril asking me to come round to his rooms that evening. He had charming chambers in Piccadilly overlooking the Green Park, and as I used to go to see him every day, I was rather surprised at his taking the trouble to write. Of course I went, and when I arrived I found him in a state of great excitement. He told me that he had at last discovered the true secret of Shakespeare's Sonnets; that all the scholars and critics had been entirely on the wrong tack; and that he was the first who, working purely by internal evidence, had found out who Mr. W. H. really was. He was perfectly wild with delight, and for a long time would not tell me his theory. Finally, he produced a bundle of notes, took his copy of the Sonnets off the mantelpiece, and sat down and gave me a long lecture on the whole subject.

'He began by pointing out that the young man to whom Shakespeare addressed these strangely passionate poems must have been somebody who was a really vital factor in the development of his dramatic art, and that this could not be said either of Lord Pembroke or Lord Southampton. Indeed, whoever he was, he could not have been anybody of high birth, as was shown very clearly by the 25th Sonnet, in which Shakespeare contrasting himself with those who are "great princes' favourites," says quite frankly —

Let those who are in favour with their stars

Of public honour and proud titles boast,

Whilst I, whom fortune of such triumph bars,

Unlook'd for joy in that I honour most.

And ends the sonnet by congratulating himself on the mean state of him he so adored.

Then happy I, that love and am beloved

Where I may not remove nor be removed.

This sonnet Cyril declared would be quite unintelligible if we fancied that it was addressed to either the Earl of Pembroke or the Earl of Southampton, both of whom were men of the highest position in England and fully entitled to be called "great princes"; and he in corroboration of his view read me Sonnets CXXIV. and CXXV., in which Shakespeare tells us that his love is not "the child of state," that it "suffers not in smiling pomp," but is "builded far from accident." I listened with a good deal of interest, for I don't think the point had ever been made before; but what followed was still more curious, and seemed to me at the time to dispose entirely of Pembroke's claim. We know from Meres that the Sonnets had been written before 1598, and Sonnet CIV. informs us that Shakespeare's friendship for Mr. W. H. had been already in existence for three years. Now Lord Pembroke, who was born in 1580, did not come to London till he was eighteen years of age, that is to say till 1598, and Shakespeare's acquaintance with Mr. W. H. must have begun in 1594, or at the latest in 1595. Shakespeare, accordingly, could not have known Lord Pembroke till after the Sonnets had been written.

　　'Cyril pointed out also that Pembroke's father did not die till 1601; whereas it was evident from the line,

　　You had a father; let your son say so,

　　that the father of Mr. W. H. was dead in 1598. Besides, it was absurd to imagine that any publisher of the time, and the preface is from the publisher's hand, would have ventured to address William Herbert, Earl of Pembroke, as Mr. W. H.; the case of Lord Buckhurst being spoken of as Mr. Sackville being not really a parallel instance, as Lord Buckhurst was not a peer, but merely the younger son of a peer, with a courtesy title, and the passage in England's Parnassus, where he is so spoken of, is not a formal and stately dedication, but simply a casual allusion. So far for Lord Pembroke, whose supposed claims Cyril easily demolished while I sat by in wonder. With Lord Southampton Cyril had even less difficulty. Southampton became at a very early age the lover of Elizabeth Vernon, so he needed no entreaties to marry; he was not beautiful; he did not resemble his mother, as Mr. W. H. did —

　　Thou art thy mother's glass, and she in thee

　　Calls back the lovely April of her prime;

　　and, above all, his Christian name was Henry, whereas

the punning sonnets (CXXXV. and CXLIII.) show that the Christian name of Shakespeare's friend was the same as his own — Will.

'As for the other suggestions of unfortunate commentators, that Mr. W. H. is a misprint for Mr. W. S., meaning Mr. William Shakespeare; that "Mr. W. H. all" should be read "Mr. W. Hall" ; that Mr. W. H. is Mr. William Hathaway; and that a full stop should be placed after "wisheth," making Mr. W. H. the writer and not the subject of the dedication — Cyril got rid of them in a very short time; and it is not worth while to mention his reasons, though I remember he sent me off into a fit of laughter by reading to me, I am glad to say not in the original, some extracts from a German commentator called Barnstorff, who insisted that Mr. W. H. was no less a person than "Mr. William Himself." Nor would he allow for a moment that the Sonnets are mere satires on the work of Drayton and John Davies of Hereford. To him, as indeed to me, they were poems of serious and tragic import, wrung out of the bitterness of Shakespeare's heart, and made sweet by the honey of his lips. Still less would he admit that they were merely a philosophical allegory, and that in them Shakespeare is addressing his Ideal Self, or Ideal Manhood, or the Spirit of Beauty, or the Reason, or the Divine Logos, or the Catholic Church. He felt, as indeed I think we all must feel, that the Sonnets are addressed to an individual — to a particular young man whose personality for some reason seems to have filled the soul of Shakespeare with terrible joy and no less terrible despair.

'Having in this manner cleared the way as it were, Cyril asked me to dismiss from my mind any preconceived ideas I might have formed on the subject, and to give a fair and unbiassed hearing to his own theory. The problem he pointed out was this: Who was that young man of Shakespeare's day who, without being of noble birth or even of noble nature, was addressed by him in terms of such passionate adoration that we can but wonder at the strange worship, and are almost afraid to turn the key that unlocks the mystery of the poet's heart?

Who was he whose physical beauty was such that it became the very corner-stone of Shakespeare's art; the very source of Shakespeare's inspiration; the very incarnation of Shakespeare's dreams? To look upon him as simply the object of certain love-poems is to miss the whole meaning of the poems: for the art of which Shakespeare talks in the Sonnets is not the art of the Sonnets themselves, which indeed were to him but slight and secret things — it is the art of the dramatist to which he is always alluding; and he to whom Shakespeare said —

Thou art all my art, and dost advance

As high as learning my rude ignorance,

he to whom he promised immortality,

Where breath most breathes, even in the mouths of men, —

was surely none other than the boy-actor for whom he created Viola and Imogen, Juliet and Rosalind, Portia and Desdemona, and Cleopatra herself. This was Cyril Graham's theory, evolved as you see purely from the Sonnets themselves, and depending for its acceptance not so much on demonstrable proof or formal evidence, but on a kind of spiritual and artistic sense, by which alone he claimed could the true meaning of the poems be discerned. I remember his reading to me that fine sonnet —

How can my Muse want subject to invent,

While thou dost breathe, that pour'st into my verse

Thine own sweet argument, too excellent

For every vulgar paper to rehearse?

O, give thyself the thanks, if aught in me

Worthy perusal stand against thy sight;

For who's so dumb that cannot write to thee,

When thou thyself dost give invention light?

Be thou the tenth Muse, ten times more in worth

Than those old nine which rhymers invocate;

And he that calls on thee, let him bring forth

Eternal numbers to outlive long date —

and pointing out how completely it corroborated his theory; and indeed he went through all the Sonnets carefully, and showed, or fancied that he showed, that, according to his new explanation of their meaning, things that had seemed obscure, or evil, or exaggerated, became clear and rational, and of high artistic import, illustrating Shakespeare's conception of the true relations between the art of the actor and the art of the dramatist.

'It is of course evident that there must have been in Shakespeare's company some wonderful boy-actor of great beauty, to whom he intrusted the presentation of his noble heroines; for Shakespeare was a practical theatrical manager as well as an imaginative poet, and Cyril Graham had actually discovered the boy-actor's name. He was Will, or, as he preferred to call him, Willie Hughes. The Christian name he found of course in the punning sonnets, CXXXV. and CXLIII.; the surname was, according to him, hidden in the seventh line of the 20th Sonnet, where Mr. W. H. is described as —

A man in hew, all HEWS in his controwling.

'In the original edition of the Sonnets "Hews" is printed with a capital letter and in italics, and this, he claimed, showed clearly that a play on words was intended, his view receiving a good deal of corroboration from those sonnets in which curious puns are made on the words "use" and "usury." Of course

I was converted at once, and Willie Hughes became to me as real a person as Shakespeare. The only objection I made to the theory was that the name of Willie Hughes does not occur in the list of the actors of Shakespeare's company as it is printed in the first folio. Cyril, however, pointed out that the absence of Willie Hughes's name from this list really corroborated the theory, as it was evident from Sonnet LXXXVI. that Willie Hughes had abandoned Shakespeare's company to play at a rival theatre, probably in some of Chapman's plays. It is in reference to this that in the great sonnet on Chapman, Shakespeare said to Willie Hughes —

But when your countenance fill'd up his line,

Then lack'd I matter; that enfeebled mine —

the expression "when your countenance filled up his line" referring obviously to the beauty of the young actor giving life and reality and added charm to Chapman's verse, the same idea being also put forward in the 79th Sonnet —

Whilst I alone did call upon thy aid,

My verse alone had all thy gentle grace;

But now my gracious numbers are decay'd,

And my sick Muse doth give another place;

and in the immediately preceding sonnet, where Shakespeare says —

Every alien pen has got my USE

And under thee their poesy disperse,

the play upon words (use=Hughes) being of course obvious, and the phrase "under thee their poesy disperse," meaning "by your assistance as an actor bring their plays before the people."

'It was a wonderful evening, and we sat up almost till dawn reading and re-reading the Sonnets. After some time, however, I began to see that before the theory could be placed before the world in a really perfected form, it was necessary to get some independent evidence about the existence of this young actor, Willie Hughes. If this could be once established, there could be no possible doubt about his identity with Mr. W. H.; but otherwise the theory would fall to the ground. I put this forward very strongly to Cyril, who was a good deal annoyed at what he called my Philistine tone of mind, and indeed was rather bitter upon the subject. However, I made him promise that in his own interest he would not publish his discovery till he had put the whole matter beyond the reach of doubt; and for weeks and weeks we searched the registers of City churches, the Alleyn MSS. at Dulwich, the Record Office, the papers of the Lord Chamberlain — everything, in fact, that we thought might contain some allusion to Willie Hughes. We discovered nothing, of course, and every day the existence of Willie Hughes seemed to me to become more problematical. Cyril was in a dreadful state, and used to go over the whole question day after day, entreating me to believe; but I saw the one flaw in the theory, and I refused to be convinced till the actual existence of Willie Hughes, a boy-actor of Elizabethan days, had been placed beyond the reach of doubt or cavil.

'One day Cyril left town to stay with his grandfather, I thought at the time, but I afterwards heard from Lord Crediton that this was not the case; and about a fortnight afterwards I received a telegram from him, handed in at Warwick, asking me to be sure to come and dine with him that evening at eight o'clock. When I arrived, he said to me, "The only apostle who did not deserve proof was St. Thomas, and St. Thomas was the only apostle who got it." I asked him what he meant. He answered that he had not merely been able to establish the existence in the sixteenth century of a boy-actor of the name of Willie Hughes, but to prove by the most conclusive evidence that he was the Mr. W. H. of the Sonnets. He would not tell me anything more at the time; but after dinner he solemnly produced the picture I showed you, and told me that he had discovered it by the merest chance nailed to the side of an old chest that he had bought at a farmhouse in Warwickshire. The chest itself, which was a very fine example of Elizabethan work, he had, of course, brought with him, and in the centre of the front panel the initials W. H. were undoubtedly carved. It was this monogram that had attracted his attention, and he told me that it was not till he had had the chest in his possession for several days that he had thought of making any careful examination of the inside. One morning, however, he saw that one of the sides of the chest was much thicker than the other, and looking more closely, he discovered that a framed panel picture was clamped against it. On taking it out, he found it was the picture that is now lying on the sofa. It was very dirty, and covered with mould; but he managed to clean it, and, to his great joy, saw that he had fallen by mere chance on the one thing for which he had been looking. Here was an authentic portrait of Mr. W. H., with his hand resting on the dedicatory page of the Sonnets, and on the frame itself could be faintly seen the name of the young man written in black uncial letters on a faded gold ground, "Master Will. Hews."

'Well, what was I to say? It never occurred to me for a moment that Cyril Graham was playing a trick on me, or that he was trying to prove his theory by means of a forgery.'

'But is it a forgery?' I asked.

'Of course it is,' said Erskine. 'It is a very good forgery; but it is a forgery none the less. I thought at the time that Cyril was rather calm about the whole matter; but I remember he more than once told me that he himself required no proof of the kind, and that he thought the theory complete without it. I laughed at him, and told him that without it the theory would fall to the ground, and I warmly congratulated him on the marvellous discovery. We then arranged that the picture should be etched or facsimiled, and placed as the frontispiece to Cyril's edition of the Sonnets; and for three months we did nothing but go over each poem line by line, till we had settled every difficulty of text or meaning. One unlucky day I was in a print-shop in Holborn, when I saw upon the counter some extremely beautiful drawings in silver-point. I was so attracted by them that I bought them; and the proprietor of the place, a man called Rawlings, told me that they were done by a young painter of the name of Edward Merton, who was very clever, but as poor as a church mouse. I went to see Merton some days afterwards, having got his address from the printseller, and found a pale, interesting young man, with a rather common-looking wife — his model, as I subsequently learned. I told him how much I admired his drawings, at which he seemed very pleased, and I asked him if he would show me some of his other work. As we were looking over a portfolio, full of really very lovely things — for Merton had a most delicate and delightful touch — I suddenly caught sight of a drawing of the picture of Mr. W. H. There was no doubt whatever about it. It was almost a facsimile — the only difference being that the two masks of Tragedy and Comedy were not suspended from the marble table as they are in the picture, but were lying on the floor at the young man's feet. "Where on earth did you get that?" I said. He grew rather confused, and said — "Oh, that is nothing. I did not know it was in this portfolio. It is not a thing of any value." "It is what you did for Mr. Cyril Graham," exclaimed his wife; "and if this gentleman wishes to buy it, let him have it." "For Mr. Cyril Graham?" I repeated. "Did you paint the picture of Mr. W. H.?" "I don't understand what you mean," he answered, growing very red. Well, the whole thing was quite dreadful. The wife let it all out. I gave her five pounds when I was going away. I can't bear to think of it now; but of course I was furious. I went off at once to Cyril's chambers, waited there for three hours before he came in, with that horrid lie staring me in the face, and told him I had discovered his forgery. He grew very pale and said — "I did it purely for your sake. You would not be convinced in any other way. It does not affect the truth of the theory." "The truth of the theory!" I exclaimed; "the less we talk about that the better. You never even believed in it yourself. If you had, you would not have committed a forgery to prove it." High words passed between us; we had a fearful quarrel. I dare say I was unjust. The next morning he was dead.'

'Dead!' I cried,

'Yes; he shot himself with a revolver. Some of the blood splashed upon the frame of the picture, just where the name had been painted. By the time I arrived — his servant had sent for me at once — the police were already there. He had left a letter for me, evidently written in the greatest agitation and distress of mind.'

'What was in it?' I asked.

'Oh, that he believed absolutely in Willie Hughes; that the forgery of the picture had been done simply as a concession to me, and did not in the slightest degree invalidate the truth of the theory; and, that in order to show me how firm and flawless his faith in the whole thing was, he was going to offer his life as a sacrifice to the secret of the Sonnets. It was a foolish, mad letter. I remember he ended by saying that he intrusted to me the Willie Hughes theory, and that it was for me to present it to the world, and to unlock the secret of Shakespeare's heart.'

'It is a most tragic story,' I cried; 'but why have you not carried out his wishes?'

Erskine shrugged his shoulders. 'Because it is a perfectly unsound theory from beginning to end,' he answered.

'My dear Erskine,' I said, getting up from my seat, 'you are entirely wrong about the whole matter. It is the only perfect key to Shakespeare's Sonnets that has ever been made. It is complete in every detail. I believe in Willie Hughes.'

'Don't say that,' said Erskine gravely; 'I believe there is something fatal about the idea, and intellectually there is nothing to be said for it. I have gone into the whole matter, and I assure you the theory is entirely fallacious. It is plausible up to a certain point. Then it stops. For heaven's sake, my dear boy, don't take up the subject of Willie Hughes. You will break your heart over it.'

'Erskine,' I answered, 'it is your duty to give this theory to the world. If you will not do it, I will. By keeping it back you wrong the memory of Cyril Graham, the youngest and the most splendid of all the martyrs of literature. I entreat you to do him justice. He died for this thing — don't let his death be in vain.'

Erskine looked at me in amazement. 'You are carried away by the sentiment of the whole story,' he said. 'You forget that a thing is not necessarily true because a man dies for it. I was devoted to Cyril Graham. His death was a horrible blow to me. I did not recover it for years. I don't think I have ever recovered it. But Willie Hughes? There is nothing in the idea of Willie Hughes. No such person ever existed. As for bringing the whole thing before the world — the world thinks that Cyril Graham shot himself by accident. The only proof of his suicide was contained in the letter to me, and of this letter the public never heard anything. To the present day Lord Crediton thinks that the whole thing was accidental.'

'Cyril Graham sacrificed his life to a great Idea,' I answered; 'and if you will not tell of his martyrdom, tell at least of his faith.'

'His faith,' said Erskine, 'was fixed in a thing that was false, in a thing that was unsound, in a thing that no Shakespearean scholar would accept for a moment. The theory would be laughed at. Don't make a fool of yourself, and don't follow a trail that leads nowhere. You start by assuming the existence of the very person whose existence is the thing to be proved. Besides, everybody knows that the Sonnets were addressed to Lord Pembroke. The matter is settled once for all.'

'The matter is not settled!' I exclaimed. 'I will take up the theory where Cyril Graham left it, and I will prove to the world that he was right.'

'Silly boy!' said Erskine. 'Go home: it is after two, and don't think about Willie Hughes any more. I am sorry I told you anything about it, and very sorry indeed that I should have converted you to a thing in which I don't believe.'

'You have given me the key to the greatest mystery of modern literature,' I answered; 'and I shall not rest till I have made you recognise, till I have made everybody recognise, that Cyril Graham was the most subtle Shakespearean critic of our day.'

As I walked home through St. James's Park the dawn was just breaking over London. The white swans were lying asleep on the polished lake, and the gaunt Palace looked purple against the pale-green sky. I thought of Cyril Graham, and my eyes filled with tears.

# 2

It was past twelve o'clock when I awoke, and the sun was streaming in through the curtains of my room in long slanting beams of dusty gold. I told my servant that I would be at home to no one; and after I had had a cup of chocolate and a petit-pain, I took down from the book-shelf my copy of Shakespeare's Sonnets, and began to go carefully through them. Every poem seemed to me to corroborate Cyril Graham's theory. I felt as if I had my hand upon Shakespeare's heart, and was counting each separate throb and pulse of passion. I thought of the wonderful boy-actor, and saw his face in every line.

Two sonnets, I remember, struck me particularly: they were the 53rd and the 67th. In the first of these, Shakespeare, complimenting Willie Hughes on the versatility of his acting, on his wide range of parts, a range extending from Rosalind to Juliet, and from Beatrice to Ophelia, says to him —

What is your substance, whereof are you made,

That millions of strange shadows on you tend?

Since every one hath, every one, one shade,

And you, but one, can every shadow lend —

lines that would be unintelligible if they were not addressed
to an actor, for the word 'shadow' had in Shakespeare's
day a technical meaning connected with the stage. 'The best
in this kind are but shadows,' says Theseus of the actors in
the Midsummer Night's Dream, and there are many similar
allusions in the literature of the day. These sonnets evidently
belonged to the series in which Shakespeare discusses the nature
of the actor's art, and of the strange and rare temperament
that is essential to the perfect stage-player. 'How is it,' says
Shakespeare to Willie Hughes, 'that you have so many
personalities?' and then he goes on to point out that his beauty
is such that it seems to realise every form and phase of fancy, to
embody each dream of the creative imagination — an idea that
is still further expanded in the sonnet that immediately follows,
where, beginning with the fine thought,

O, how much more doth beauty beauteous seem

By that sweet ornament which TRUTH doth give!

Shakespeare invites us to notice how the truth of acting, the
truth of visible presentation on the stage, adds to the wonder of
poetry, giving life to its loveliness, and actual reality to its ideal
form. And yet, in the 67th Sonnet, Shakespeare calls upon Willie
Hughes to abandon the stage with its artificiality, its false mimic
life of painted face and unreal costume, its immoral influences
and suggestions, its remoteness from the true world of noble
action and sincere utterance.

Ah, wherefore with infection should he live

And with his presence grace impiety,

That sin by him advantage should achieve

And lace itself with his society?

Why should false painting imitate his cheek,

And steal dead seeming of his living hue?

Why should poor beauty indirectly seek

Roses of shadow, since his rose is true?

It may seem strange that so great a dramatist as Shakespeare, who realised his own perfection as an artist and his humanity as a man on the ideal plane of stage-writing and stage-playing, should have written in these terms about the theatre; but we must remember that in Sonnets CX. and CXI. Shakespeare shows us that he too was wearied of the world of puppets, and full of shame at having made himself 'a motley to the view.' The 111th Sonnet is especially bitter:—

O, for my sake do you with Fortune chide,

The guilty goddess of my harmful deeds,

That did not better for my life provide

Than public means which public manners breeds.

Thence comes it that my name receives a brand,

And almost thence my nature is subdued

To what it works in, like the dyer's hand:

Pity me then and wish I were renew'd —

and there are many signs elsewhere of the same feeling, signs familiar to all real students of Shakespeare.

One point puzzled me immensely as I read the Sonnets, and it was days before I struck on the true interpretation, which indeed Cyril Graham himself seems to have missed. I could not understand how it was that Shakespeare set so high a value on his young friend marrying. He himself had married young, and the result had been unhappiness, and it was not likely that he would have asked Willie Hughes to commit the same error. The boy-player of Rosalind had nothing to gain from marriage, or from the passions of real life. The early sonnets, with their strange entreaties to have children, seemed to me a jarring note. The explanation of the mystery came on me quite suddenly, and I found it in the curious dedication. It will be remembered that the dedication runs as follows:—

TO THE ONLIE BEGETTER OF

THESE INSUING SONNETS

MR. W. H. ALL HAPPINESSE

AND THAT ETERNITIE

PROMISED

BY

OUR EVER-LIVING POET

WISHETH

THE WELL-WISHING

ADVENTURER IN

SETTING

FORTH.

T. T.

Some scholars have supposed that the word 'begetter' in this dedication means simply the procurer of the Sonnets for Thomas Thorpe the publisher; but this view is now generally abandoned, and the highest authorities are quite agreed that it is to be taken in the sense of inspirer, the metaphor being drawn from the analogy of physical life. Now I saw that the same metaphor was used by Shakespeare himself all through the poems, and this set me on the right track. Finally I made my great discovery. The marriage that Shakespeare proposes for Willie Hughes is the marriage with his Muse, an expression which is definitely put forward in the 82nd Sonnet, where, in the bitterness of his heart at the defection of the boy-actor for whom he had written his greatest parts, and whose beauty had indeed suggested them, he opens his complaint by saying —

I grant thou wert not married to my Muse.

The children he begs him to beget are no children of flesh and blood, but more immortal children of undying fame. The whole cycle of the early sonnets is simply Shakespeare's invitation to Willie Hughes to go upon the stage and become a player. How barren and profitless a thing, he says, is this beauty of yours if it be not used:—

When forty winters shall besiege thy brow

And dig deep trenches in thy beauty's field,

Thy youth's proud livery, so gazed on now,

Will be a tatter'd weed, of small worth held:

Then being ask'd where all thy beauty lies,

Where all the treasure of thy lusty days,

To say, within thine own deep-sunken eyes,

Were an all-eating shame and thriftless praise.

You must create something in art: my verse 'is thine, and BORN of thee'; only listen to me, and I will 'BRING FORTH eternal numbers to outlive long date,' and you shall people with forms of your own image the imaginary world of the stage. These children that you beget, he continues, will not wither away, as mortal children do, but you shall live in them and in my plays: do but —

Make thee another self, for love of me,

That beauty still may live in thine or thee.

I collected all the passages that seemed to me to corroborate this view, and they produced a strong impression on me, and showed me how complete Cyril Graham's theory really was. I also saw that it was quite easy to separate those lines in which he speaks of the Sonnets themselves from those in which he speaks of his great dramatic work. This was a point that had been entirely overlooked by all critics up to Cyril Graham's day. And yet it was one of the most important points in the whole series of poems. To the Sonnets Shakespeare was more or less indifferent. He did not wish to rest his fame on them. They were to him his 'slight Muse,' as he calls them, and intended, as Meres tells us, for private circulation only among a few, a very few, friends. Upon the other hand he was extremely conscious of the high artistic value of his plays, and shows a noble self-reliance upon his dramatic genius. When he says to Willie Hughes:

But thy eternal summer shall not fade,

Nor lose possession of that fair thou owest;

Nor shall Death brag thou wander'st in his shade,

When in ETERNAL LINES to time thou grow'st:

So long as men can breathe, or eyes can see,

So long lives this, and this gives life to thee; —

the expression 'eternal lines' clearly alludes to one of his plays that he was sending him at the time, just as the concluding couplet points to his confidence in the probability of his plays being always acted. In his address to the Dramatic Muse (Sonnets C. and CI.), we find the same feeling.

Where art thou, Muse, that thou forget'st so long

To speak of that which gives thee all thy might?

Spend'st thou thy fury on some worthless song,

Darkening thy power to lend base subjects light?

he cries, and he then proceeds to reproach the Mistress of Tragedy and Comedy for her 'neglect of Truth in Beauty dyed,' and says —

Because he needs no praise, wilt thou be dumb?

Excuse not silence so, for 't lies in thee

To make him much outlive a gilded tomb

And to be praised of ages yet to be.

Then do thy office, Muse; I teach thee how

To make him seem long hence as he shows now.

It is, however, perhaps in the 55th Sonnet that Shakespeare gives to this idea its fullest expression. To imagine that the 'powerful rhyme' of the second line refers to the sonnet itself, is to mistake Shakespeare's meaning entirely. It seemed to me that it was extremely likely, from the general character of the sonnet, that a particular play was meant, and that the play was none other but Romeo and Juliet.

Not marble, nor the gilded monuments

Of princes, shall outlive this powerful rhyme;

But you shall shine more bright in these contents

Than unswept stone besmear'd with sluttish time.

When wasteful wars shall statues overturn,

And broils root out the work of masonry,

Nor Mars his sword nor war's quick fire shall burn

The living record of your memory.

  'Gainst death and all-oblivious enmity

Shall you pace forth; your praise shall still find room

Even in the eyes of all posterity

That wear this world out to the ending doom.

So, till the judgement that yourself arise,

You live in this, and dwell in lovers' eyes.

It was also extremely suggestive to note how here as elsewhere Shakespeare promised Willie Hughes immortality in a form that appealed to men's eyes — that is to say, in a spectacular form, in a play that is to be looked at.

For two weeks I worked hard at the Sonnets, hardly ever going out, and refusing all invitations. Every day I seemed to be discovering something new, and Willie Hughes became to me a kind of spiritual presence, an ever-dominant personality. I could almost fancy that I saw him standing in the shadow of my room, so well had Shakespeare drawn him, with his golden hair, his tender flower-like grace, his dreamy deep-sunken eyes, his delicate mobile limbs, and his white lily hands. His very name fascinated me. Willie Hughes! Willie Hughes! How musically it sounded! Yes; who else but he could have been the master-mistress of Shakespeare's passion, 1 the lord of his love to whom he was bound in vassalage, 2 the delicate minion of pleasure, 3 the rose of the whole world, 4 the herald of the spring 5 decked in the proud livery of youth, 6 the lovely boy whom it was sweet music to hear, 7 and whose beauty was the very raiment of Shakespeare's heart, 8 as it was the keystone of his dramatic power? How bitter now seemed the whole tragedy of his desertion and his shame! — shame that he made sweet and lovely 9 by the mere magic of his personality, but that was none the less shame. Yet as Shakespeare forgave him, should not we forgive him also? I did not care to pry into the mystery of his sin.

His abandonment of Shakespeare's theatre was a different matter, and I investigated it at great length. Finally I came to the conclusion that Cyril Graham had been wrong in regarding the rival dramatist of the 80th Sonnet as Chapman. It was obviously Marlowe who was alluded to. At the time the Sonnets were written, such an expression as 'the proud full sail of his great verse' could not have been used of Chapman's work, however applicable it might have been to the style of his later Jacobean plays. No: Marlowe was clearly the rival dramatist of whom Shakespeare spoke in such laudatory terms; and that

Affable familiar ghost

Which nightly gulls him with intelligence,

was the Mephistopheles of his Doctor Faustus. No doubt, Marlowe was fascinated by the beauty and grace of the boy-actor, and lured him away from the Blackfriars Theatre, that he might play the Gaveston of his Edward II. That Shakespeare had the legal right to retain Willie Hughes in his own company is evident from Sonnet LXXXVII., where he says:—

Farewell! thou art too dear for my possessing,

And like enough thou know'st thy estimate:

The CHARTER OF THY WORTH gives thee releasing;

My BONDS in thee are all determinate.

For how do I hold thee but by thy granting?

And for that riches where is my deserving?

The cause of this fair gift in me is wanting,

AND SO MY PATENT BACK AGAIN IS SWERVING.

Thyself thou gayest, thy own worth then not knowing,

Or me, to whom thou gavest it, else mistaking;

So thy great gift, upon misprision growing,

Comes home again, on better judgement making.

Thus have I had thee, as a dream doth flatter,

In sleep a king, but waking no such matter.

But him whom he could not hold by love, he would not hold by force. Willie Hughes became a member of Lord Pembroke's company, and, perhaps in the open yard of the Red Bull Tavern, played the part of King Edward's delicate minion. On Marlowe's death, he seems to have returned to Shakespeare, who, whatever his fellow-partners may have thought of the matter, was not slow to forgive the wilfulness and treachery of the young actor.

How well, too, had Shakespeare drawn the temperament of the stage-player! Willie Hughes was one of those

That do not do the thing they most do show,

Who, moving others, are themselves as stone.

He could act love, but could not feel it, could mimic passion without realising it.

In many's looks the false heart's history

Is writ in moods and frowns and wrinkles strange,

but with Willie Hughes it was not so. 'Heaven,' says Shakespeare, in a sonnet of mad idolatry —

Heaven in thy creation did decree

That in thy face sweet love should ever dwell;

Whate'er thy thoughts or thy heart's workings be,

Thy looks should nothing thence but sweetness tell.

In his 'inconstant mind' and his 'false heart,' it was easy to recognise the insincerity and treachery that somehow seem inseparable from the artistic nature, as in his love of praise that desire for immediate recognition that characterises all actors. And yet, more fortunate in this than other actors, Willie Hughes was to know something of immortality. Inseparably connected with Shakespeare's plays, he was to live in them.

Your name from hence immortal life shall have,

Though I, once gone, to all the world must die:

The earth can yield me but a common grave,

When you entombed in men's eyes shall lie.

Your monument shall be my gentle verse,

Which eyes not yet created shall o'er-read,

And tongues to be your being shall rehearse,

When all the breathers of this world are dead.

There were endless allusions, also, to Willie Hughes's power over his audience — the 'gazers,' as Shakespeare calls them; but perhaps the most perfect description of his wonderful mastery over dramatic art was in A Lover's Complaint, where Shakespeare says of him:—

In him a plenitude of subtle matter,

Applied to cautels, all strange forms receives,

Of burning blushes, or of weeping water,

Or swooning paleness; and he takes and leaves,

In either's aptness, as it best deceives,

To blush at speeches rank, to weep at woes,

Or to turn white and swoon at tragic shows.

. . . . . . . .

So on the tip of his subduing tongue,

All kind of arguments and questions deep,

All replication prompt and reason strong,

For his advantage still did wake and sleep,

To make the weeper laugh, the laugher weep.

He had the dialect and the different skill,

Catching all passions in his craft of will.

Once I thought that I had really found Willie Hughes in Elizabethan literature. In a wonderfully graphic account of the last days of the great Earl of Essex, his chaplain, Thomas Knell, tells us that the night before the Earl died, 'he called William Hewes, which was his musician, to play upon the virginals and to sing. "Play," said he, "my song, Will Hewes, and I will sing it to myself." So he did it most joyfully, not as the howling swan, which, still looking down, waileth her end, but as a sweet lark, lifting up his hands and casting up his eyes to his God, with this mounted the crystal skies, and reached with his unwearied tongue the top of highest heavens.' Surely the boy who played on the virginals to the dying father of Sidney's Stella was none other but the Will Hews to whom Shakespeare dedicated the Sonnets, and who he tells us was himself sweet 'music to hear.' Yet Lord Essex died in 1576, when Shakespeare himself was but twelve years of age. It was impossible that his musician could have been the Mr. W. H. of the Sonnets. Perhaps Shakespeare's young friend was the son of the player upon the virginals? It was at least something to have discovered that Will Hews was an Elizabethan name. Indeed the name Hews seemed to have been closely connected with music and the stage. The first English actress was the lovely Margaret Hews, whom Prince Rupert so madly loved. What more probable than that between her and Lord Essex's musician had come the boy-actor of Shakespeare's plays? But the proofs, the links — where were they? Alas! I could not find them. It seemed to me that I was always on the brink of absolute verification, but that I could never really attain to it.

From Willie Hughes's life I soon passed to thoughts of his death. I used to wonder what had been his end.

Perhaps he had been one of those English actors who in 1604 went across sea to Germany and played before the great Duke Henry Julius of Brunswick, himself a dramatist of no mean order, and at the Court of that strange Elector of Brandenburg, who was so enamoured of beauty that he was said to have bought for his weight in amber the young son of a travelling Greek merchant, and to have given pageants in honour of his slave all through that dreadful famine year of 1606–7, when the people died of hunger in the very streets of the town, and for the space of seven months there was no rain. We know at any rate that Romeo and Juliet was brought out at Dresden in 1613, along with Hamlet and King Lear, and it was surely to none other than Willie Hughes that in 1615 the death-mask of Shakespeare was brought by the hand of one of the suite of the English ambassador, pale token of the passing away of the great poet who had so dearly loved him. Indeed there would have been something peculiarly fitting in the idea that the boy-actor, whose beauty had been so vital an element in the realism and romance of Shakespeare's art, should have been the first to have brought to Germany the seed of the new culture, and was in his way the precursor of that Aufklarung or Illumination of the eighteenth century, that splendid movement which, though begun by Lessing and Herder, and brought to its full and perfect issue by Goethe, was in no small part helped on by another actor — Friedrich Schroeder — who awoke the popular consciousness, and by means of the feigned passions and mimetic methods of the stage showed the intimate, the vital, connection between life and literature. If this was so — and there was certainly no evidence against it — it was not improbable that Willie Hughes was one of those English comedians (mimae quidam ex Britannia, as the old chronicle calls them), who were slain at Nuremberg in a sudden uprising of the people, and were secretly buried in a little vineyard outside the city by some young men 'who had found pleasure in their performances, and of whom some had sought to be instructed in the mysteries of the new art.' Certainly no more fitting place could there be for him to whom Shakespeare said, 'thou art all my art,' than this little vineyard outside the city walls. For was it not from the sorrows of Dionysos that Tragedy sprang? Was not the light laughter of Comedy, with its careless merriment and quick replies, first heard on the lips of the Sicilian vine-dressers? Nay, did not the purple and red stain of the wine-froth on face and limbs give the first suggestion of the charm and fascination of disguise — the desire for self-concealment, the sense of the value of objectivity thus showing itself in the rude beginnings of the art? At any rate, wherever he lay — whether in the little vineyard at the gate of the Gothic town, or in some dim London churchyard amidst the roar and bustle of our great city — no gorgeous monument marked his resting-place. His true tomb, as Shakespeare saw, was the poet's verse, his true monument the permanence of the drama. So had it been with others whose beauty had given a new creative impulse to their age. The ivory body of the Bithynian slave rots in the green ooze of the Nile, and on the yellow hills of the Cerameicus is strewn the dust of the young Athenian; but Antinous lives in sculpture, and Charmides in philosophy.

## 3

After three weeks had elapsed, I determined to make a strong appeal to Erskine to do justice to the memory of Cyril Graham, and to give to the world his marvellous interpretation of the Sonnets — the only interpretation that thoroughly explained the problem. I have not any copy of my letter, I regret to say, nor have I been able to lay my hand upon the original; but I remember that I went over the whole ground, and covered sheets of paper with passionate reiteration of the arguments and proofs that my study had suggested to me. It seemed to me that I was not merely restoring Cyril Graham to his proper place in literary history, but rescuing the honour of Shakespeare himself from the tedious memory of a commonplace intrigue. I put into the letter all my enthusiasm. I put into the letter all my faith.

No sooner, in fact, had I sent it off than a curious reaction came over me. It seemed to me that I had given away my capacity for belief in the Willie Hughes theory of the Sonnets, that something had gone out of me, as it were, and that I was perfectly indifferent to the whole subject. What was it that had happened? It is difficult to say. Perhaps, by finding perfect expression for a passion, I had exhausted the passion itself. Emotional forces, like the forces of physical life, have their positive limitations. Perhaps the mere effort to convert any one to a theory involves some form of renunciation of the power of credence. Perhaps I was simply tired of the whole thing, and, my enthusiasm having burnt out, my reason was left to its own unimpassioned judgment. However it came about, and I cannot pretend to explain it, there was no doubt that Willie Hughes suddenly became to me a mere myth, an idle dream, the boyish fancy of a young man who, like most ardent spirits, was more anxious to convince others than to be himself convinced.

As I had said some very unjust and bitter things to Erskine in my letter, I determined to go and see him at once, and to make my apologies to him for my behaviour. Accordingly, the next morning I drove down to Birdcage Walk, and found Erskine sitting in his library, with the forged picture of Willie Hughes in front of him.

'My dear Erskine!' I cried, 'I have come to apologise to you.'

'To apologise to me?' he said. 'What for?'

'For my letter,' I answered.

'You have nothing to regret in your letter,' he said. 'On the contrary, you have done me the greatest service in your power. You have shown me that Cyril Graham's theory is perfectly sound.'

'You don't mean to say that you believe in Willie Hughes?' I exclaimed.

'Why not?' he rejoined. 'You have proved the thing to me. Do you think I cannot estimate the value of evidence?'

'But there is no evidence at all,' I groaned, sinking into a chair. 'When I wrote to you I was under the influence of a perfectly silly enthusiasm. I had been touched by the story of Cyril Graham's death, fascinated by his romantic theory, enthralled by the wonder and novelty of the whole idea. I see now that the theory is based on a delusion. The only evidence for the existence of Willie Hughes is that picture in front of you, and the picture is a forgery. Don't be carried away by mere sentiment in this matter. Whatever romance may have to say about the Willie Hughes theory, reason is dead against it.'

'I don't understand you,' said Erskine, looking at me in amazement. 'Why, you yourself have convinced me by your letter that Willie Hughes is an absolute reality. Why have you changed your mind? Or is all that you have been saying to me merely a joke?'

'I cannot explain it to you,' I rejoined, 'but I see now that there is really nothing to be said in favour of Cyril Graham's interpretation. The Sonnets are addressed to Lord Pembroke. For heaven's sake don't waste your time in a foolish attempt to discover a young Elizabethan actor who never existed, and to make a phantom puppet the centre of the great cycle of Shakespeare's Sonnets.'

'I see that you don't understand the theory,' he replied.

'My dear Erskine,' I cried, 'not understand it! Why, I feel as if I had invented it. Surely my letter shows you that I not merely went into the whole matter, but that I contributed proofs of every kind. The one flaw in the theory is that it presupposes the existence of the person whose existence is the subject of dispute. If we grant that there was in Shakespeare's company a young actor of the name of Willie Hughes, it is not difficult to make him the object of the Sonnets. But as we know that there was no actor of this name in the company of the Globe Theatre, it is idle to pursue the investigation further.'

'But that is exactly what we don't know,' said Erskine. 'It is quite true that his name does not occur in the list given in the first folio; but, as Cyril pointed out, that is rather a proof in favour of the existence of Willie Hughes than against it, if we remember his treacherous desertion of Shakespeare for a rival dramatist.'

We argued the matter over for hours, but nothing that I could say could make Erskine surrender his faith in Cyril Graham's interpretation. He told me that he intended to devote his life to proving the theory, and that he was determined to do justice to Cyril Graham's memory. I entreated him, laughed at him, begged of him, but it was of no use. Finally we parted, not exactly in anger, but certainly with a shadow between us. He thought me shallow, I thought him foolish. When I called on him again his servant told me that he had gone to Germany.

Two years afterwards, as I was going into my club, the hall-porter handed me a letter with a foreign postmark. It was from Erskine, and written at the Hotel d'Angleterre, Cannes. When I had read it I was filled with horror, though I did not quite believe that he would be so mad as to carry his resolve into execution. The gist of the letter was that he had tried in every way to verify the Willie Hughes theory, and had failed, and that as Cyril Graham had given his life for this theory, he himself had determined to give his own life also to the same cause. The concluding words of the letter were these: 'I still believe in Willie Hughes; and by the time you receive this, I shall have died by my own hand for Willie Hughes's sake: for his sake, and for the sake of Cyril Graham, whom I drove to his death by my shallow scepticism and ignorant lack of faith. The truth was once revealed to you, and you rejected it. It comes to you now stained with the blood of two lives — do not turn away from it.'

It was a horrible moment. I felt sick with misery, and yet I could not believe it. To die for one's theological beliefs is the worst use a man can make of his life, but to die for a literary theory! It seemed impossible.

I looked at the date. The letter was a week old. Some unfortunate chance had prevented my going to the club for several days, or I might have got it in time to save him. Perhaps it was not too late. I drove off to my rooms, packed up my things, and started by the night-mail from Charing Cross. The journey was intolerable. I thought I would never arrive. As soon as I did I drove to the Hotel l'Angleterre. They told me that Erskine had been buried two days before in the English cemetery. There was something horribly grotesque about the whole tragedy. I said all kinds of wild things, and the people in the hall looked curiously at me.

Suddenly Lady Erskine, in deep mourning, passed across the vestibule. When she saw me she came up to me, murmured something about her poor son, and burst into tears. I led her into her sitting-room. An elderly gentleman was there waiting for her. It was the English doctor.

We talked a great deal about Erskine, but I said nothing about his motive for committing suicide. It was evident that he had not told his mother anything about the reason that had driven him to so fatal, so mad an act. Finally Lady Erskine rose and said, George left you something as a memento. It was a thing he prized very much. I will get it for you.

As soon as she had left the room I turned to the doctor and said, 'What a dreadful shock it must have been to Lady Erskine! I wonder that she bears it as well as she does.'

'Oh, she knew for months past that it was coming,' he answered.

'Knew it for months past!' I cried. 'But why didn't she stop him? Why didn't she have him watched? He must have been mad.'

The doctor stared at me. 'I don't know what you mean,' he said.

'Well,' I cried, 'if a mother knows that her son is going to commit suicide —'

'Suicide!' he answered. 'Poor Erskine did not commit suicide. He died of consumption. He came here to die. The moment I saw him I knew that there was no hope. One lung was almost gone, and the other was very much affected. Three days before he died he asked me was there any hope. I told him frankly that there was none, and that he had only a few days to live. He wrote some letters, and was quite resigned, retaining his senses to the last.'

At that moment Lady Erskine entered the room with the fatal picture of Willie Hughes in her hand. 'When George was dying he begged me to give you this,' she said. As I took it from her, her tears fell on my hand.

The picture hangs now in my library, where it is very much admired by my artistic friends. They have decided that it is not a Clouet, but an Oudry. I have never cared to tell them its true history. But sometimes, when I look at it, I think that there is really a great deal to be said for the Willie Hughes theory of Shakespeare's Sonnets.

國家圖書館出版品預行編目資料

王爾德短篇小說集II／王爾德（Oscar Wilde）著；陳筱宛譯
——初版——臺中市：好讀，2022.12
冊；　公分，——（典藏經典；69）
〔中英雙語版〕
ISBN 978-986-178-644-5（平裝）
873.57　　　　　　　　　　　　　　111020282

**好讀出版**

典藏經典 69

# 王爾德短篇小說集 II

作　　者／王爾德 Oscar Wilde
譯　　者／陳筱宛
總 編 輯／鄧茵茵
文字編輯／簡伊婕
美術編輯／廖勁智
內頁編排／王廷芬
行銷企劃／劉恩綺
發 行 所／好讀出版有限公司
　　　　　台中市407西屯區工業30路1號
　　　　　台中市407西屯區大有街13號（編輯部）
TEL:04-23157795 FAX:04-23144188 http://howdo.morningstar.com.tw
（如對本書編輯或內容有意見，請來電或上網告訴我們）
法律顧問　陳思成律師

讀者服務專線／TEL：02-23672044 / 04-23595819#213
讀者傳眞專線／FAX：02-23635741 / 04-23595493
讀者專用信箱／E-mail：service@morningstar.com.tw
網路書店／http：//www.morningstar.com.tw
郵政劃撥／15060393（知己圖書股份有限公司）
印刷／上好印刷股份有限公司
如有破損或裝訂錯誤，請寄回知己圖書更換

二　　版／西元 2022 年 12 月 15 日
定　　價／220 元

線上讀者回函
獲得好讀資訊

Published by How Do Publishing Co., LTD.
2022 Printed in Taiwan
All rights reserved.
ISBN 978-986-178-644-5